# THE

# Secret Tunnel

# THE
# Secret Tunnel

James Lear

CLEIS PRESS

Published in the United States by Cleis Press Inc.,
P.O. Box 14697, San Francisco, California 94114.

Printed in the United States.
Cover design: Scott Idleman
Cover photograph: copyright © 2008 by Louis LaSalle,
    www.louislasalle.com
Text design: Frank Wiedemann
Cleis logo art: Juana Alicia

First Edition.
10 9 8 7 6 5 4 3 2

Library of Congress Cataloging-in-Publication Data

Lear, James, 1960-
The secret tunnel / James Lear. -- 1st ed.
    p. cm.
ISBN 978-1-57344-329-6 (pbk. : alk. paper)
1. Gay men--Fiction. 2. Railroad trains--Fiction. 3. Murder--Fiction.
4. Great Britain--Fiction. I. Title.

PR6069.M543S43 2008
823'.914--dc22

                                        2008019378

# I

THE FLYING SCOTSMAN RUNS 392 MILES DOWN THE EAST coast of Great Britain, between Edinburgh and London, in eight and a quarter hours, nonstop. It is one of the most famous trains in the world—as famous as the Twentieth Century Limited, the Orient Express, and *le Train Bleu*— a train steeped in tradition and history and romance. For many passengers, a trip on the Flying Scotsman is as exciting as anything they might find at journey's end. For some, it's worth finding an excuse to go to London or Edinburgh simply to enjoy the ride.

For me, the Flying Scotsman has additional attractions. As an avid reader of detective fiction (and a would-be amateur sleuth), I find all train trips exciting and potentially thrilling. Did not Agatha Christie, fast emerging as the leading British crime writer, title her latest novel *The Mystery of the Blue Train*? And then, for a lover of men, there are the fellow passengers, everything from soldiers to lords, the railway staff—the sooty, greasy engineers, the impeccable stewards, the pert young porters—all of us thrown together, far from home, for a few hours, never to see each other again. I never set off without a sense of excitement, a tingling in my head, in my heart, and in my pants. Just the thought of rail travel—all that steam, the pumping pistons, the fiery furnace, the tunnels and cuts—gives me a hard-on.

I was traveling from Edinburgh to London to see my old friend from Cambridge, Harry Morgan, for the first time since his marriage just over two years ago, in the autumn of 1925. Harry—or "Boy," as we always called him at Cambridge, on account of his youthful looks and enthusiastic personality—was now a respectable family man with a promising future in banking. True, I had fucked him on the eve of his wedding, and could not help thinking, as I watched him walk down the aisle in his beautifully tailored morning suit, that just a few hours previously his legs were over my shoulders and my dick up his ass. Was he doing the right thing by marrying Belinda Eagle? Could he ever really be happy? The answer, I knew, was yes. It depressed me at the time, and it depressed me still, even though I had found happiness with another man, Vincent West. But there was something about my friendship with Boy Morgan, forged in the hopelessly romantic atmosphere of Cambridge, tempered during our almost lethal adventures that long-ago weekend in Drekeham Hall, that I could never relinquish. Perhaps it was the knowledge that he would never fully be mine, that it was to women that he would always turn for love and security, however much he liked fucking, and being fucked, by me. Perhaps it was that still boyish personality that spilled out from every word of his letters. I wondered if he had kept the looks that went with the character, or married life had fattened and aged him. I half hoped that it had.

So it was with mixed feelings that I was traveling to London on a gloomy winter morning in 1928—that Vince and I were to have traveled together—to attend the christening of Boy's firstborn child, a daughter to whom I was to be godfather. The invitation had been sent to both of us by Belinda, accompanied by a personal note from Morgan to me, in which he begged me to come, despite the distance, hinting—or was this my imagination?—that there was more than baptism in the cards. But, at the last minute, Vince had canceled; work would not let him leave Edinburgh, and I would have to travel alone. I was half cross, and half excited. Perhaps more than half.

I left home at nine in the morning, in plenty of time for the ten o'clock departure. It was one of those winter days that never really gets light, when the sky changes from a dull dark gray to a dull light gray and then, as if exhausted by the effort, fades to black. Those days are gloomy all over the world, no doubt—but there is something particularly grim about the Scottish winter. Perhaps it is the Edinburgh rock that absorbs all the light—that mixture of basalt and sandstone that even in brilliant sunshine looks dull. Perhaps it is the fine drizzly fog that shrouds the city, cutting out what little daylight manages to penetrate the high uniform clouds. Whatever the reason, I stomped into Waverley Station in a mood that suited the weather. I was angry and indignant; woe betide the insolent porter or clumsy passenger who crossed my path.

I blamed Vince for spoiling our holiday, and thoroughly enjoyed playing the wounded party, knowing full well that it was not his fault that he had to work throughout the long weekend we had planned. God knows, I had canceled enough dinners, theater trips, and parties because I had to stay late at the hospital, where I was now a junior doctor, well on the way to qualification—and Vince seldom, if ever, complained. But now that he was obliged to accompany a prominent author on a lightning tour of Scotland—a prestigious job, fiercely contested by his colleagues, and a sure stepping stone to full editorship—all I could do was rant. He had told me over dinner, which I'd ruined by sulking, and tried to reason with me in bed, but I turned my back and turned off the light.

There had been time, this morning, for a moody rapprochement. We were both awake at five, even though it was still night. The leisurely clip-clop of the milkman's horse approached our window, passed under it, and receded, the jingle of bottles in metal crates barely audible in the attic where we slept. I counted the footsteps as they came and went, and felt very forlorn. Vince must have been doing the same thing, as he sighed and shifted, pulling the blankets over his shoulder. I didn't feel like talking, as I knew we'd only get into the same round of recriminations and explanations that had ruined the evening, but I did feel like fucking. I'm nearly always rock hard in the small hours, sometimes painfully so, from sleep or dreams or the need to pee—but on this occasion I was also aware of the fact that I was about to be separated from my lover for three nights, and wanted to leave at least one load up his ass.

I moved across the mattress, which creaked and twanged—we had become inured to these nocturnes—and threw an arm around him. He had his back to me, so I had no trouble pressing my cock against his buttocks. It was not quite flesh on flesh—unromantic it may be, but the chilly Edinburgh nights, not to mention the need for some vestige of propriety, meant that we habitually wore pajamas in bed. Even though we had our own self-contained flat on the top two floors of the house, there was always the chance that the landlady might let herself in on some pretext and, finding two naked men in bed together, go running to the police with hysterical tales of sodomites in the attic. She was a great churchgoer, our Mrs. McPhee, and only put up with our cohabitation because I was a doctor, and an American to boot, and therefore allowed my eccentricities. Vince, as an Englishman, was only just this side of the Devil himself, but our promptly paid rent stilled her wagging tongue.

My dick made contact with Vince's ass through two layers of flannel—but even so I could feel the rubbery firmness of his round buttocks, which I had parted so many times in the two years we'd been together. He sighed again at the contact, and pressed back into me, twisting his neck so that our tongues could meet. We kissed hard, our unshaven faces scratching, our nighttime breath sour. I reached down and started fumbling with the drawstring of his pajama bottoms; Vince had a bad habit of tying them in a double bowknot, something he'd learned at boarding school and had never been able to unlearn, and when I was in a hurry—as I was now—the knot tended to stick. Thankfully, he had a fly through which I could draw his cock, and I caressed it until he was just as hard as I was. I was ready to rip a hole in the seat of his pants, and started tugging at the fabric, but Vince had other ideas.

Throwing the blankets and sheets to the floor, he pushed me onto my back, pulled down my pants (no knotting for me) and started sucking my dick as if it was breakfast. Vince had become, in the last two years and under my exacting tuition, an extremely accomplished lover, and he fucked like a god—but if there was one thing at which he really excelled, it was sucking cock. If he continued, I would come in his mouth, which he loved—but I wanted to punish his ass first, as a way of expressing my displeasure at his "abandonment" (as I thought of it) and, simultaneously, letting him know that I loved him more than ever. Sex, for me, is equally capable of expressing positive and negative emotions, often at the same time.

Vince knew what I had in mind, and eased off when he felt my cock hardening even further in his mouth. He pulled the jacket over his head; I could see the outlines of his pale, athletic body in the faint glow of the streetlamps that penetrated the curtains. He straddled me, shifted my legs up, gripped my cock, and wriggled out of his pajama pants. I

11

was still wet from his sucking; that was all the lubrication he was going to get. We both wanted this to be a rough ride.

And it was. Vince wasted no time lowering himself onto me, and I provided the necessary pressure by bracing my pelvis upward to shove my cock right into the base. When the hair above my dick met the hair around his crack, I was ready to start pumping. We had done this often enough to establish a rhythm quickly—fucking really is one of those activities that "practice makes perfect"—and soon his motions were synchronized with my thrusts, taking me deep inside him. His prick was bouncing up and down, slapping against his taut stomach, and when I grabbed the head I could feel sticky fluid, which I gathered between my thumb and forefinger and brought to my mouth. This was not going to take long.

When I'm fucking Vince, I like to make him come first, because in his postorgasmic state the last few thrusts as I come send him into a kind of trance. And so I wrapped a fist around his dick and started jerking him off. I could tell he was getting close; with one hand he was pinching his nipple, with the other he was reaching back to feel my dick stretching his ass lips. Some hard fucking would do the rest. The bed was creaking so loudly that it must have been audible all over the house.

The first shot of his spunk went above my face and hit the headboard; the next caught me on the chin and ran down my neck. I kept fucking and jerking until I knew he had no more to give me and then, grabbing him by the upper arms, threw him onto his back, never letting my cock slide out of his ass. I let him take my full weight through my cock, just balancing on my toes and elbows, and fucked him as hard as I could. He sighed and moaned and then went silent as I covered his mouth with mine, smearing his face with his own spunk, and squirted far up into his guts.

"That'll teach you to work when I want you to come

with me," I said, half in jest, wiping my sticky cock all over his chest. I got shakily to my feet and left him to recover alone.

By the time I had washed and dressed, Vince was in the kitchen making a pot of tea and cutting slices of bread for my breakfast. We ate and drank in silence, but it was an amicable silence compared to the frostiness of the previous evening. I watched his throat working as he swallowed his tea, marveled at the paleness of his skin where his bathrobe fell open. When it was time to leave, I stood behind his chair, kissed him on the neck, and thrust one hand into his robe, pulling it open. Soon he was hard again, as was I inside my spiffy black pants—but I did not have time for another elaborate farewell. I grabbed some butter from the dish, smeared it around his cock and balls. He rested his feet on the table, pushing aside plates and mugs, which clattered to the floor, and, leaning back against me, allowed me to finger him and caress his cock until he was squirming his way to another orgasm. There was less outcome this time, but still enough to make a fan pattern across his belly.

I kissed him deeply, told him I loved him, and left the house. And I did love him, do love him, but as I walked through cold, wet streets toward the station it was not Vince I was thinking of. I was thinking of Boy Morgan, and what we might do together. I was thinking of Boy's slim hips, his strong shoulders, his long, slender cock twitching in my hand... He would be so glad to see me, and Belinda would be preoccupied with the baby. And Vince—well, Vince had decided not to come with me. I was a free agent. We had made no promises to one another, Vince and I; we were not married, like Morgan and Belinda, we had never said that we would forsake all others. It would not be my fault if Morgan seduced me. And what Vince didn't know wouldn't hurt him...

Yes, after so short a period of domestic happiness with

Vince, I had all the adulterer's self-justifying excuses at my fingertips—and I knew it. Which, more than anything, more than the weather or the crowds or the prospect of traveling alone, explained my foul mood as I stomped into Waverley Station to catch the ten o'clock train to London—the Flying Scotsman.

I was so looking forward to taking this legendary journey with Vince that I had splurged on a first-class compartment, thinking of the fun we could have during the eight and a quarter hours between Waverley and Kings Cross. I still had his ticket in my jacket pocket; there had been no time to arrange a refund. Perhaps if I had not been so grumpy last night, or had spent less time fooling around this morning, I might have got my money back, but now it would go to waste.

"Can I help you with that, sir?"

I did not need help, and was about to tell the porter that I was more than capable of carrying a single suitcase—and then I looked at him. He can't have been more than 18, at least if his smooth chin and fresh complexion were anything to go by, but he had the broad shoulders and sturdy thighs of a man. The cross words died on my tongue, and I put my suitcase down on the ground.

"Going to London, sir?" He had the typical Edinburgh lilt, which I had finally learned to understand after a year of dealing with colleagues and patients, who thought my constantly repeated "Pardon me?"s were a sign of idiocy.

"Yes, I am. Thank you." It was an idiotic question—where else was I likely to be going?—but I was pleased with the little salute that he gave me, pushing his cap back slightly so I could see his thick brown hair tumbling over his forehead. He swung the case onto his cart, and I watched his shoulders bunching and flexing in his tight little jacket. I allowed him to walk ahead of me so that I could feast my eyes on his absurdly round butt. He looked around, smiled, and winked.

"Tickets, please."

The conductor was a mean-looking, surly son of a bitch, one of those to whom a uniform gives an excuse to be a bastard to everyone. When he saw my first-class ticket, his expression changed from generalized contempt to a sort of reluctant deference.

"Thank you," I snapped, taking the ticket back.

"I take it," said the porter—which was music to my ears, until he went on—"that you have a carriage reserved?"

"Indeed I do." I handed him the reservation.

"This way, sir! Let's get you comfortable."

"There's really no need," I said, as we reached the carriage door. "I think I can manage from here."

"No trouble, sir." He had thick eyebrows for a lad of his age, and they were traveling up toward the peak of his cap.

"All right." If he wanted a large tip, he was going to have to earn it. "Take it away."

He hefted my case onto his shoulder, held the carriage door open, and followed me up the steps.

"In the rack, sir?"

"Yes, if you can reach."

"Just about, sir." He raised himself up on tiptoe—he wasn't tall, only about five foot five—and managed to get the edge of the case into the steel luggage rack. His jacket rose way up his back, and I was able to appreciate the narrowness of his waist.

"Is that all, sir?" He stood at ease, smiling.

I glanced at my watch, and saw that we had a good quarter of an hour before the train was due to leave. "Actually, I've just remembered I need to get a couple of things out for the trip."

"Yes, sir?"

"So would you mind getting it down again?"

"Certainly, sir. Anything you say."

He reached up again and grabbed the handle of the suitcase, and then, in pulling it down, lost his balance. He would have fallen had I not place my hands on his hips.

"Oops."

"Thank you, sir."

I did not remove my hands. "Just put it down on the seat."

This necessitated that he lean forward, which of course pressed his ass into my crotch.

There were passengers and railway staff all around us, so any further intimacies were problematic.

"I think you'll have a very comfortable ride, sir," he said, turning to face me. "As you can see, there are blinds on all the windows."

"Ah, indeed. Perhaps you could show me how they work."

"With pleasure, sir."

He pulled down buff-colored shades over the external windows, and fastened them at the bottom with a shiny steel button.

"And what about these?" I gestured toward the windows that separated the carriage from the corridor.

"Like so, sir." Within seconds, he'd obscured the view.

"Very good. Now what else can you show me?"

He turned around and started unbuckling his belt, and soon I was getting a good view of two very handsome hemispheres.

"First class," I said.

He looked over his shoulder. "Want to fuck me, sir?"

"I'd like nothing better, boy." My cock was like an iron bar again. "But is it a good idea?"

"Sounds like a good idea to me."

"Isn't it a bit...public?"

As if on cue, a whistle blew just yards away. He stood up,

flushed in the face, and pulled up his pants. "Aye. I suppose so."

"Do you make a habit of seducing passengers like this, boy?"

"No, sir."

"Only the first-class ones, I suppose, who might pay well."

He looked crestfallen.

"I don't blame you. I'd happily pay five pounds to get my cock up your ass."

"You're American, aren't you, sir?"

"Yes, I am."

"Is it true what they say?"

"What might that be?" I'd heard a lot of folklore about Americans, not least the prevalent notion that we were all multimillionaires.

"That you have really big cocks."

This sounded so comic, in his Scottish accent, his face red, his eyes shining, that I had to bite the inside of my mouth to stop myself from laughing.

I grabbed his hand and placed it on my crotch. "Why don't you find out for yourself?"

His eyes grew even wider.

"I... I think it must be true."

"I guess it is."

The whistle blew again, and we heard footsteps outside the carriage. The door handle turned, and we sprang apart.

"There you are, Arthur." It was that mean conductor again. "There are passengers waiting to be attended to."

"He hasn't quite finished attending to me yet, thank you. Now, would you mind putting the case back up on the rack?"

"Yes, sir."

The conductor hung around in the doorway.

"Was there something?" I asked, in my most arrogant Yankee tone.

"No, sir." Oh, the emphasis on that last word! "Hurry up, Arthur." He walked away, scowling.

"Thank you, sir."

"Will I see you again, Arthur?"

"It's a long way to London."

"Here." I pulled out my wallet and gave him a ten-shilling note. "A little payment on account."

"Thank you, sir. That's very generous."

"Don't worry, Arthur. You'll earn every penny."

"What's your name, sir?"

"Mitchell. Edward Mitchell. But my friends call me Mitch."

He pocketed the bill and gave my cock a last squeeze. "Thanks, Mitch." He winked over his shoulder and was gone.

I took a book out of my case—I was greatly looking forward to reading Agatha Christie's latest novel, *The Big Four*, and had been saving it especially for the trip—hoisted the luggage aloft, and settled into my seat.

At ten o'clock sharp, the Flying Scotsman puffed and jolted its way out of Waverley Station in a great cloud of steam, and as I watched the hills of Edinburgh recede I reflected that this was my second view that morning of Arthur's Seat.

# II

READERS OF MY PREVIOUS ADVENTURES MAY RECALL THAT, after the completion of studies at Cambridge, I intended to return to my native Boston to pursue a career as a doctor. But plans change—and when an opportunity arose at the Edinburgh Royal Infirmary, I jumped at it. There were many reasons for this, the main one, of course, being Vincent West, to whom I was devoted and with whom I wanted to live, wherever it may be. We planned to move to America, where, I naively assumed, he would be able to walk into a good job—but, in fact, Uncle Sam was against us, and it would have been easier to get a camel through the eye of a needle than to get Vince through US immigration. When I made the mistake of losing my temper at the American embassy, the officials started asking all sorts of awkward questions about the nature of our friendship, and hinted that the police might be interested. We retired, hurt, and began to consider a future in the United Kingdom, where doctors were in short supply and I could earn enough to keep both of us in reasonable comfort. Vince got a good job in an Edinburgh publishing house, and we both loved our new Caledonian existence.

But there were other reasons why I was drawn to that rocky city, less romantic but no less real. For it was here in Edinburgh, around 50 years ago, that Arthur Conan Doyle had embarked on his medical and literary careers. Here he had trained at the University, and here he had published his first story. I saw Edinburgh entirely through Conan Doyle's eyes, scanning its narrow side streets for evidence of crime, hanging around the Castle eyeing what I thought might be suspicious types—and, of course, eyeing the soldiers, who came and went in noisy, bekilted groups. Both Vince and I developed a taste for these rough and ready Scottish lads, and we occasionally invited one of them back to our lodgings for supper. The fact that I was American, and a doctor, seemed to make it easy for them to engage in acts that they might have thought disgusting otherwise. The money didn't hurt, either.

The only crimes I stumbled across in Edinburgh were, alas, those committed by Vince and myself and our occasional guests in our apartment on Nicolson Street—and we made very sure that there were no snooping "detectives" around when we got down to those particular felonies. That aside, life rolled along without incident; I did well at the hospital, and Vince did well at the publishers, we made some good friends, enjoyed plays and concerts and long walks on weekends. It was an agreeable existence, illuminated by our deepening love for each other, and by our regular, inventive, and extremely athletic sex life.

But once a sleuth, always a sleuth—or so I told myself. My brush with crime in Drekeham Hall, and my brilliant (I thought) methods of discovering the villain, had given me an appetite for amateur detection that was far from satisfied. I slaked it on detective fiction, of which there was no shortage. I devoured every new Agatha Christie as it appeared, and had become completely obsessed by the personality and methods of her detective hero, Hercule Poirot, the fastidious Belgian with the superfluity of "little grey cells." I loved, also, Lord Peter Wimsey, the gorgeous aristocratic hero of Dorothy L. Sayers's novels—and I fantasized, while reading about his deeds, about how this blond athlete might take to a dark-haired, muscular, American assistant with specialized medical knowledge. We could do great things together...

My family kept me supplied with lurid crime magazines, the covers of which adorned our walls. Conan Doyle I still revered and reread, and found all sorts of erotic undertones in his novels and stories which I'm sure would have disgusted him, but which delighted me. Vince said that he half expected to find me masturbating over Sherlock Holmes novels, so intently did I read them—and, although I laughed it off, it was in fact true. I had frequently read between the lines so deeply that I would finger myself just as Holmes and Watson fingered the villain, shooting my load as the police shot their guns. Detection and erection did more than rhyme, in my book.

While my medical career was going according to plan— in another year I'd be fully qualified—my detective career had stalled. Without crime there could be no detection, and Edinburgh seemed to be a sort of crime-free Utopia. I suspected all sorts of villainy, and Vince often accused me, with good reason, of deliberately seeing the worst in people just to feed my own appetite for mystery. However, I have always believed that readiness and preparation are the key to success in life, so I kept my powers of observation and "deductive reasoning," as Holmes would have it, in good order.

To that end, I found myself studying my fellow passengers as they passed up and down the corridor outside my carriage, settling themselves in for the trip. There was the overdressed dowager type with her mousy traveling companion, bustling along like a glorious galleon with a dingy little dinghy in its wake. They looked respectable enough, but who knew the truth? The dowager could be a man in women's clothes—I'd encountered such things, both in life and in fiction—perhaps on the run from the police, or heading to London for some piece of skulduggery. Her companion, shabby as she looked, could be the daughter of an aristocratic family, kidnapped and drugged, brainwashed into a state of semiconscious slavery, a pawn in a daring ransom drama... They passed by, followed by my little porter friend, almost buried under a crazy burden of hatboxes and suitcases. I don't suppose they'd get to see Arthur's seat as I had, I thought, rubbing my crotch. How could I get him in a dark corner before we reached London? Perhaps the first-class lavatories would do... There would be room enough in there to bend him over and give him what he wanted, and of course there would be the great advantage of a lock on the door...

As usual, I had drifted from practicing my detective skills into some time-wasting sexual fantasy. I sat up straight, took my hands from my lap, and looked at the next passersby, a highly respectable family, led by an immaculately dressed young blond father in his gray suit and hat, followed by a meek, pretty mother in an over-fussy gown, and three young girls of diminishing sizes. The father looked angry, the wife near tears. A simple misunderstanding over the whereabouts of their seats, perhaps, or an argument over the trivia of childcare—or something more sinister? He appeared to be the very epitome of middle-class British manhood, with his pale skin and blond hair—but could he not, in fact, be a Bolshevik spy in disguise, accompanied by his equally dangerous whore and a group of homicidal midgets in knee socks and satin sashes? They had crossed the North Sea at night, beached the boat somewhere on the Firth of Forth, and were now heading to London, perhaps bent on assassination...

"Well, for God's sake, get her into a dry pair!" said the

father as he passed the door, his face like thunder.

"Yes, dear," said the wife, her voice trembling.

There was an unmistakable odor of infant urine as the youngest and smallest of the daughters passed by. Had she really wet her pants? Or was this just another example of their dastardly cunning?

Next came a group of three young men—this was much more to my taste than toddlers in damp pants—in animated discussion, carrying their own luggage toward the rear of the train. They were all dressed stylishly, one of them—the best-looking, with his black hair and dark, regular features—in an excellent tweed suit that must have cost a pretty penny. The other two, good-looking in a more obvious, less appealing way, were weighed down with cameras and briefcases. They looked like reporters to me; they had that sneaky, over-observant air about them. Were they trailing someone, hoping to uncover a scandal? Was their black-haired companion in fact a junior minister entrusted with secret documents of state? And were the reporters really reporters—or thieves? They looked slick, a little too slick, perhaps. Highly paid cat burglars, put on the train expressly to acquire the documents, disappearing before we reached Kings Cross?

"She's not so good-looking in real life," said one of them, the shorter of the two, a smooth-faced fellow with pale green eyes.

"I suppose the studio lights do a lot," said the handsome guy in tweed.

They passed by, one of them—the taller of the two "reporters"—casting a last look at me over his shoulder. Desire? Or something more sinister?

I got up and stepped into the corridor, partly to stretch my legs, partly to investigate the bathroom facilities. Those of us who look for adventure in public places do well to check the locks on doors, the dimensions of cubicles, the arrangements for washing. Also, I needed to piss.

The door was locked, the "Engaged" sign showing, so I waited, looking out the window at the still dark sky, wondering if those heavy gray clouds presaged rough weather or simply another gloomy winter day. Minutes passed. The door remained locked. Just my luck: someone was settling down for a good long dump. I wandered up to the dining car, which was already starting to fill with people requiring coffee. The steward, an immaculately dressed man somewhere in his sixties, laid out the crockery and silverware with exquisite precision. Each knife, each fork, placed just so; each plate, each cup, with the London and North Eastern Railway crest facing forward. He looked up at me, smiled, blushed, and patted the back of his neat white hair. A useful ally and confidant for later in the trip? Or an accomplished poisoner, even now plotting the death of a prominent passenger?

Now I really needed to get to the lavatory, and retraced my steps. It was still occupied, and I had raised my knuckles to rap discreetly on the door when I was stopped by a loud bang and the sound of a raised voice, hastily dropped, from within. Had someone beaten me to it, and got Arthur the porter in there for a quick fuck before we had even reached the border? I thought not; the voice sounded threatening, and there was nothing rhythmic about that single bang to suggest pleasant physical activity.

I knocked on the door. Total silence.

"I say," I began—I had picked up such Anglicisms from Vince, and found they worked well in such delicate situations—"are you going to be long in there?"

The lock rattled, and the "Engaged" sign slid around to "Vacant." The mean conductor slipped out of the compartment and pulled the door closed behind him.

"I beg your pardon, sir," he said, sneering and, I noticed, sweating slightly. "The lavatory is out of order. I suggest you use another."

I tried hard to see through the narrow gap between the door and the frame, but he pulled it shut.

"What's wrong?" I asked. "Perhaps I can fix it."

"No, sir. I'm about to lock this facility. Please go further down the train."

I smelled a rat. "I've paid for a first-class ticket," I said, now allowing my New World directness full range, "and I intend to have first-class service."

I heard another, softer, thump from inside the cubicle.

"There's someone in there, isn't there?"

"No, sir." He looked shifty now.

"What have you been doing?" I felt more kindly disposed to him now, assuming that he had been enjoying himself, either with a girl or a young man; with my track record, I could hardly judge him.

"Nothing."

"I am quite prepared to overlook your…indiscretion…if you will simply vacate the facility and allow me to use it."

"It's out of order," he said faintly, but he knew the battle was lost. I put my hand on the doorknob and turned it. Inside, cowering against the wall, was just what I had hoped to see—an attractive young man in a state of disarray. But his disarray was not one that suggested sexual activity. His collar was torn, as if from rough handling around the neck, and there was blood trickling from one nostril.

"Good God," I said, "what has been going on here?"

"I caught a stowaway, sir," said the conductor, grimly. He looked like a prison officer about to lead a condemned man to his cell. "We have to deal with this sort of scum every day."

The young man didn't look like scum, even though it was clear that he was not well off; his frayed cuffs and patched jacket suggested to me an impoverished student rather than a crook. He was short, not much over five foot four, and rather stocky, though far from fat. He had brown hair cut short over a high forehead, wide blue eyes, and freshly shaven cheeks, already turning slightly blue with stubble. He dabbed at the blood with a handkerchief.

"Are you all right, friend?" I asked.

"There's no point talking to him, sir," said the conductor. "He's some kind of foreigner."

"As am I," I said. "And I should have thought that, as a guest in your country, he deserves to be treated with some respect."

"He's traveling without a ticket."

"And do you regularly beat up people who appear to be traveling without a ticket?"

"It's my job."

The stowaway was looking from one of us to the other, trying to figure out if he was about to go from the frying pan to the fire. I thought it was time to reassure him.

"So," I said, slowly and clearly, as if speaking to an idiot, "you do not have a ticket?"

"*Non*. I 'ave lost 'im."

He spoke good enough English, though heavily accented. French, I guessed.

"That's what they all say, these stowaways," said the conductor, puffing out his chest. "Now, if you'll let me get on with my job, sir."

"No," I said, ignoring him and addressing the man. "You haven't lost your ticket. Didn't they tell you?" I reached into my jacket pocket and produced Vince's unused ticket. "I was holding it for you." The conductor—and, indeed, the young man—looked baffled.

"What is your name?"

"Bertrand Damseaux."

"That's precisely what it says here," I said, referring to a piece of paper that actually listed a few books I was hoping to get in London. "I was expecting to meet you at the station. Where were you?"

Both the conductor and the boy had figured out that some deception was taking place, but it was in neither's interest to expose me. The conductor, if he'd called me a liar, would have lost his job. And to the boy, I represented deliverance.

"Come along, Bertrand," I said. "Your carriage awaits."

"But—" said the conductor.

"First class," I said.

The boy came out, skirting the conductor as if he feared another blow, and followed me down the corridor. I ushered him into the compartment, closed the door behind us, and pulled down the blinds. I still needed to piss, but not so urgently that it would delay me from getting to the bottom of a potentially interesting story.

"*Alors*, Bertrand," I said, and quickly realized that I had exhausted most of my conversational French, as I had no immediate need to remark on the weather, order a beer, or borrow a pen from my aunt.

"Sir."

He stood, awkwardly fiddling with a loose button on his jacket.

"If you play with it, it'll drop off. Did your mother tell you nothing?"

He looked up at me through wet lashes, trying to figure out if he'd understood me correctly, and then broke into a huge smile.

"That's better," I said. "And I see that you understand English perfectly well."

"Yes, sir," he said. "My accent, it is very pronounced."

"But charming."

"*Merci*."

I held his look, and realized that my chance companion could help me pass the time very pleasantly. The ticket would not go to waste after all.

"Please, sit down."

He did as bidden.

"So, Bertrand," I said, sitting opposite him and leaning back, crossing my legs, "you were traveling without a ticket."

"Yes."

"You hadn't lost it, had you?"

"No."

"You were, in fact, hoping to get a free ride to London."

He blushed and looked down at his feet.

"Don't worry, kid. I've done the same myself, riding the buses in Boston. But that's a far cry from stowing away all the way to London."

"Yes, sir. I am ashamed."

"You didn't really think you'd get away with it, did you?"

"I did not know."

"That was very foolish. You must have a very good reason for going to London."

"Yes, sir."

"It's none of my business, of course."

"I am supposed to see my uncle."

"Ah. I see." I was relieved to hear that there was no talk of a sweetheart or wife.

"He was to have given me news of my father's will."

"Your father's... Oh. I see. I'm sorry."

"He has been ill for many years, sir. It is a relief for us all. And I hope also he has left me some money."

I was taken aback by this pragmatic approach to bereavement.

"You and your father were not...close?"

"No, sir. He detested me."

"Ah. How unfortunate." I could think of nothing more to say.

"Thank you, sir, for your assistance."

"You're most welcome."

"Now I will leave you in peace." He stood up.

"*Au contraire*, Bertrand," I said. "I'm traveling alone. I would appreciate your company between here and London." I uncrossed my legs and planted my feet a yard apart on the carriage floor. I could see his eyes flicking down toward my crotch.

"With pleasure, sir."

I half thought of getting him to show his gratitude with a quick blow job right then and there, but there was too much traffic in the corridor to make this possible. Well, his time would come.

"Now, sit down, make yourself comfortable, and let me go to the bathroom."

He did as he was told; I liked that.

"And don't run away."

"Of course not, sir. I am...*à votre service*."

"I'm delighted to hear it."

For a moment, I entertained the thought of inviting him to "serve" me in the bathroom, but I imagined he'd had enough rough treatment for one morning.

When I returned, he was sitting neatly, patiently, his jacket sleeves pulled down to conceal his shirt cuffs.

"I have been poor too, Bertrand," I lied. "There's nothing to be ashamed of. Your clothes may not be stylish, but you look good in them." And you'll look even better out of them, I thought, imagining his solid little body, wondering if his heavy beard growth was a reliable indicator of overall hirsuteness.

"Thank you, sir. It is true. I am poor."

"Tell me all about it." I settled back again, legs apart. I intended to become erect as he was talking to me, and I wanted him to see.

"I am Belgian," he began.

"No shit!"

"Sir?"

"You're Belgian! Like Hercule Poirot?"

"*Qui est-il, ce Poirot?*"

"The detective—the hero of Agatha Christie's novels."

He looked blank. "*Je ne le connais pas.*"

"Forgive me. Continue."

"My family lives in Waterloo, the scene of a famous battle."

"Indeed."

"And I am the youngest of three sons."

I resisted the temptation to ask if they were all as fuckable as he was, but the thought alone was increasing the bulge in my pants.

"I am sent to Scotland as an agent for my father's business of export–import, as it is I who have the better English from the others." That was debatable, I thought, but kept it to myself.

"And for many months now, no money is coming from Belgium to me, and now I am... I do not know how to say. *Fauché comme les blés.*"

"Flat broke."

"Flat broken," he essayed. "Yes. My pockets are empty."

I put one hand into my pants pocket and plumped up my basket. He noticed the gesture; he could hardly fail to.

"Now I hear from my uncle that father is died, and I must come to London to hear read the will."

"In the hope that there is some money for you?"

"*Bien sûr.* And to discover what is my future."

"I see." It was a sad enough tale, and I suspected that there was much more that he was not telling me. I had already painted his father as a cruel, coldhearted tyrant, his mother as a warm, passionate woman broken down by years of domestic bullying—poor Bertrand caught between the two, despised by a father who, perhaps, recognized that his youngest son would never carry on the family name...

"And you, sir?"

"Me?"

"For what do you go to London?"

"Ah. To see an old friend."

"Old?"

"I mean, he's young, but I have known him for a long time."

He was glancing down between my legs more frequently. "And he is your particular friend?"

"No." I thought the time had come for frankness. "I left my particular friend at home in Edinburgh."

"Ah."

"And you have his ticket."

"I see."

"And, perhaps, you can take his place in other ways."

"As I said, sir, I am very grateful to you."

"How grateful?"

Checking the window—the blinds were still down—he knelt between my legs and looked up at me.

"I see. You really are very grateful, aren't you?"

"Yes."

"Have you ever sucked a man's cock before, Bertrand?"

"I…" He blushed and cast his eyes down. I took him by the chin and made him look at me.

"Have you ever wrapped those pretty lips around a hard dick?" With my thumb I rubbed his mouth; he sucked on it, running his tongue in little circles around the sensitive pad. If he could do this to my thumb, then my cock was in for a first-class service. I gave him my index finger and then my middle finger, delighting in the way his mouth stretched to accommodate them. I could feel all around the inside of his face—his white teeth, his soft tongue and hard gums, the yielding lining of his cheeks. Grabbing hold of his lower teeth, I pulled him down into my crotch. He made no resistance, and was soon rubbing his face against the hardness that he encountered there.

"You're going to be a very good traveling companion, aren't you?"

He mumbled something incomprehensible, possibly in French, and started burying his nose in my pants.

This was going too far, too fast, I suddenly realized, as a breeze from the carriage window made the blinds billow, rendering us all too visible. Horny as I was, I was not suicidally stupid, and I knew all too well the penalties that attended the kind of activity we were about to engage in. Fortunately for us, there was no one around at that time, otherwise we might both have been met at Kings Cross by the police.

"We'll have to wait," I said, removing my fingers from Bertrand's warm, wet mouth. I wiped them on my handkerchief.

He got up, brushed down his pants—which were already worn at the knee, perhaps from similar attempts—and sat opposite me again, this time with a big smile on his face.

"When I see you, I hoped that you were like me. Another who loves men."

"Oh yes, Bertrand. I love men." And I've loved plenty, I felt like adding, but I did not wish to ruin what, to him, was a special moment.

"All my life I have waited for such a friend."

I really didn't need the complication of this young Belgian falling in love with me. I was more than happy to fuck his brains out, to watch that handsome, trusting face skewered on my dick, but I did not want to break his heart.

"You must know," I said, laying a hand on his knee, "that I am not free."

"Ah, for that," he said, with that typical Continental puff of dismissal, "I know I can not hope. But for the present, I hope we can be...*intime*."

"Yes, Bertrand, I hope very much to be *intime* with you."

I lowered my voice. "If there was a sleeper car on this train, I'd take you there right now."

"And what would you do there, sir?"

"I would fuck you."

"Yes," he said, shifting in his seat as if he could already feel my dick up his ass, "you would."

"And I hope, somehow, that I will." I was mentally calculating the chances of fucking Bertrand, and Arthur the porter, and perhaps that mean son of a bitch of a conductor, in the course of a one-way journey to London. I guessed that I could make it. My powers of recovery were still prodigious, and I was more than capable of getting hard and coming three times in 24 hours. Well, four, of course, if I counted Vince, whom I remembered with a guilty pang. Four times. Yes, I'd done it before. I could doubtless do it again. And there was something about a train trip, and the chance encounters that it threw in one's way, that made me feel like I could do more if necessary. And then, of course, there was Boy Morgan to attend to in London... Could I manage five?

Bertrand was staring raptly at me. "*Avant Londres...*" His mouth hung a little open, as he contemplated what was in store for him.

"Yes. There's a long way to go, yet."

Little did I know how long.

When we were both sitting decently, I raised the blinds; no point in arousing suspicion so early in the trip.

"You can start off by telling me exactly what happened in the toilet. What was that man doing to you?"

Bertrand rubbed his chin. " 'E 'it me."

"I guessed that. Anything else?"

"I am ashamed."

"You mean there were things of a different nature?"

"Yes. He is *un monstre.*"

"I have no doubt," I said, thinking of the conductor's high-handed treatment of me and the porter even before we left Waverley. Well, if I was looking for an adventure, there was a ready-made villain. A sadist in uniform, taking advantage of young, defenseless men, to whose rescue I seemed destined to come... Already I was hard again at the thought of my own nobility.

"When he come into the third-class carriage checking tickets, I run up here, and he follow me," Bertrand said. "I hide in the *toilette*, I lock the door, but he 'ave a special key. The door open, and he come in and find me."

"What were you doing?"

"I was pretending to have a shit, of course." The vulgarity sounded almost elegant in his accent. "I sit with my pants at my... What are these? *Mes chevilles?*"

"Your ankles." The things you'll be resting on my shoulders when I fuck you, I thought.

"*Bon*, my ahnkles."

"So he found you there, bare-assed, without a ticket."

"And he take advantage of me."

"I can't blame him."

"If it 'ad been you, sir, I would not 'ave minded."

"Please, don't call me sir. My name is Mitch."

"Ah, thank you. Meetch." He tried the name a couple of times, and seemed satisfied. "But from 'im, yeuch, *dégueulasse...*"

"He's not so bad-looking," I said, and it was true: the conductor was tall and well made, with a strong jawline and heavy, masculine features.

"*Non*, not so bad," said Bertrand, "but he is cruel. He call me names, he call my mother names, he insult my country—not even my country, but France, even though I try to explain—"

"There's no point in trying to explain geography to that type."

"*D'accord*. Then he become violent, he push me back so I am exposed." He blushed and looked down; I found the image of his nakedness under the cruel glare of the tyrannical conductor extremely arousing.

"Then what?"

"He get out his thing."

"His thing? You mean his cock?"

"*C'est ça.* I did not mean his *poinçonneuse.*"

"And he made you...touch it?"

"He waved it at me, calling me names, making it hard."

"Was it very big?" Some detective I was, already speculating about the dimensions of my villain's dick.

"Yes. It was big and very dark and angry. He take my hair and pull me toward it, and when I keep my mouth shut and will not suck him, then he hit me, *comme ça.*" He mimed a vicious backhand across the face. "It make me to bleed at the nose."

"But all you had to do was suck his dick and you'd have got a free ride to London."

"*Jamais*, for such as he."

"Was he so repellent to you?"

"I never will, for one that I do not first like well."

I felt somewhat chastened, as I had frequently obliged men whom I liked far from well, if they were not entirely repulsive to me. I thought it best not to tell Bertrand this just yet, as he seemed to be developing a slight case of hero worship.

"Of course not. That would be very wrong. But under other circumstances...?"

"For you, I give everything. *Ma bouche, mon cul.*"

I did not need a dictionary for this. Oh, for a sleeper car...

I was about to pull down the blinds again, when a bell rang in the corridor.

"Coffee! Fresh coffee!"

"Ah! *Enfin!*" said Bertrand. "Perhaps the coffee will be drinkable, no?"

"I wouldn't count on it."

"But it is necessary in any case. Shall we?" He stood up, and I could see that he was just as hard as I was. In standing and adjusting my pants and getting out of the carriage, I managed to ascertain it with a good squeeze.

"No, you go first," I said, as he held the door for me. "I want to know what I've got to look forward to."

He blushed again, but smiled, and preceded me to the dining car, deliberately stopping in his tracks so that I had no choice but to bump up against him.

# III

THE COFFEE WAS FAR FROM BAD, ALTHOUGH BERTRAND made all sorts of faces while forcing it down. I hoped he wasn't so fussy about swallowing other things. We were lucky to get a seat in the dining car—the smiling steward showed us to the last remaining table, thoroughly annoying the married couple with three children, who preceded us in the queue. He claimed, entirely falsely, that we had "made a reservation."

"You're very busy this morning," I said. "What's the special occasion?"

"Don't you know, sir?" He lowered his voice. "We have stars on board."

"Who's that?"

"Ah!" He gestured toward a lavishly set table at the front of the carriage, gleaming with crystal and silver, dazzling with white linen. "Wait and see!"

He busied himself with other passengers, occasionally looking over his shoulder to give us a wink and a twinkle.

"He is a nosey Parker," said Bertrand. He was obviously proud of his idiomatic English, and beamed at me.

I wanted to fuck him right there on the table, ruining the steward's pristine place setting. I pressed my leg against his, and enjoyed watching him blush.

"So," I said, "who do you think they are? These stars?"

He shrugged. "I have no idea."

"That would explain the newspapermen." I remembered the pair in the flashy suits. "I thought there was something going on." I thought nothing of the kind, actually, and had been entirely engrossed in imagining all sorts of nonsense about perfectly innocent passengers, while there was headline news under my very nose. "But why," I said, determined to sniff out a mystery, "are they eating in the public dining car, when doubtless they have their own private carriage?"

A voice, surprisingly close to my ear, answered.

"They wish to be seen."

I turned my head quickly, and caught a flash of steel-gray hair, a clear blue eye, the faint scent of citrus—soap, or cologne.

"Excuse me?"

"We're going to take some photographs of them having their lunch. I hope it won't inconvenience you too much."

He was a tall man, powerfully built, in a well-tailored navy-blue suit. His hair was neatly cut, his face clean-shaven and slightly tanned. He was, perhaps, 45 or 48—at least 20 years my senior—but he was in impressive shape, from his broad shoulders to his solid midriff and powerful thighs.

"Forgive me for eavesdropping," he said, his voice suggesting upper-middle-class south-of-England origins. "It's rather hard not to overhear conversations in such close quarters."

"That's quite all right."

He gave me a card; his hand was large, square, and brown, hairy on the back, his cuffs immaculate.

THE BRITISH-AMERICAN FILM COMPANY LIMITED
Wardour Street, London

## PETER DICKINSON
Publicity director

"Pleased to meet you, Mr. Dickinson." And I was pleased, already wondering if he could be persuaded to join me in the enjoyments I had planned. While I am, by instinct, more inclined to fuck than be fucked, I have a weakness for masculine older men, a type which Peter Dickinson epitomized. And to tell the truth, I was also somewhat excited by the fact that he was part of the movie world.

The steward brought more coffee, which we drank while Mr. Dickinson hovered around our table, being a little more attentive (to me, at least) than the occasion really demanded. Bertrand looked sulky; like most Europeans, I guessed, he thought that the movies were beneath him.

"Do you have any objection to being in photographs, Mr....?"

"Mitchell. Edward Mitchell."

"Mr. Mitchell. And your...friend?" He said the word as if he had only just decided not to say "servant."

"This is Bertrand. Say *bonjour*, Bertrand."

Bertrand managed to offer a hand and mumble, "Bertrand Damseaux."

"So, who do we have the pleasure of dining with today? Janet Gaynor? Ivor Novello?"

"You like Ivor Novello, Mr. Mitchell?"

Even Bertrand perked up at this point.

"You don't mean—"

"Sadly, no. Mr. Novello is not working with us at present."

"No," said Bertrand, "he is at this moment making a film of *The Vortex*, for Gainsborough Studios."

"Ah, Monsieur Damseaux is a film enthusiast, I see."

Bertrand made that characteristic shrug. "I like Novello."

"You have excellent taste," said Dickinson.

"Unlike this coffee," said Bertrand, grimacing.

"No, gentlemen, today I am looking after Miss Daisy Athenasy."

"Good grief," I said. "Daisy Athenasy? The star of *Dead Man's Kiss*?" Vince and I had seen the film in Edinburgh one wet Sunday afternoon, and I vaguely remembered a blonde actress with dark, bee-stung lips and a somewhat bovine expression, vamping and mugging her way through scenes of peril.

"The very same."

"An excellent film," I lied. I'd spent much of the screening with my fingers up Vince's ass, and my mouth on his neck.

"Well, her latest, which we're shooting now, is much better. It's a rollicking new version of the classic *Rob Roy*."

"Ah," said Bertrand, "with Hugo Taylor. *Bien*."

"You are very well informed, monsieur. Do you read the film magazines?"

"I glance at them," said Bertrand, looking rather pleased with himself.

Hugo Taylor! Everyone had heard of Hugo Taylor—at least, everyone in our circles. He was the darling of the West End stage, the life and soul of every theatrical party and gossip column, and, according to the rumors, one of us. Perhaps this was wishful thinking—he was exceptionally handsome, with his dark, Celtic looks, his laughing eyes, and his clean, athletic limbs. Vince and I had even cut his picture out of the paper, and speculated about how we would entertain him should he ever visit Edinburgh.

"Ah, you are a fan, Mr. Mitchell?"

"Well, I wouldn't describe myself as a fan. I mean, I'm a doctor."

"Indeed? A medical man? How reassuring. It's always good to know there's a doctor on board."

"Let us hope that I am not needed."

"Of course."

"But is Mr. Taylor...?"

"On the same train as us? He certainly is. That was what you were going to ask, wasn't it?"

"Yes."

"Mr. Taylor and Miss Athenasy will be here in a short while." Heads were turning all over the carriage. Dickinson lowered his voice. "Which accounts for the sudden popularity of LNER's catering, which, frankly, is not up to much."

"*C'est vrai,*" said Bertrand, still grimacing over his coffee.

"However, a picture is a picture, and it will be nice for the readers of the film magazines to see that stars take their meals just like ordinary folk. I shall seat them here." He gestured to the next table, already laid with crystal, silver, and china. "You will be visible behind them as they eat."

"But isn't it a little early for lunch? It's barely eleven."

"Ah," said Dickinson, tapping his nose, "that's the magic of the movies. They won't really be eating their lunch, I'm afraid. That was a step too far for Miss Athenasy. They will be served in their private carriage."

"Bah," said Bertrand. (He really did say "Bah," a noise I had never actually heard before.) "They are snobs."

"Perhaps, monsieur. But they also need some privacy. A rest from the glare of publicity."

"Publicity which you are paid to provide." Bertrand was spoiling for a fight; it amused me.

"Let us say, publicity which I am paid to control." Dickinson was smiling, tapping the tips of his fingers together. I suspected that he could eat boys like Bertrand for breakfast. "Speaking of which, you must excuse me, gentlemen. We have some unwanted guests."

The two flashily dressed young men had materialized in

the carriage, drawing attention to themselves by trying to look inconspicuous.

"Ah! So I was right," I said. "They are reporters."

"Correct," said Dickinson. "And they should not be on this train at all."

"It is a free country, I think, is it not?" said Bertrand.

"Yes, unfortunately for me. They are on the scent of a story that I do not wish them to report."

"I see. Concerning Miss Athenasy and Mr. Taylor?"

"Of course. The newspapers are determined to create scandal."

"How awful."

"And people will say that there's no smoke without fire."

"But surely," I said, "there is no fire between Daisy and Hugo?"

"Aah," said Dickinson, getting to his feet, "there we are straying into confidential realms. I must disturb you no longer. Thank you for your cooperation." He smiled, a dazzling display of perfect white teeth, and bowed slightly to us both.

"What a charming man," I said.

"I do not like him."

"Bertrand, it's a little early in our friendship to be jealous."

Bertrand looked flustered. "I did not mean that... Not only that, *en tout cas*."

"Don't worry." I leaned forward and whispered, "My cock is all yours."

"It is good."

"Damn right."

"But also, I do not like him because...because I do not like him. He has *un air suspect*."

"Oh come on. He's fine!"

"As you will. I do not trust him."

"Just because he's in the film business—"

"*Non*, not only this. Perhaps I am, as you say, jealous. But also there is instinct."

"Prejudice, you mean. You know nothing about him."

"And you know nothing about me, Mitch."

"I know enough. You are poor and you would like to be honest."

"Is that why you were so kind to me?"

"Not entirely," I said, gripping his leg. "It was also because I wanted to fuck you."

"This is well," he said, his face clearing. When Bertrand smiled, the world seemed like a better, kinder place. "Perhaps, after lunch?"

"I'd like nothing better than to get your sweet ass up on the table right here and now, and fuck you in full view of British-American's cameras."

"*Ah, mais les fourchettes! Les verres!*"

"It'll have to wait, then, till I can provide you with a more comfortable landing."

"It will be worth it, Mitch."

I was caressing his leg, which necessitated leaning over the table in an awkward position. We were disturbed by a discreet cough from the steward.

"Will you be taking luncheon, gentlemen? If so, I will reserve a table for you."

I sat up straight and muttered something about dropping my napkin.

"Our sole is very good, and I think you would like the spit-roasted chicken, if I may make a suggestion."

"You certainly can."

"And perhaps a glass of hock?"

"Ah, *non, pfff*," said Bertrand. "No German wine."

"Forgive me, sir."

"*Un bourgogne blanc, s'il vous plaît.*"

"Certainly, sir. Shall we say one o'clock? That should

give you time to…work up an appetite." The steward rolled his eyes and turned on the balls of his feet.

"I wonder what dishwater he will bring us?" said Bertrand.

"It must be a burden, having such a discerning palate."

"Sadly, my income does not match my tastes."

"Then happily, you are my guest. Nothing will give me greater pleasure than to treat you to a decent lunch and a good bottle of wine."

"Nothing?"

"Well…" I was about to resume my sub-table groping when I was distracted by an outbreak of chattering and shushing from the door of the carriage. Heads turned, eyes flickered, and comments were made behind hands.

Dickinson led the way, a camera slung around his neck. Behind him came a slim young man in an exquisite pearl-gray double-breasted suit, with a flower in his buttonhole and a rather loud necktie, his suspiciously long hair carefully waved and pomaded and—could it be?—somewhat unnaturally golden. He carried a clipboard and pen and appeared to be some sort of secretary. Next came what looked like a glittering cloud, all wisps and sparkles, which eventually revealed itself to be Miss Daisy Athenasy in a swansdown-trimmed gown and a mineful of diamonds. She walked like a racehorse, her haunches describing figure eights, and smiled benignly at all of us. She looked as if she had just been aroused from a deep sleep of exotic dreams, and was not yet fully awake.

She was followed by—oh, it was really him!—Hugo Taylor, immaculate in a charcoal lounge suit, a lavender tie, and a beautiful pearl tiepin. His black hair was carefully combed, but not so carefully as to make him look effeminate. His face was perfectly symmetrical, almost pretty, an impression that was mitigated by his famously athletic body. Taylor's trademark, both on stage and screen, was his regular use of gymnastic stunts—backflips, forward rolls, handstands, cartwheels—often without a shirt. The orchestra seats, during a Hugo Taylor show, were full of adoring fans of both sexes. Now he simply walked, but with such elegance and poise that I found myself sighing. Bertrand had stars in his eyes. We must have looked like a couple of schoolgirls. Taylor caught our gaze, smiled, and acknowledged us with a tilt of the head. I felt momentarily thrilled, before realizing that his every waking hour must be dogged by people such as me.

"For heaven's sake, Bertrand," I said, feeling slightly embarrassed. "Control yourself."

The steward showed the stars to their table, and, when they were seated, the rest of the passengers tried to look as if nothing out of the ordinary was happening, in that peculiarly British way. In America, conversations would have been struck up, autographs requested and given, life stories recounted at tedious length. But here, in the chilly north, a decent reserve was maintained. The stern-looking dowager snorted at her mousy traveling companion and continued to sip tea and nibble a biscuit. The young mother shushed her three daughters, who were staring, rapt, at Daisy, while their father scowled and stared out the window. Even the steward made a pretense of polishing the silverware, although I could tell from his high color and sparkling eyes that he was almost breathless with excitement. I imagined he too was a great admirer of Hugo Taylor.

The foppish young secretary fluttered around Miss Athenasy, arranging her gown, calming and pampering her like a pedigree cat. Dickinson whispered a word in Taylor's ear; Taylor nodded.

"Mr. Mitchell, Monsieur Damseaux," said Dickinson, "allow me to introduce you." We scrambled to our feet, as if under orders; the rest of the passengers fumed silently into their coffee cups. "Miss Daisy Athenasy." She smiled sleepily, extended a hand laden with sparkling stones; we both pressed the fingertips. "Mr. Hugo Taylor." Taylor stood, and gave us both manly handshakes. Was that a little extra warmth, a little extra pressure, that he communicated to me? What exactly had Dickinson whispered in his ear? Was there to be a private party, later, in Taylor's carriage? Taylor, Dickinson, Bertrand, and me...

I was aware of a presence behind me, and turned to see a huge hulking form in a black suit, the shirt collar way too tight around the bull neck, dark eyes under a beetling brow watching our every move.

"It's okay, Joseph," said Taylor. "I don't think they're going to murder us."

The gorilla grunted and took a seat beside—not at—the table.

"Joseph is a necessary evil, gentlemen," said Taylor, with a subtle smile on his face. "The studio believes that the world is full of lunatics just waiting for an opportunity to bump me off, or to abduct Miss Athenasy and do unspeakable things to her lily-white body."

"Oh Hugo, darling, really." Daisy drawled. "Your imagination disgusts me."

"As you can see, Miss Athenasy and I are the very best of friends."

"Now then, Hugo," interrupted Dickinson, who did not want this carefully orchestrated luncheon to turn into a public mudslinging match, "perhaps you would like to sit down?"

"Of course. I shall behave. Fear not, Mr.... What was your name again?"

"Dickinson. Peter Dickinson."

"I wish the studio would just give us one publicity manager," said Taylor. "It's very confusing for simple folk like actors to be learning new names all the time."

"I'm with you for the duration, Hugo."

"Good. Now let's get this show on the road, as they say."

Dickinson prepared his camera and signaled his readiness to shoot.

"Apologies for the interruption, ladies and gentlemen," said Taylor, addressing the carriage. "We shall simply take a few photographs and leave you in peace."

"Well, really," said the dowager. "I call that an impertinence."

Her companion, who had been watching Taylor with brimming eyes, the pupils like potholes, looked mortified.

Bertrand and I resumed our seats. Wine had materialized in our glasses—presumably to make it look more like luncheon—and we tasted it. It was a little early in the day for me, but I was grateful for the drink.

"*Pas trop mal*," said Bertrand, smacking his lips. Here was a boy almost indecently ready to be corrupted by the finer things in life.

Food was served to the stars, and they made a decent pretense of putting it onto forks and letting it hover around their mouths. They toasted each other (I noticed that Miss Athenasy, at least, was really drinking) and laughed and chatted. It looked convincing. They looked good, and Dickinson worked quickly and efficiently to capture the scene. The rest of the passengers had given up all pretense, and were openly staring—all except the dowager, who decided now was the time to start loudly dictating a letter to her companion.

There was a scuffle at the door. Joseph leaped to his feet and barged down the carriage.

"Bloody reporters," muttered Dickinson, darkly. I pitied the poor creatures, being manhandled by the Neanderthal Joseph; they were, after all, only trying to do their job. But I was so starstruck, and so taken with Peter Dickinson, that I said nothing. I wondered, vaguely, if Joseph would be part of the party... I rather liked the idea of watching him fuck Bertrand... The contrast in their height would be amusing... How many men was I planning to have? I was losing count...

The camera clicked and flashbulbs popped, silverware clinked and jingled, and all too soon this unreal meal was over. Daisy and Hugo left as they had arrived, in a haze of swansdown and diamonds. Taylor looked back over his shoulder and gave us all a cheery salute. The steward started clearing their plates; not a mouthful of food had been swallowed.

"No, darling," I heard the mother saying to one of her daughters, "just because Daisy Athenasy doesn't eat up like a good girl, that doesn't mean you can leave your greens."

Dickinson and Joseph accompanied the stars to their carriage; only the secretary remained.

"Well, they're settled now," he said, pulling up a chair. "May I, gentlemen?" He had an open, friendly face, the skin a little too smooth and shiny, the eyebrows possibly plucked—but there was a look in his eye that I could not mistake. Here was a fellow traveler, in more senses than one.

"*D'accord*." Bertrand seemed less hostile now, with a couple of glasses of wine inside him.

"So, gents, what did you make of my charges?"

"They seem very nice," I said.

"Nice?" the secretary spluttered, and wiped his mouth on my napkin, which he plucked from my lap. "No, I wouldn't describe Hugo and Daisy as nice."

"Well, she seemed a bit...tired."

"Yes. Miss Athenasy is frequently tired."

"Ah." I suspected some dark secret but was too tactful to ask an employee to spill the beans.

"She has a little help when she gets in front of the cameras. You know..." He mimed sniffing.

"You mean she dopes?"

48

"Please, Mr. Mitchell!"

I whispered, "Is that why she doesn't eat anything?"

"Among other reasons. Like all actresses, she is obsessed with her weight."

"She is already too thin," said Bertrand. "In Belgium, women have flesh on their bones."

"Not that it would interest you too much," I said, watching the secretary's face for a reaction. He cocked an eyebrow but made no comment. Bertrand blushed and looked at his hands.

"I'm sure she will eat in their private carriage," I said.

"Yes," said the secretary, "she will certainly be eating something. Or someone."

What was he trying to tell me? There was some scandal afoot, of that I was sure. Perhaps not a crime, as such, or a proper murder mystery, but at least something worthy of my powers of deductive reasoning.

I thought for a moment and then said, "Joseph?"

His eyebrows rose even further. "Are you a mind reader?"

"Me? No. Just a doctor."

"I see. The diagnostic mind. You'd make a very good..."

"Yes? What?"

He looked slightly flustered. "I was going to say detective."

"But how extraordinary! That is exactly what I want to be!"

"You? A detective? Why on earth?"

"Oh, I have a passion for crime fiction."

"Me too! Allow me to introduce myself." He pulled out a card—everyone on this train had cards—bearing a coat of arms and the name "Francis Laking, bart." I knew enough about English customs to realize that this was a minor aristocrat.

"Sir Francis." I held out my hand; he took it in a soft, limp grip. "Edward Mitchell."

"Oh, really! You can dispense with the sirs and madams.

It's Francis, if you insist, but everyone, I mean really every-one, calls me Frankie."

"And Frankie, you can call me Mitch."

"And who is this enchanting creature?" People were looking around, but Frankie didn't care; he seemed to love the attention.

"This is Bertrand Damseaux, my...traveling companion."

"*Enchanté.*" Frankie took Bertrand's hand, and would have kissed it had it not been snatched back. "Well, now, Mitch. As a budding detective, what do you make of our fellow passengers? Have you nosed out a mystery? Are they all they appear to be, do you imagine? Or are they traveling in disguise?"

This was a matter more suited to my taste than movie stars. "Quite possibly. Look at those two, for instance." I nodded toward the ample dowager and her cringing com-panion. "What do you think of them?"

Frankie glanced around. "That old trout? I'd say that's Two-Pistols Pete, the scourge of Whitechapel, on his way back from robbing a bank in Morningside. In drag."

"And he's accompanied by Finger Flynn the Gelignite King."

"*Ah, mon dieu...*" Bertrand looked disgusted.

"Brilliant disguises, I think we must agree," said Frankie, with a smirk. "They almost look like real women."

"Almost," I said, "but not quite."

"Yes. The moustache is a bit of a giveaway. And what of the young family? Relatives of the Tsar, perhaps, fleeing from persecution..."

"I feel certain that the children are highly trained midget assassins, dressed up like little girls," I said. "Any moment now they will leap over the table and murder that old queen of a steward."

"And this one?" asked Bertrand, nodding toward the door. It was the handsome young man with the black hair and the beautiful tweed suit, whom I'd remarked before in company with the two reporters. "If this was a crime novel, what would he be?"

"Ah, an interesting case," said Frankie. "I understand that he is a diamond merchant."

"No!"

"Apparently so. From South Africa."

"How do you know?"

"I heard him talking to those newspapermen."

"Me too... Wow, a diamond merchant. You should introduce him to Miss Athenasy," I said. "She'd clean him out!"

"I'm sure she'd love to," said Frankie, "but her husband is already kicking up a fuss about the amount she spends on jewelry."

"The poor man. He must have very deep pockets."

"Indeed he does. He owns the British-American Film Company."

"*D'accord*," said Bertrand. "Monsieur Herbert Waits."

"The very same," said Frankie. "I shall have to watch myself with you, monsieur. You know my employer's business better than she knows it herself."

"Monsieur Waits discovered Mademoiselle Athenasy in a music hall, *n'est-ce pas*?"

"Indeed he did. She was part of an acrobatic trio, the Tri-Angles. Very supple, our Miss Athenasy, or plain Daisy Dawkins as she was in those days."

"And he made her into a star."

"Yes, he did. She got him up the aisle so fast I don't think the old man knew what had hit him. And before you knew it, she was getting lead roles in British-American productions. Now, Miss Athenasy has many talents, I am sure, but acting is not among them."

"This is true," said Bertrand.

"Which means that, in order to stop the picturegoing public from staying away from her films in droves, we have to make her more interesting in other ways. You know, her clothes, her sporting activities, her love life."

"I see. And at present you and Mr. Dickinson are engineering a little romance between her and Hugo Taylor."

"Unlikely as it may seem, yes. The public will swallow it hook, line, and sinker, and they will trundle obediently along to see *Rob Roy*, however dreadful it is."

"And what role does Miss Athenasy take in *Rob Roy?*" I asked, racking my brain for a vampish blonde in Scott's novel.

"Diana Vernon, of course."

"Good lord," I said, remembering the bold, high-spirited heroine of the book. "She's not exactly as I pictured her."

"Well, a wig and a bit of rouge can work wonders."

"And Hugo Taylor is Rob Roy?"

"Naturally. It's very romantic."

"But in the book—"

"They don't get together. Of course they don't. But this isn't the book."

"It is a travesty," said Bertrand, helpfully.

"It is indeed, my fine French friend."

"*Belge*," said Bertrand, sulking again. He was going to have to be taught a lesson in manners.

"In any case," said Frankie cheerfully, "not many people actually read Walter Scott, thank God. I am quite ready to admit that I got no further than chapter three, and have never been so bored in my life. I prefer something with a bit of...action."

"Me too," I said.

"We understand each other, do we not? Now, in the film, for instance, there are lots of fights. Hugo Taylor leaps into action in a kilt and no shirt."

"Ah," breathed Bertrand.

"That interested you, *mon petit*. And there are some excellent gallops across the moors, which we filmed on location in the Trossachs, and a very splendid swordfight on the battlements of Edinburgh Castle, for which we have shot the exteriors. The rest will be completed in the studios when Mr. Taylor has settled into his next West End run. Which, as Monsieur Damseaux will tell us, is...?"

"A revival of *La Dame aux Camélias*, with Tallulah Bankhead."

"Correct! Would you like a job, monsieur?"

Even Bertrand looked interested now. "*Vraiment?*"

"Let us just say *peut-être* at this stage. We can discuss it in London. And now, gentlemen, you must excuse me. I must attend to my charge. A pleasure to make your acquaintance."

We shook hands. "Thank you for the inside information. And don't worry. We'll be discreet."

"Indeed. Keep an eye on the diamond merchant for me. I don't want him bankrupting British-American if at all possible." He beamed at us both and left.

"There!" I said. "Charming. And generous too. He offered you a job."

"That, we shall see."

"And I think he would like to fuck you, too."

"Also that, we shall see."

"Ever had two men at the same time, Bertrand? Up that neat little ass?"

"Oh, Mitch," he said, in a way that could easily have meant yes or no.

I was about to drag him back to the carriage and damn the consequences, when the diamond merchant sat down at a nearby table and we had leisure to observe him. The first thing I noticed, as he pulled a nice-looking gold cigarette case out of his jacket pocket, was a large diamond ring on his right hand. The stone was substantial, sunk discreetly into a plain gold band, but it signaled wealth far more effectively than the flashy settings favored by Miss Athenasy.

This was a rock of consequence, worn, I had no doubt, by a man of consequence. The young mother was staring open-mouthed. Her husband too was glaring at the handsome diamond merchant, watching him like a hawk.

"Hey, check out the ring!" I said.

"Hmm," said Bertrand, impressed. "*Ça, c'est un bijou.*"

"And he's not bad-looking."

"I find him very good."

"Oh, you do, do you?"

"I do."

"Better than me?"

"*Non, mais…* Better than your friend Dickinson, for example."

"I see."

The diamond merchant lit a cigarette—even his cigarettes had gold bands—and ordered a brandy. He looked out the window at the scenery flashing by, his eyes flickering, tired. It must be tough to be that wealthy, I thought. Perhaps I could help to take his mind off his troubles.

"Tell me, Mitch," said Bertrand, reading my thoughts, "is there anyone on this train that you do not want to fuck?"

"I'm not crazy about the dowager."

"Ah. Well, that is some relief. You are not altogether without discrimination."

"Come on, Bertrand. Let's get back to that carriage and pull down the blinds again."

"You will get me into trouble."

"You're already in trouble, boy. A little more won't hurt you. Much."

The excitement of the morning, the wine, the company, and the constant rhythmic bumping of the train had made me reckless, and I was quite prepared to risk discovery in order to get my rocks off with Bertrand, even if it was only in his mouth; it wouldn't take long, and would serve as an amusing hors d'oeuvre to lunch. But just as we were getting amorous in our carriage, with the blinds pulled down and our tongues in each other's mouths, there was a tap at the door.

Damn these railway personnel! I disengaged my mouth and shouted, "Go away!"

"It's me, Mr. Mitchell. Peter Dickinson."

Bertrand scowled and shook his head, but I was eager to admit him to the party. I adjusted my clothes, but didn't take too much trouble to hide the bulge in my pants.

"Come in, Peter."

He shut the door behind him and leaned his back against it. This would prevent any unwanted entry; why hadn't I thought of that? Bertrand could have been sucking me without fear of discovery.

"Gentlemen. I just wanted to thank you for your cooperation earlier." He was sizing us both up—our flushed faces, our bulging crotches. "I hope I am not interrupting."

"Nothing that you're not welcome to join in. Wouldn't you say, Bertrand?"

"If he wants." I think Bertrand was secretly excited at the idea of having two men, as I had earlier suggested. He was determined not to be friendly to Dickinson, but he would welcome his cock, I suspected.

"That's very good of you, Mr. Mitchell." He rubbed his groin.

"Mitch."

"Mitch. Come here, Mitch."

I stood in front of him. The train lurched a little, and our bodies were pressed together, hard cock to hard cock. I felt his chest, his stomach; they were firm and warm.

"What do you want to do, Mitch? You want me to fuck you? Or shall we both fuck your little friend?"

"Whatever you like."

"*Venez, monsieur*," he said to Bertrand. "Let's see what we've got."

Bertrand stood up.

"Turn around." There was mastery in his voice; he was obviously used to being obeyed.

"Now, show us your arsehole."

"*Quoi?*"

"*Ton cul. Ton trou.*"

"Ah!"

Bertrand unbuttoned his pants, lifted his shirt, and exposed a round, downy backside for our inspection.

"Very nice indeed," said Dickinson. "What do you think, Mitch?"

"A fine piece of ass."

"You said it. Now, Bertrand, how about sitting down on that seat and getting your legs in the air for me?"

Bertrand did as he was told—it was a bit of a struggle, as he was still encumbered by pants and underpants, which were bunched up over his shoes and socks. He put his hands behind his knees and pulled his legs up. His thighs were delightfully hairy.

"Now, Mitch, mind that door."

I leaned against the door, one hand rubbing my crotch. Bertrand was ready: his cock was hard, lying on a thick bed of soft dark fuzz.

"I could fuck him right here and now," said Dickinson, running his hand up and down the lengthening stiffness in his pants.

"Well? What are you waiting for?"

"In case you haven't noticed, gentlemen, we are slowing down."

I had noticed nothing of the sort. All I could think of was Dickinson's cock, Bertrand's ass, and my cock and ass in any of several delightful combinations.

"*Merde!*" said Bertrand, struggling to get up. "We are stopping. *Qu'est ce qui se passe?*"

"We have a few minutes." Dickinson spat into his hand,

slicked up his fingers and pushed them against Bertrand's asshole.

"We are not... Mmmf!... Scheduled to stop... Aaah!" Dickinson's finger was inside him, fucking him, wetting the black hair around the tight pink hole.

"There has been a slight change of schedule, I believe," said Dickinson, cupping my groin, squeezing my dick. "A minor engineering problem. I am assured we will not be long."

The train was slowing more.

Bertrand was uneasy. "But, monsieur, if someone were to come in... Oh! Ça!" Dickinson fingered him more vigorously. I noticed a drip of precum at the tip of Bertrand's cock.

"You can see how much he likes it."

"And now?" Dickinson moved his finger in further, and Bertrand closed his eyes. "I like a tight little arse," said Dickinson. "He's hot inside, Mitch. He's going to be a good fuck."

"I know it."

He continued fingering Bertrand, now introducing his index finger as well.

"Shall we make him come?" said Dickinson, with a leer.

"Do it."

I heard the squeal of the brakes and the hiss of the steam, voices and whistles from outside. Doors slammed, and there were footsteps in the corridor.

"Alas, gentlemen." Dickinson retrieved his fingers, leaving Bertrand's ass gaping at fresh air, "that will have to wait." He opened the door and stuck his head out. Bertrand struggled to pull his pants up. "Duty calls. I'm sure you will find some way to pass the time." He slipped out, closing the door softly behind him. Bertrand buttoned himself up; the poor boy looked physically ill.

"I was on the edge," he said. "One more push and I think I would have... Sploof!"

"Well, don't you dare sploof inside your pants. When you do it, I want to see it. And taste it."

"Oh, you..." he tutted, but from his shy little smile I could tell that he was relishing the prospect of coming for me.

The train had stopped completely. We lifted the blinds and saw the hustle and bustle of York station.

# IV

This was not according to schedule. The Flying Scotsman's nonstop service from Edinburgh to London had only recently been introduced, amid much ballyhoo, and was regarded as one of the wonders of the transportation world. Stopping at York—which the train had always done before—was a disappointment for all the passengers, not least for Bertrand, who was ready to take at least one hot, hard length up his tight hairy asshole.

The dowager passed by our window, looking like a disgusted camel.

"Really," we heard her say, "one sincerely hopes that they will offer a refund of some sort. See to it, Chivers."

"Yes, ma'am." The little companion, walking a pace behind her mistress, shot her a look of such sharp loathing I almost expected to see the glitter of a blade burying itself in the dowager's fox-fur wrap.

They were not the only ones to step down from the train, despite the best efforts of the conductor and the station staff to keep them contained. A little man in a uniform was running up and down the platform with a bullhorn. "Ladies and gentlemen, please stay on board the train— We will be departing shortly— Please, ladies and— Please— We shall—"

He was jostled by a press of people spilling from the carriages, all eager to stretch their legs and get a good look at each other. Our conductor, the one from whom I had rescued poor Bertrand, passed by the window with a grim expression on his face. He glanced in, saw us pressed against the glass, and turned away in disgust.

"*Cochon de merde*," muttered Bertrand.

"Come on, let's get some fresh air." I was, in truth, more interested in mixing with a group of kilted soldiers who had piled out of the third-class carriage at the end of the train.

"Fresh air! This obsession with fresh air!" Bertrand said, putting on his shabby overcoat.

"You couldn't wait to get your clothes off just now."

"Ah, but there was something to warm me," he said. "Now I am cold."

We stepped down onto the platform; there was still frost in the shadows, and our shoes crunched on the gravelly surface. I strolled toward the soldiers, four sturdy lads stamping their boots and blowing into their cupped hands. I knew very well that Scottish soldiers were a friendly bunch—some of our overnight guests had proved just how friendly they could be—so I was looking forward to a little flirtatious banter with these tall, thickset creatures with their long wool socks and bare, hairy knees.

Bertrand trotted after me, and as we passed them one of the soldiers made a protracted kissing sound, followed by low male laughter.

I stopped and turned. "Good morning, gentlemen." Bertrand walked on.

"Morning, sir." The ringleader was a handsome-looking brute, with a strong jawline and a broken nose. His cap was pushed far down his forehead; the back of his head was practically shaved. According to the stripes on his jacket, he was a sergeant.

"Nice to stretch the legs," I said. "Cigarette, anyone?" I offered my case. It was duly admired.

"That looks like silver."

"It is silver."

"You're American."

"And you're Scottish."

"What about your wee friend?"

"He's Belgian."

"I fought in Belgium," said the ringleader, "and I still bear the scars of that war." He lifted up his kilt and showed a deeply indented scar on his left thigh. I bent to inspect it.

"You're lucky to have kept the leg."

"Aye. Plenty didn't."

"Ever get any pain?"

"You a doctor?" he asked.

"Or just enjoying the view?" put in another, digging his pals in the ribs.

"Both, in fact."

"I get a twinge now and again," he said, dropping the skirt. I stood up, reluctantly. There had been a noticeable blast of heat from under his kilt, and I felt like warming my hands.

"Otherwise, you're in good health?"

"Aye, sir." He lit his cigarette from my lighter. "Rude health."

"I'm glad to hear it."

"Perhaps you'd like to examine me, doctor?" This came from one of the younger soldiers, a snub-nosed redhead.

"Why, soldier, what's wrong with you?"

"Well," he said, in a foolish, childish voice, "I keep getting these awful swellings down there."

The sergeant clipped him around the ear. "Don't be so fuckin' cheeky, boy. Sorry, sir."

"That's fine. I don't mind high spirits."

"Is that so? The lads do have very high spirits, don't you, lads?"

There was a general, throaty murmuring of "aye."

"And what are the four of you doing in London?" I asked him. "Duty, or pleasure?"

"Bit of both, sir. We're on guard duty at the Palace."

"Indeed. Then perhaps I shall come and look you up."

The sergeant leaned toward me; I smelled whiskey on his breath. "Or come to the carriage later, and look us up there."

He took a final drag on his cigarette and flicked the stub away with finger and thumb. It landed on the platform in a shower of sparks, hissing on a patch of frost.

Bertrand was beckoning furiously from the end of the platform.

"Goodbye, boys. Hope to see more of you later."

They laughed, waved, moved on. Perhaps, in a group like this, they would be unwilling to do more than talk dirty. But if I could single one of them out—the quiet, dark-haired one, perhaps, or the brute of a sergeant...

Bertrand was hopping from one foot to the other. "*Vas-y! Pour l'amour de dieu*, Mitch..."

"What is it? I was just talking to those—"

"Listen."

"What?"

"*Écoute!* In there!" He jerked his thumb toward the shed at the end of the platform.

"What is it?"

"Go! Hear!"

He grabbed my arm and walked me toward the shed. There was something, he was right—a rhythmic thumping, and what sounded like groaning. Was there an animal tethered in there—a station dog, perhaps—trying to get out? Or was it...

"It is the engineer, I think."

"The engineer?"

"And the... What is it you call him? *Le chauffeur.* He who makes the fire."

"The stoker."

"*Oui, c'est ça,* the stokkeur. They have gone in together."

"And now they're making these strange noises."

"*Bien sûr.* I think, perhaps..."

"You're not suggesting that they stopped the train at York just so they could nip into the shed for a fuck, are you?"

"Why not?"

"Are they good-looking?"

"The engineer is not bad. He is blond, with blue eyes. The stokkeur, he looks like a gypsy."

I was intrigued—but unfortunately neither of us was tall enough to see through the tiny, filthy window at the top of the shed door. I looked around for something to stand on—a bucket, perhaps—to no avail.

"Lift me up, Bertrand."

"Are you mad?"

"Then let me lift you."

"I do not wish to— Ah, hold on— No, stop!"

I grabbed his thighs and hoisted him in the air, burying my face in his crotch. He wobbled dangerously, then braced himself against the shed wall.

"*Oh, là,*" he said. "*Mais... Oh!*"

"What can you see?" I asked—rather indistinctly, as I had a mouthful of warm cloth.

"Well, really... *Oh, mon dieu...*"

I could make a good guess at what Bertrand was watching, as he started stiffening in his pants. I pressed my face into him. It's amazing what you can get away with on a crowded railway station platform in broad daylight.

"Let me down. *Assez.*"

He sprang to the ground and landed nimbly.

"Well? What did you see?"

Bertrand shrugged. "He was sucking him."

"Who? Who was sucking whom?" In recounting such things, mere pronouns are inadequate.

"*Le blond*. The engineer. He was on his knees, sucking the chauffeur."

"My God. Quick. Pick me up. I want to see—"

"Mitch—"

"I wanna see his cock—"

"Mitch, for God's sake—" Bertrand was clearing his throat.

"What's the matter? You've seen it. it's only fair that I—Oh. Right." It was the conductor, bearing down on us with a face like thunder.

"What are you doing, gentlemen?"

"Just getting a little light exercise, if it's any of your business, which I doubt," I replied. "We are traveling to London for a gymnastics competition."

He knew very well the kind of gymnastics we were practicing for, but he was in no position to comment.

"Please, could you get back on the train, sir? We are about to depart."

"It doesn't look like it." Nearly all the passengers were out on the platform—even Daisy Athenasy and Hugo Taylor, surrounded by people. The soldiers were sniffing around Miss Athenasy like dogs; Hugo Taylor was chatting with "my" sergeant.

"Come on, Bertrand. Let's go and talk to our friends."

"This is private railway property, sir."

"Private? Yes, we saw just how private it was. Come, Bertrand."

We left the conductor steaming, his back to the shed door.

Frankie was flitting around the stars, trying to keep the

soldiers' hands off Daisy's dress, trying at the same time to get a good look at their legs.

"Oh, chaps, thank God you're here! Give me a hand getting Daisy back on the train!"

"Is she…" I made a face, crossing my eyes and sticking out my tongue to suggest intoxication.

"Just a touch," said Frankie. "Come on, Daisy dear. Back on the nice warm train. You'll catch your death out here. Hugo, could you give me a— Oh, this is hopeless." Hugo Taylor had detached himself from the throng with the sergeant, and they were strolling up the platform, deep in conversation. How nice life must be for the rich and famous…

"Where the hell is Joseph?" growled Daisy Athenasy, tottering on her heels. "Joseph! I want Joseph!"

"Joseph is on the train, I'm sure." Frankie assured her. "And so is nice Mr. Dickinson. So shall we— Ups-a-daisy, Daisy! Honestly," he added, turning to me as Miss Athenasy staggered onto the carriage step, "I could murder that bloody Peter Dickinson. Never there when you want him, always there when you don't."

"Let me help." I took Daisy by the elbow and pushed her onto the train. She slipped, screamed, but managed to right herself. I wondered just how much of whatever-it-was she had taken.

"Will she be all right?"

"Oh, yes," said Frankie. "She's always like this. She only stayed sober for the photographs because I hid her stuff. She raised merry hell."

"Is she injecting?"

"Not if I can help it." He lowered his voice. "So far, she has restricted herself to sniffing. Not a very ladylike habit, in my opinion, especially when she falls asleep with a runny nose. Oh, the things I have to do in my job. Hello, looks like we're about to get going again."

"Look, Mitch!" Bertrand pointed to the engine, where

the engineer and the stoker were scuttling out of the shed and back on board. The engineer's face was smudged with black—perhaps from the stoker's pants, but perhaps just from soot...

"All aboard!" yelled the conductor. "All aboard!" yelled the station attendant with the bullhorn. Little Arthur, the porter, ran past me, his heels practically kicking his ass, and helped heave the dowager back into her carriage. I heard the words "disgrace" and "write to the chairman" before her voice was drowned, only just, by the engine's whistle. The soldiers were the last to board, leaping on as the train was moving off, their kilts flying in the air, giving me ample opportunity to admire their strong, hairy thighs... And we were off again.

It was just in time. The first puffs of steam only emphasized how black the sky was getting. Before we were even clear of York station, flakes of snow were beginning to whirl and flurry outside the windows.

Bertrand wanted to go back to our compartment, presumably to pick up where we had left off—inspired, perhaps, by what he had seen through the shed window. I was inclined to humor him, especially if he was in the mood to suck cock, but I was distracted by several things. First, there was absolutely no apparent reason why the train had stopped at York; no explanation had been given, there had been no sign of mechanics working on the train or the track, and it seemed improbable that we had only been delayed so that the engineer could suck his stoker's dick. Second, I was puzzled by the behavior of the stars, out on the platform without their publicist or their burly bodyguard, Joseph, attended only by Frankie, who would not be much use in the event of an attack. Third, where were the newspapermen? Surely they would have taken advantage of such a God-given opportunity to accost Hugo and Daisy with their impertinent questions. And yet, I had not seen them. Were

Dickinson and Joseph dealing with them in some sinister way, while the rest of the passengers were distracted? Had the engineer and the stoker vacated the engine just so that Dickinson and Joseph could feed their victims' bodies to the flames? It seemed highly unlikely, but I did find myself sniffing the air for the telltale aroma of roasting flesh.

No, the air was clean—shit! Not clean enough. I pulled my head back into the carriage with a big flake of soot in my eye. It hurt like hell.

"Oh, fuck!"

"Here." Bertrand pulled out a handkerchief. "Put your head back. *Comme ça.*" He wiped the soot from my eye, which was streaming.

"There's something in it! God, it hurts!"

"Look up... Look down... *Voilà.* Just...one...moment..." He dabbed at my eye with a corner of the handkerchief, and removed a large piece of dirty grit. The delicate operation had brought us into close quarters; his hand was on the back of my head, and he was practically sitting on my knee.

"Ah. Thank you. That's better."

He did not move. "Mitch. When can we..."

"You horny little bastard."

"I want you so badly. Inside me. Look." He nodded down to the front of his pants, where there was an obvious swelling. "Please."

"But I want to see what's going on—"

"It won't take long. Just fuck me."

This was too much to resist, so, once more, we headed toward the bathroom. And once again the door was locked.

"*Putain!*"

"You must be patient." I pressed myself against him. "It's worth waiting for." I could feel his ass pushing back against me; his eagerness was making me hot as hell. I kissed the back of his neck, his ear.

"*Vite! On arrive!*"

There was a rattling and thumping from within the bathroom. We disengaged ourselves, and Bertrand hurried back to the compartment. The toilet door opened a crack, and I saw the diamond merchant's handsome profile emerge—and then withdraw, as if he was checking the lay of the land. This intrigued me, and I concealed myself inside an empty carriage.

The door opened again, and the diamond merchant stepped out—followed by the young father from the dining car. They muttered something to each other and walked away in opposite directions.

I stepped out of my hiding place, feigning complete surprise when I collided with the diamond merchant.

"Oh! I'm so sorry."

He practically jumped out of his skin. "Jesus!"

"I said I'm sorry. I didn't mean to alarm you."

He calmed down immediately. "That's quite all right. You just... I was... I apologize."

What had been going on in that bathroom? Was the diamond dealer in fact a diamond smuggler? It was too much to hope that, as Bertrand had mockingly said, every single man on the Flying Scotsman was queer—and besides, the young father was married. But then again, as Vince frequently said, so was Oscar Wilde. No, it was a transaction of a different sort that had been going on, surely. I remembered how the young father had glowered at the diamond merchant in the dining car. Obviously they had arranged to meet on the train, and they were trying to maintain a discreet distance in order to avoid suspicion. Now, despite their plans, I had caught them in the act. Not the act I would like to have caught them in—the contrast between the diamond merchant's dark hair and the young father's blond coloring was enough to get me interested—but something that appealed to my appetite for mystery and detection. Where there were diamonds involved, there was almost bound to be trouble.

"Very unusual to stop at York, isn't it?" I said. I wasn't going to let him go just yet, and played the part of the garrulous American traveler.

"Yes, very unusual. I suppose there was some problem on the line." I tried to place his accent; it was definitely English, but there was a slight twang in there. South African, as Frankie had suggested? I knew the diamond business was big there. Or Australian? Definitely not American, nor Scottish, but there my certainty stopped.

"Looks like we're coming in for some heavy weather," I said. This was an understatement; the light was failing fast, and sleet was rattling against the windows.

"Yes. I hope it doesn't mean delays…" He scowled, his dark eyebrows joining in the middle.

"You got an appointment to keep in London?"

"What? Oh, yes, of course."

"And what line of business might you be in, if you don't mind me asking?" This was the sort of question an Englishman would never ask, at least not on such casual acquaintance, but we Americans were, it seemed, a byword for impertinence.

"Oh… International trade. Buying and selling. Import-export." I suppose one doesn't just say "I'm a diamond dealer" to a complete stranger.

"That's a mighty fine ring you're wearing, if I may say so." He was gripping the handrail by the window, his knuckles white, his large hand bunching into a fist. Despite his manners, it was easy to see that he was eager to get away from me. The ring—that thick gold band with the single, deep-set sparkler—looked like a brass knuckle.

"Thank you." He quickly moved his hand, stuck it in his pocket.

"An engagement ring?"

"What?" He was starting to sound annoyed. "No. Nothing of the sort."

"I'm glad to hear it."

"Are you?" he replied. "Well. If you will excuse me, Mr....er..."

I extended a hand. "Mitchell. Dr. Edward Mitchell, of Boston and Edinburgh, at your service."

"A medical doctor?"

"Yes, sir."

We shook. The thick gold band dug into my fingers.

"And you are...?"

"Rhys. David Rhys." He seemed less unfriendly now that he knew I was a medical man.

"Rhys. That would be... No, don't tell me. Oh, darn it. Is it—"

"Welsh. It's Welsh. I'm Welsh."

"Of course. I've been trying to place the accent."

He smiled for the first time; the corners of his eyes creased up, and he flashed his teeth. "Is it that obvious? I've not lived there for a long time."

"It's very pleasant," I assured him. "And I suppose that explains your dark coloring as well."

"Yes. I'm what they call a Celt. Pale skin, dark hair. You could have Celtic blood as well, Dr. Mitchell."

"Me? I don't know. My people were English, as far as I know. And I tan like a Negro in the summer, when I'm outdoors, swimming and riding and playing tennis."

"Although not so much in Scotland, I assume."

"Not as much as I would like."

We were getting on well, I thought, but he suddenly seemed to recall something, and resumed his frosty manner.

"I must leave you in peace, Dr. Mitchell."

"Not on my account. It's a pleasure to—"

"Good morning."

He turned his back and stalked down the corridor. A

footstep behind me betrayed the approach of Peter Dickinson. Had Rhys been running away from him?

"Ah, Mitch," said Dickinson. "How is poor Bertrand? Have you been able to take care of him yet?"

"No."

"I wouldn't leave it too long. Such conditions can worsen rapidly. Although, as a doctor, you would understand that, I'm sure."

"Indeed."

He lowered his voice and spoke close to my ear; again, that intoxicating smell of citrus cologne and warm male flesh tickled my nostrils. "And I might add in this case: physician, heal thyself. We don't want you to be...uncomfortable, do we?"

"I might need a hand. It can be a tricky procedure—"

"It's not a hand that you need, Mitch." He cupped his groin. "It's this."

"Yeah..."

"All yours..." He took my hand and drew it down. His crotch was warm—almost hot. I could feel a big pair of balls and a large, semihard dick. I squeezed gently.

"How about now?" I nodded toward the vacant toilet. "I can get Bertrand as well if you want."

"Two for the price of one? I'm tempted, Mitch. As you can probably tell." I'd brought him to full erection by now. "But, sadly, I am needed elsewhere."

"Daisy?"

"Daisy, Hugo, the full traveling freak show."

"Sounds like fun."

He rolled his eyes; I didn't stop feeling him up. "Oh, you have no idea."

"Did you deal with those reporters?"

He closed his eyes. "Oh, shit, that feels good. I'm going to come in my pants if you carry on like that."

"Go right ahead."

"Be a terrible shame to waste it, wouldn't it? I'd rather squirt it in your mouth, or up your little friend's arse."

"That can be easily arranged." My mouth was watering, and I was hungry for a taste of Dickinson. "Come on. It won't take long."

"Patience, Mr. Mitchell. I want more than a furtive suck in a train toilet. You're worth more than that."

The sound of whistling approached down the corridor. "Now," said Dickinson, making his cock throb in my hand, "if it was this little piece, I might consider it."

Arthur, the porter, bounced into view, carrying a tray with a white cloth over it. I relinquished my grip on Dickinson's crotch.

"Gentlemen!" said Arthur. "If you will excuse me."

"Is that going to Miss Athenasy and Mr. Taylor's carriage, lad?"

"Yes, Mr. Dickinson, sir."

"Just one moment."

Dickinson lifted the cloth. A delicious smell wafted out— of steak, and fried potatoes and mushrooms. If my mouth had not already been watering at the thought of Dickinson's hefty cock, that would have done the job.

"Is it satisfactory, sir?"

"Perfectly, Arthur. Come and see me later for a tip."

"Thank you, sir."

Obviously I was not the only passenger from whom Arthur was expecting to make a profit. Dickinson replaced the cloth, and patted Arthur on the ass. "Good lad."

"Oh, sir."

"Off you go."

Arthur squeezed his way between us, and hurried down the corridor, leaving a savory waft in his wake.

"There are some very tidy pieces of arse on this train, Mitch. Your little Bertrand, and my little Arthur..."

I had hoped he would be "my" little Arthur, but it seemed

churlish to argue the point. Perhaps, at some point, we could trade. Now there was an idea.

"Better make sure that all is well with my charges. See you later, Mitch, I have no doubt."

He smiled and followed Arthur to the private carriage.

"Hsssssssst!"

Was it the brakes, or the wind?

"Hsssssssst!"

No, it was Bertrand, peeking out from our compartment, sounding—insofar as a hiss can convey meaning—extremely unhappy. I joined him.

"I see you, manipulating him."

"Oh. Watching, were you?"

"I do not like that man, I tell you."

"Bet you didn't mind watching me feeling his cock, though? Eh?"

"Bah... You are too...too much..."

"I bet it turned you on, Bertrand. Let me see." I grabbed him; he too was hard in his pants, although nowhere near as large as Dickinson. "As I suspected. You're as bad as I am, my friend."

"It is not fair, Mitch. I want you."

"And you will have me."

"But when?"

It was a good question. Every time I tried to make out with Bertrand, we were interrupted. I was not used to forces conspiring against me in this way. Normally, I see an opportunity, and I take it. I do not like to defer gratification. It makes me irritable.

"Okay. Now."

"*Enfin*. And where?"

"The bathroom."

"Oh, that bathroom... *C'est toujours occupé*. I prefer here."

"And I prefer not to be caught in the act and locked up

in Pentonville Prison, thank you very much."

"These English laws... *Barbares*..."

"That may be, but unless you have time to lobby Parliament for a very rapid piece of legislation, I'm afraid you're going to have to accompany me to the bathroom. If you want this, that is." I grabbed his hand and brought it to my fly.

"Yes," said Bertrand, ever the pragmatist. "This I want very much."

"So come on."

This time, thank God, the bathroom was free, and we locked ourselves in. The wind was howling outside, and it was practically dark; snow and sleet rattled on the windows. But we did not care about the weather. The moment the door was locked, I pulled Bertrand toward me, leaned down, and kissed him on the mouth. His lips parted, and my tongue forged ahead.

After so long a delay, I was ready to devour Bertrand. My lust was so extreme that I could barely contain myself: I wanted to fuck his mouth, fuck his ass, kiss him, lick him, and bite him all at the same time. I wanted two dicks, two mouths, and at least three pairs of hands for all that I had in mind. But when I opened my eyes and saw him staring up at me with what can only be described as devotion, I tempered my fury. The door was locked; we had a little time. If anyone else wanted to get in, that was their bad luck. They could piss second class, for once.

We continued to kiss, tasting the coffee and the wine that we had recently drunk, tasting each other. I cupped the back of Bertrand's head with my hand, rubbing his short brown hair, massaging the tendons in his neck. With my other hand, I squeezed his buttocks; they were firm and full, just how I like them. I remembered how hairy he was down there, how his ass lips sucked on Dickinson's finger, and thought how good my dick would look in the same place.

I broke the kiss.

"I want to fuck you, Bertrand."

His mouth hung open, wet with spit. His face was so trusting, so open, it almost seemed a shame to be using him in this way. Were it not for the fact that he clearly wanted my dick inside him as much as I wanted to put it there, I might have hesitated. Might.

"First, I will suck you." I'm not sure whether this direct statement was just the European way, or if his English was inadequate to express anything more complicated, but in any case he dropped to his knees and started unbuttoning my fly. I helped him by unbuckling my belt and pulling out my shirttail. I was as hard as could be inside my underpants; the fabric was stretched to its full extent. As soon as the bulge was exposed, Bertrand pressed his face into it, rubbing it all over his cheeks, running up and down the length of my cock with his lips. I put both hands on his head, caressing him, pulling him into me.

It was not long before the cotton barrier was too much for him, and he broke away, looking up to me to make the next move. I pulled my pants and underpants down, and my cock sprang free. After such a long and unwelcome confinement, it seemed to jump for joy.

"Oh, Mitch..."

"There it is, Bertie. All yours."

"It's so big..."

I never tire of being told that my dick is big; what man would? In truth, it is not a real monster, and there was at least one bigger on this train—Dickinson's. But it was big enough, bigger than Bertrand's, for instance, and to his eyes, and from that angle, it must have looked enormous.

"Can you take it?"

He said nothing, but smothered my cock in kisses, up and down the shaft, over the head, underneath and down to the balls. He squeezed it, weighed it in his hands, measured the girth with his fingers. He was clearly delighted with me, and I with him.

"Now open your mouth and suck me. I want to see your lips stretched around it."

He didn't need to be asked twice. His pretty mouth opened, and his pink tongue protruded a little, as a kind of welcome mat. I let the head of my cock rest on that warm, wet platform for a moment, and then moved forward. His lips closed around me and I was in.

Oh, his mouth felt good! Like plunging into a cool pool on a hot day, or a warm bath on a cold day. It felt like coming home tired from work, like a pint of beer after a long trip, like a feather bed after a night out. My dick got harder, thicker, and his lips opened in a larger O around me. I rubbed his ears and pulled him further down. He gagged a little—I let him come up for breath—but then, like the cocksucker he clearly was, he went straight down again.

My head was starting to spin, and I wanted more, more, more. I stuck a foot into Bertrand's crotch and started roughly pushing at his cock; he got the message, and undressed himself in that quarter. I could see his thick, stubby little dick jutting straight out from a thick bush of hair, and I wanted to feel it too. Fortunately, this being a first-class facility, there was a sizable marble surface around the washbasin, large enough for a man of Bertrand's dimensions to lie on, if not fully stretched out.

"Get up."

He got to his feet, reluctantly.

"Strip."

He took off his jacket, and I pulled the shirt over his head. His torso was stocky, sturdy, a little fleshy, but not unpleasantly so. From his chest downward, he was hairy.

"Jump up here." I patted the marble surround.

"Oof! It is cold!" He sat, naked except for his shoes and socks, his pants and underpants bunched around his ankles, and we kissed again. I grabbed his cock, which was even harder than mine, and started gently jerking him.

"Ohhhh…" he sighed. "That is good."

"Now suck me again."

I positioned myself against the wall, so he could recline awkwardly and get his head down to cock level. Soon I was fucking his mouth, but now I was able to caress his hairy body and play with his hard cock and tight little balls. It would not take much to make him come, and I enjoyed keeping him on the threshold, withholding release.

I spat on a finger, and worked my way around to his ass; he obligingly crooked his upper leg to give me greater access. His hole yielded easily, and he felt just as warm and welcoming at that end as he did around my cock.

"I must fuck you, Bertrand. I need to get my cock in your ass."

"Mmmmfff…" However much he wanted it as well, he was reluctant to relinquish what was in his mouth. I half thought of coming down his throat, fingering and jerking him off at the same time… But who knew if I would get another chance to get up his ass? I would never forgive myself if I passed up what could be my only opportunity to fuck him.

I pulled him up. His face was red, and wet from saliva, sweat, and my precum. Both of us were close. I had to fuck him fast.

I lifted him down, kissing him again as I did so, and pushed him into a kneeling position, his elbows resting on the toilet lid. In this way, there was just room for me behind him. I slicked up my cock, and positioned the sticky head between his cheeks.

"Have you been fucked before, Bertrand?"

"Please… Do it to me."

"Have you?"

"It doesn't matter."

I realized he had not.

"It will hurt. I don't have anything to make it hurt less." There was hair cream in my luggage, and a jar of Vaseline, of course—but I was not prepared to risk my chances by going to get them. I thought of using soap, of which there was a pretty fragranced bar by the sink, but did not want to sting the delicate interior of his rectum.

"I don't mind. I want you."

"Okay. Just try to breathe deeply…"

I spat copiously into my hand, slathering the thick saliva over my hard penis until it glistened. I spat again and worked it around the opening of his ass. Was it my imagination, or was he drawing my fingers inside him? He was ready. I was going to hurt him, but I hoped he would soon think it was worth the pain.

"Mitch…"

I pressed forward, so the tip of my cock was inside him. God, he felt so hot!

"Yes, Bertrand?"

"Mitch, I… Oh, *mon dieu…*"

I pushed in further, and the whole head disappeared into his hairy pink hole.

"I… Oh… Oh! Mitch… I…"

I pushed gently but firmly, and another inch slid inside.

"Is it good? Does it hurt?"

"It hurts, but it is good. Oh Mitch, I have to tell you… I…"

"What, Bertrand?" I gave him another inch, and another; he was whimpering now.

"I… I…"

I pressed in further, all the way to the base. He had every inch of me. He was entirely mine, and I entirely his. His face, pressed against the lid of the toilet seat, was dark red, working with emotion.

"Mitch… I love you…"

The words were hardly out of his mouth when the train gave a violent lurch, throwing me forward, and farther, harder, up Bertrand's ass. He yelped, but stifled the cry with his fist. I had hurt him a lot, I think, but he was determined to take it.

And then there was another shuddering lurch, and the screaming squeal of brakes, a violent hiss of steam, and the train came to a sudden stop, and all the lights went out.

It was totally, utterly dark. Pitch black. From outside the window, not a ray of light penetrated the carriage. I saw nothing, only heard my breathing and Bertrand's stifled moans, smelled his hot body and the scent of my own rut mingled with the floral bouquet of the soap.

We had stopped, and it seemed the outside world had stopped as well.

But it was too late. Not everything could stop. I kept pumping Bertrand's ass, my orgasm finally claiming its release. I fucked him hard and rough in the dark—I made him shout out, whether in pain or pleasure I was not sure, and I pumped a heavy load inside him. Gripping his cock, I jerked him in time with my last few thrusts, and felt hot jets squirting out of him.

And then we lay, panting, in the utter darkness, going nowhere.

# V

We struggled to our feet and got dressed in the dark, cleaning ourselves as best we could with toilet paper. I had come inside Bertrand, so I wiped his ass and shoved some tissue inside his underpants to soak up any leakage, but he had shot all over the place. For a small man, he produced a large load. It was impossible to see where it had gone, but every time I touched him or his pants my hand seemed to encounter yet another sticky glob.

"What happened?" His voice trembled, possibly through fear of the dark, possibly because he had just been fucked so hard that his legs were shaking.

"I don't know. But I think we must be in a tunnel." It was impossible to be sure; the window was heavily frosted, so I could not see if there were walls around us.

"*Viens*. We must get out of here. It is too…ooooffff… claustrophobic."

I slid back the bolt and pushed the door; it did not move. I tried again, harder; it yielded maybe a quarter of an inch, but no further. We were trapped.

"I think there's been an accident, Bertrand." I put my hands on his shoulders, felt him shudder. "You must be calm."

"I detest the dark...and closed spaces..."

"You'll be fine. You're with me." I kissed him on the mouth, holding him until the trembling stopped.

"*Bien.* Now I am a man again."

The door would not budge. I imagined all sorts of horrors: a collision in the tunnel, the carriage mangled, wreckage outside the door trapping us inside. It was difficult to gauge how hard the impact had been; we had been fucking so vigorously that we'd probably have ignored an earthquake.

I pressed my ear to the door and listened. There was no sound at all. No creaking and groaning of twisted metalwork, no obvious sounds of fire. No moaning or crying of other passengers. Either they were all dead, or they were all right.

I heard running footsteps approaching, and I called out, "Hey! Hello! There are people trapped in here." The footsteps came to a halt, and I banged on the door. "Hey! In here! Can you help us?" Still the door would not yield—and the footsteps proceeded, quieter this time, not running, betrayed only by the softest of thuds.

"What the fuck is going on?" I said.

"I don't know... It is like a nightmare." Bertrand sounded bad again.

I fumbled for my lighter and flicked it on. In the wavering light of the flame, I saw his ashen face and wet eyes. His mouth, where I had kissed and fucked it, was red. He relaxed a little in the light.

"We're going to be okay, Bertrand. Don't go crazy. Everything is fine."

"*J'ai peur...* I'm sorry, it is ridiculous. I am an adult. I should not be afraid of the dark, like a child in the nursery. I am ashamed of myself."

I kissed him again. "Don't be. You can't help it." The strangeness of the situation, and Bertrand's extreme vulnerability, were making me hard again. "Why don't you just close your eyes and suck me for a while. Forget everything else."

"May I?"

"You may." I extinguished the lighter, which was starting to burn my fingers, and unbuttoned myself, guiding Bertrand's hand to my cock. He caressed me and sank gratefully to his knees, burying his face in my groin. Thus occupied, he was quiet and comforted. In truth, I found this distraction a comfort as well. There was something eerie about the silence, the darkness, and those inexplicable footsteps...

Bertrand sucked very well. Very enthusiastically. Perhaps he thought we were about to die, and wanted to go with a dick down his throat...

There was a bang on the door.

"Is there anyone in there?" A man's voice.

"Yes. I'm okay," I replied.

"Are you hurt?"

"No..."

"I thought I heard someone groaning."

Shit: I had been so transported by the darkness, the silence, and the intensity of Bertrand's sucking that I had forgotten to silence myself.

"I'm trapped. The door won't open."

"Hang on."

The door handle rattled and turned—and the door swung open. The light of a candle dazzled my eyes—and behind it, the face of the mean conductor, the one who had abused Bertrand before.

Bertrand—who was down on his knees, his face still buried in my groin, my cock hitting the back of his throat. The conductor took everything in at a glance, looked around him, and stepped into the lavatory. He placed the candlestick by the sink.

I pulled out of Bertrand's mouth; he looked around, dazed.

There was not much room with three men in a bathroom designed for single occupancy, and as Bertrand struggled to his feet we all came into close physical contact.

"Your friend was not so accommodating earlier on."

"That could be because you hit him."

The conductor scowled at me; in the candlelight, his face looked positively sinister. He was tall, and powerfully built; in a fight, he might be match even for me, a champion college wrestler.

"I was mistaken. I thought he was... Well, never mind. I apologize."

My cock was still hanging out of my open fly, and although it was going down rapidly, it still looked large; Bertrand's vacuum-pump mouth had seen to that. The conductor was eyeing it.

"You can do better than that," I said. "You can show us how sorry you are."

"Sir, at this time—"

"Come on." I took my cock between finger and thumb, and shook it at him. "Suck it."

"There are other matters—"

"More important? Than this? I don't think so."

"Sir, I—"

Bertrand stood with his arms folded across his chest, a smile on his face. "Yes," he said, "to see you suck it would be good. Please. After you."

The conductor looked—what? Frightened? Disgusted? It was hard to tell. But he did as he was told, and with a bit of shifting around managed to get his head at my groin level. I grabbed his hair, and pushed him into me. He started licking my shaft, my balls, kissing the head—and then he opened up and took me. Bertrand, who was fast revealing himself as one of the greediest, cock-hungriest boys I had ever met, was busy exploring the conductor's pants.

More footsteps running down the corridor.

"Mr. Simmonds! Mr. Simmonds! Where are you, sir?"

It was young Arthur's voice.

"In here!" I cried, wondering how we were going to fit Arthur into our cramped quarters. I felt certain that we would find a way.

The conductor—Simmonds, as I now knew him to be—spat out my cock. "What are you doing? You fool—"

He sprang to his feet, grabbed the candlestick, and barged out of the cubicle. "Arthur! There you are! I've been looking for you!"

"Are you all right, Mr. Simmonds? You look flushed."

"I'm just helping a couple of passengers who were...er... trapped in the toilet. Now, look lively. What's going on?"

I stuffed my cock back in my pants, adjusted my clothes, and pushed the door open. There stood Arthur, wide-eyed, carrying a storm lantern.

"Mr. Mitchell, sir! Are you hurt?"

"No, Arthur, I'm fine. Mr. Simmonds has been most... helpful. What's happening?"

Bertrand tumbled out of the toilet and into the corridor, and stood for a while taking deep gulps of air. Arthur looked puzzled, and glanced from one to another.

Simmonds took control.

"We are stuck in the tunnel, gentlemen. The signal turned red very suddenly. We stopped as quickly as we could, but the engineer thinks we may have damaged one of the wheels. He's trying to ascertain now whether it's safe to proceed."

"Where are we?"

"Near Grantham. In the Stoke Tunnel."

"Are we safe?"

"We're quite safe, sir. The tunnel is very long, but there are signals all the way along the track. No train will come anywhere near us. I'm sure we'll be moving again shortly."

"What happened to the lights?" asked Bertrand, who

found the surrounding gloom far less attractive than I did.

"The electrics overloaded when the engineer put the brakes on, I suppose," said Simmonds.

"So," I said, still hard in my pants, "we have nothing to do but wait."

"Exactly, sir. If I were you, I would go back to your compartment and sit tight."

"Oh—I prefer the company in here..." I gestured back to the toilet.

Simmonds cleared his throat, made some excuse about talking to the engineer, and fled.

"You're a doctor, aren't you, sir?"

"Yes, Arthur."

"I think, if you don't mind my saying so, that it might be a good idea if you were to see a few of the passengers. One or two of them were hurt when the train stopped."

"You're right. I should have thought of that myself. Lead the way."

"Certainly, sir." Arthur held up his lantern. "If I might just say something..."

"What, Arthur?"

"The young gentleman." He nodded toward Bertrand. "He might just need to wipe his sleeve."

A huge blob of semen sat on Bertrand's arm, soaking into the fabric.

"*Merde alors!*" He rubbed it in, and we made our way along the train.

"Shit!"

I thought I had seen a ghost. Up ahead in the dark corridor was a fluttering white shape. As we drew near, it resolved itself into the more familiar contours of Daisy Athenasy. Her face was white, her lips a dark, purplish color; she looked exactly as she did on the screen, in black and white. Glamorous—but to me, as a doctor, alarmingly ill.

She staggered as if drunk. I wondered if she had taken an overdose.

"Miss Athenasy!"

I barged past Arthur and caught Daisy just as she was about to fall to the floor. Her eyelids were closing. I felt her hand; it was freezing cold.

"Miss Athenasy, what is the matter?"

"Oh! Help me!" She looked up into my eyes, just as I'd seen her do on screen. "Help me, please…" And then she went limp. I placed her carefully on the floor, and pressed my ear to her chest; her heart was beating, a little fast perhaps, but nothing worse. She was not dying.

"Bertrand, fetch my bag from the compartment." I always carry a few basic medical supplies with me.

Bertrand groped his way along the corridor, while Arthur entered the private carriage.

"Oh, my God. Mr. Mitchell, sir… Oh, my God."

There, in the private compartment, illuminated only by the candles on the dining table, sat Hugo Taylor, his head in his hands, blood dripping from a wound in his scalp, seeping between his fingers, running down his hands, and soaking into his brilliant white cuffs.

"Mr. Taylor!"

He looked up and flinched.

"It's all right, Mr. Taylor. It's me. Mitch. I'm a doctor."

"Oh, thank God. I thought…"

"What?"

"Nothing." He held up his bloodstained hands. "Bloody train lurched and brought me rather violently into collision with that." He nodded toward the corner of the zinc-topped cocktail cabinet that was bolted to one wall of the carriage. "Who would have thought the old man had so much blood in him?"

"Let me see. Arthur! Hold the lantern close."

I parted Taylor's thick black hair and found the wound,

86

an inch above the hairline on the right-hand side of his skull. It was messy, but not deep. It did not look as if it had been made by a sharp metal corner.

"You'll survive. What happened exactly?"

"I don't know. I was arguing with Daisy, as per. I just got up to leave, because I couldn't stand any more of her nonsense, when I was thrown off my balance and hit the bloody whatsit."

"Was it a direct hit?"

He looked up into my face. "No... I more sort of... Well, I was sort of dragged across it, if you see what I mean."

"Because it looks more like it was done with a blunt instrument. A blackjack, or a sandbag, or something."

"I've never actually seen a blackjack, outside of a film set. Do such things really exist?"

"I guess so. Ah, here's Bertrand. I'm going to get a dressing on that. Stop the bleeding." Arthur left us with the lantern, and went off to illuminate the rest of the train as best he could.

I soon had the wound cleaned and dressed—Taylor did not wince, even when I put on the stinging antiseptic. He looked like a war hero—a role he had often played on stage and screen. He stood up, obviously felt faint for a moment, but rallied quickly and shook my hand.

"Thank you, Mr. Mitchell."

"Call me Mitch."

"I will." There was a faint moan from the corridor. "Oh, dear. Looks like the Sugar Plum Fairy is coming back to her senses." He lowered his voice. "The few that she has." He stepped out. "That's it, Daisy dear. Pick yourself up. You'll crush your lovely gown. Everything's fine. Hugo's fine. You're fine. Let's get you into bed."

Daisy got to her feet, using Taylor's body as a sort of climbing frame, and hobbled into the carriage.

"Oh! Your poor head!"

"Nothing to worry about. Come on. Thank you, gentlemen. I hope you will let me buy you dinner in London. As a way of saying thank you."

"It would be our very great pleasure," I said, trying to put as much innuendo into the words as possible.

The compartment door was pulled shut—leaving us on the outside.

"He is charming, this Hugo Taylor," said Bertrand.

"Damn right he is. And he knows it."

There were several sprains and cuts to attend to, but nothing too severe. The soldiers had made themselves useful, calming people down, getting them back to their seats, distributing lanterns and clearing luggage from the entryways.

The sergeant looked pleased to see me, and I was certainly pleased to see him. "Everything under control, sergeant?"

"Yes, sir. Nothing I can't handle."

"Glad to hear it."

Between us, we settled the passengers. I could offer little except reassurance and the odd bandage, but people were more frightened than injured. After 20 minutes, my work was done. Bertrand was waiting for me at the door, looking nervous and uneasy.

"What's the matter?"

"Those soldiers... They are very..."

"What?"

"*Vulgaire.*"

His cheeks were flushed, but he would say nothing more on the subject. I looked back at the carriage, which was quiet and tidy now. The passengers had settled in for what we all believed would be a long wait.

And then, suddenly, the lights came back on.

We blinked and gasped at the miracle. I thought I caught sight of a little under-kilt fumbling among the soldiers, but I may have been mistaken.

A cheer arose, in which Bertrand and I joined.

Cupping my hands around my eyes, I peered through the window to see the damp brickwork of the Stoke Tunnel all around us.

We made our way back up the train with lighter hearts. Daisy and Hugo's compartment was quiet and closed. The bathroom, scene of our recent adventure, was in use—to someone's great relief, I imagined. I hoped there was not too much evidence on the floor. We deposited my medical bag in our compartment, and went on to the first-class dining car. It was long past lunchtime, and I was hungry. I wondered if that fillet of sole and highly praised roast chicken was still on the menu. And to be honest, I needed a drink. The experience had shaken me.

We were not alone. The friendly old white-haired steward was flitting from table to table, and when he saw us he clasped a hand to his head.

"Gentlemen! I had given you up for lost! I'm afraid all the tables are taken... Unless I can find someone—"

"Here!" It was Frankie, completely unruffled, sharing a table with the young mother and her three daughters. "I'm sure we can squeeze up, if you don't mind, Mrs. Andrews."

"Not at all. Come on, Lily, you sit on my lap."

"And this little lady can sit with Uncle Frankie." He picked up the youngest of the three, a giggling pink-and-white bundle with long gold ringlets. She had inherited her coloring from her father—who, incidentally, was nowhere to be seen. I remembered his liaison with David Rhys, the diamond merchant. There was a mystery there, I was certain.

Bertrand and I seated ourselves, and were soon enjoying an aperitif. Frankie's good humor carried the day; he made the distressing experience of being stuck in a tunnel seem like an excuse for a party. Martinis were ordered, and bottles of wine. Mrs. Andrews's eyes twinkled, and the mood spread to our fellow diners. Even the dreaded dowager seemed to thaw a little, and inclined her head when Frankie lifted his glass.

"Ghastly old dragon," he murmured, "but one must be nice. She dines with my grandmother, of whom I have what you might call great expectations." He spoke aloud. "Hello, Lady Antonia. How are you coping?"

"The minute we arrive in town I shall telephone Sir Ronald, whom I have known since he was in velveteen breeches, and demand an explanation. One is not accustomed to this kind of inconvenience, and if people like one do not use their influence to stem the tide of socialism that is ruining our country then we might as well start taking our orders directly from Moscow. Chivers! Make a note of that! I shall tell Sir Ronald in person, those very words. Orders directly from Moscow, girl! Come along! What is the matter with you?"

Chivers struggled with a notebook and pencil, her cheeks pink and shiny with drink, her brow knitted.

"Oh, dear old Ronnie, it seems a shame to bother him," said Frankie, who seemed to be on familiar terms not only with the dowager and the chairman of the railway company, but also with most of the titled heads of Europe, at least if one were to believe his chatter. "He was so sweet to Mummy last year, after that business with Daddy and the Argentine chorus girl."

"Well!" The dowager looked simultaneously shocked and eager. "So it was true, then."

"Absolutely, my dear Lady Antonia. Every damn word of it."

"How shockin'."

"Yes, but you know Daddy. He was ever thus."

"Ah yes, indeed he was. Your father was always a scapegrace."

"And dear Ronnie... Well, of course, he's always been sweet on Mummy, would have married her himself given half a chance, and a jolly good match it would have been too."

"That's no way to speak of your parents, young man," said Lady Antonia—but she had a twinkle in her eye.

"I have every respect for my father, of course. At least, I have every respect for his wallet."

"Your father is a very fine man indeed. He is distantly connected to the Stuart line."

"As he never tires of telling me."

"And thus may have a legitimate claim to the throne of England, should it ever become vacant."

"You don't say!" Frankie giggled. "Imagine! I could be a princess!"

"Well, really!"

Lady Antonia looked disgusted, and took a big sip of martini, almost dipping the tip of her beaklike nose in her drink. Frankie rolled his eyes and turned to us.

"You know, she's really not as bad as she seems, old Antonia. She looks like a harridan, but she's a dear old pussycat underneath that fierce exterior. Aren't you, dear?"

"What am I?"

"A darling old pussycat."

"Well, really!" Lady Antonia bridled; Chivers flinched, as if expecting a beating. "You are the most vexin' young man I have ever encountered. How your poor Ma-mah copes I shall never know." But there was color even in her carved-wax face, and something approaching a smile hovering around the corner of her mouth.

Frankie lowered his voice and whispered in my ear. "Mad as a hatter, of course, with simply the most alarming political views. Got herself in with a group that calls itself the British Fascists. Ridiculous load of old bollocks, darling, they hate the wogs and the yids and the queers and the Bolshies, but nonetheless I hoped for a touch before we get very much further down the line. One has creditors popping out all over the place, and a few quid from the old bat would help no end."

The little girls started jumping up and down, the young-est—who was seated in Frankie's lap—landing rather heav-ily, which shut him up for a moment.

"Daddy!" they cried. "Daddy! Daddy!"

And there he was, Mr. Andrews, the serious, neat young father, with a face like thunder. He pushed the children away.

"For God's sake, Christina, can't you control them?"

His wife gathered the girls to her, and looked puzzled and hurt. What was he so angry about? I wondered about his mysterious liaison with Rhys, and my suspicions concerning their transactions in the lavatory. He certainly looked like a man with a guilty conscience. I stood, to allow him to sit with his family, just as our lunch was served.

"Oh, dear," fussed the steward. "I don't know what to do with you all. This is most awkward."

"The American gentleman may sit here, if he wishes," said Lady Antonia, gesturing with one gloved hand to a space beside Miss Chivers. "I shall not raise any objection."

"Thank you, ma'am."

"I trust he does not chew with his mouth open, nor slurp his soup."

"No, ma'am," I said, my republican self-respect rising at this shocking display of old-world rudeness. "Nor does he swing from the trees, nor eat with his hands." I sat beside Chivers, who uttered a barely audible "Oh, dear!" and stared out the window at the dank brickwork.

Well, I was not going to let that old gorgon spoil my lunch—I was hungry, and when I'm hungry very little stands between my and my food. The steward served the fish, and it smelled delicious; how on earth they had managed to cook during such adverse conditions was beyond me. But there it was, a delicate, juicy fillet of sole, fragrant and steaming, with a slice of lemon and some brown bread and butter, just waiting to be devoured. My mouth watered as I speared the first piece of flesh on my fork and brought it toward my mouth…

And then, quite suddenly, the train took a violent lurch forward, causing the fish to fly off my fork and onto Lady Antonia's chest, where it lodged among her pearls. Drinks flew in all directions, the steward stumbled, dumping another plate of fish over Mr. Andrews's head, and the little girls set up an earsplitting wail.

"What the fuck!" I yelled, before remembering myself.

The movement stopped, and started again suddenly, as if we were being shunted from behind. It was a sickening sensation. And then, just as I began to fear that a collision of some sort was inevitable, the engine lurched again and began to pull us forward. The tunnel fell away on either side, and we were in daylight once again. Despite the buffeting that we had all taken, we were greatly heartened by being in the open air. Snow was still falling, whirling around the windows, and the ground was covered by a good inch, which shone brightly even in the failing winter light.

"At last!" said Frankie. "We're on the move again. Maybe we will reach London today after all."

"Would someone kindly tell me what is going on?" said Lady Antonia, for all the world as if this were a conspiracy against her personally. "This is most inconvenient." She was unaware of the large flake of sole which was dangling from her pearl necklace. Chivers, on the other hand, seemed hypnotized by it.

"Don't sit there gawping, girl, go and see to our cases. I should not be at all surprised if they were smashed to smithereens, and my personal effects are being fingered by urchins from the third-class carriages." She pronounced the word in a way I had never heard before: *keddiges*.

Chivers hurried away, gripping the seat edges as she went, fearful of falling should the train lurch again.

Young Mr. Andrews picked bits of fish out of his hair, and mopped fragrant, fishy juices from his neck; he w going to need a bath as soon as we got to London, and was going to smell very unpleasant in the interim. The steward was doing his best to mop up the sea of wine and cocktails that was slopping over the tabletop.

"I'm so sorry, ladies and gentlemen. So sorry. Oh, my goodness. Oh, dear." I felt sorry for the poor old thing, and gave him a hand, and within a minute or two we had tidied up the worst of the mess.

"Luncheon is ruined," moaned the steward, almost in tears. "The chicken... All over the floor..."

"Bring us bread and cheese and bottles of wine!" commanded Lady Antonia, and for once I was in agreement with her.

We were making slow progress along the track; at this rate we would reach London in about three days. Where was the conductor? What was going on? Why was nobody keeping us informed?

I stuffed a hunk of bread and cheese into my mouth, ignoring the bulging eyeballs and tutting tongue opposite me, and wiped my mouth on a wet napkin. "If you will excuse me, your Royal Highness, I'm going to find out what the hell is going on. Unless you prefer to sit here all day stewing in your own juices."

"Well! Charming! I suppose I shouldn't be surprised. All Americans, even ones from quite good families, are painfully gauche when it comes to the finer points of etiquette..."

Her voice faded away as I marched out of the carriage. I was barely into the corridor when I saw Simmonds, the conductor, coming toward me.

"Mr. Mitchell! Please return to the dining car!"

"Whatever is going on, Simmonds? This is ridiculous. There are people hurt and frightened."

"I'm well aware of that, sir. We have hit a problem with the switch. I must ask you to return to the dining car and sit down."

"Why?"

"Because we are going to—"

The brakes screamed, and we stopped with another terrible jolt, which threw Simmonds against me. Thankfully, the lights did not go out this time. I braced myself with one leg and supported his weight; it was not an unpleasant situation, particularly as our faces were almost touching. I could smell tobacco on his breath.

"I beg your pardon, sir."

"That's okay, Simmonds." I righted him, and we both cleared our throats and fingered our collars.

"We are obliged to reverse into the tunnel again, sir. It may be bumpy. Please go into the dining car and tell everyone to sit tight. Move anything heavy or breakable and stow it. Make sure the children are safe."

"It sounds serious, Simmonds. Are we in any danger?"

He was pale, his mouth set in a grim line. "No, sir. You are in no danger. Just go to the dining car and stay out of harm's way."

I thought it best to do as I was told. Simmonds walked back down the train—and then suddenly stopped and gave a shout of fright.

I turned quickly on my heel and saw him standing frozen to the spot, just outside the lavatory.

"What is it, man? For God's sake, what is it?"

"Look, sir." He pointed to the carpet at the base of the door, where a dark red stain was spreading slowly through the pile. "Blood."

Blood it surely was: enough blood to pool on the bathroom floor and soak outward into a patch approximately one foot in diameter. That was a lot of blood.

"Who's in there?"

"I don't know, sir." Simmonds banged on the door, but we both knew it was futile. "Open up! Open up in there! What's going on?"

"You'll have to open it yourself, Simmonds. You have a passkey, don't you? Bertrand said you did."

"Of course." His hands were shaking. "Oh, God, Mr. Mitchell, what has happened?"

"Someone is hurt. Badly, by the look of it. You must let me help them."

"Please, sir—would you do it? The sight of blood... I can't..."

I reflected for a moment that he had not been so squeamish when it came to beating up poor little Bertrand, but this was no time to bear old grudges.

"Okay. Hand over the key."

But Simmonds was frantically twisting and turning, rummaging in his pockets, his jacket, looking around him on the floor.

"It's gone!"

"What is?"

"The passkey, sir. The key that opens all the carriages and the toilets. I can't find it."

"You've lost it?"

"Oh no, sir. I've never lost a key, not in fifteen years working on the railway. It's been stolen."

The whistle sounded, and with a great hiss of steam we started to move again—backward.

# VI

THERE WAS NOTHING TO DO BUT REMAIN ROOTED TO THE spot, staring at the growing stain on the carpet, a horrible crimson flower that was starting to look wet and—or was this my imagination?—starting to smell. I am familiar with the smell of blood; all doctors are. Simmonds was leaning against the corridor wall, horribly pale.

"You have to find that key, Simmonds. What happened? Where could you possibly have lost it?"

"I tell you, I didn't lose it!" His voice was high, almost a scream. "Someone must have taken it."

"But when the train jolted... Isn't it possible that you fell over, that you somehow knocked it out of your pocket?"

"I keep it on this chain." He twirled a chain from his waistcoat pocket. "It is impossible to drop it. Someone would have to have taken it off... Someone very light-fingered. I'd have seen them, surely. I'd have felt them. Unless... While we were..."

"I can assure you, Simmonds, that neither Bertrand nor I touched your key while we were in there together. We had other things on our minds."

"But how can I trust you?"

"You're right, Simmonds. You can trust nobody. You will have to decide for yourself. I, however, know that I did not take it, and I choose to believe that Bertrand didn't."

He looked suspicious. "Then who? When? And why?"

"Conductor! Conductor!' We heard footsteps running up the passage, and Dickinson burst into view. "For God's sake, what's going on?"

"We're reversing into the tunnel, sir," said Simmonds, deftly positioning himself in front of the bloodstain, so that Dickinson should not see it. "I shall be making an announcement shortly. Please return to your carriage."

"Not on your life. Daisy needs champagne. She's become quite faint. And she needs that bloody pansy of a secretary. I presume he's up there, fraternizing with his lady friends?"

"Yes, he's there."

"Christ. Fucking useless bastard." Dickinson was muttering under his breath as he barged past us into the dining car. Once again I smelled his distinctive scent, that citrus cologne that he wore—or was it a soap? A fresh smell, masculine... It made me think of blond hair and firm, set features...

"What am I going to do, Mr. Mitchell?" Simmonds pleaded. "If the first-class passengers see this, there will be full-scale panic."

"I'll be back as soon as I can. I'll keep everyone in check. Trust me, Simmonds." I put a hand on his shoulder and squeezed. Perhaps he wasn't such a bad guy after all.

There was a scuffle in the doorway as Dickinson tried to push Frankie Laking back down the train, while at the same time grabbing a bottle of champagne from an ice bucket on the table. Lady Antonia kept up her usual disapproving commentary, the steward wrung a napkin in distress, and the Andrews family stared out the window as if nothing was going on. Frankie shot through the door, nearly knocked me to the floor, and whooped as he skipped down the corridor toward Hugo and Daisy's private carriage. Dickinson came in hot pursuit.

"Keep your hands off me, you brute! I'm a virgin!"

"Shut up, you stupid fairy."

"Ladies and gentlemen," I announced, "we are currently reversing into the tunnel, as there is a problem with the switch up ahead. I am asked to tell you to remain in your seats in case of any—whoop! Jesus!"

A sideways jerk this time, and I was sent sprawling onto Bertrand, knocking the wine bucket into his lap. It was full of ice.

The children were sniveling continually now, and Mrs. Andrews, while trying to calm them, was sobbing herself. Even her husband looked a bit green around the gills, and the best he could muster was the occasional "Well, then, my dear" or "There, there." We were all frightened; one read about rail accidents, and we seemed at every moment to be on the brink of a real-life disaster.

Bertrand swore (I assume) in French, stood up, and brushed the ice cubes from his lap. They hit the floor with a bump and a clang.

A clang?

"What's that?" Something had fallen under the table; something that should not be in a wine bucket.

"It must be a knife, sir," said the steward. "Allow me."

I stopped him. There was a metal object poking out by Bertrand's shoe, black and silver and shiny. I picked it up.

A key.

I ran back to the corridor, where Simmonds stood guarding the lavatory. The bloodstain was even bigger and steamed slightly in the cold air. I held up the key.

"Where the hell was that?" Simmonds asked.

"In there."

"You found it?"

"You could say that."

"Who had it?"

"Does it matter, Simmonds? For God's sake, open the door."

He covered his eyes, grabbed the key, and jiggled it in the lock until it turned.

Rhys lay on the floor, his feet resting awkwardly on the toilet lid, his head twisted at an unnatural angle, mouth distorted and eyes open. His left hand, which was reaching toward us, fell forward slightly as I opened the door, and a wave of blood gushed out into the passage.

The ring finger was missing. It was from this fresh, glistening wound that the blood had seeped out under the door.

The stump was still bleeding, as if the heart was still pumping, but David Rhys, the diamond merchant, was dead. And the ring that had caused so much discreet admiration and excitement was gone, as well as the finger that had worn it—severed, I guessed, with a knife that was not exactly of surgical sharpness. The cut was ragged, and the bone had been broken, rather than cut or sawn, as we would do in an operating room.

Simmonds retched.

"Put your head out the window for a moment, Simmonds. Breathe deeply."

We had stopped again—back in the tunnel, the wretched black tunnel, where the air was far from fresh—but I really did not want Simmonds vomiting on the scene of the crime. It was already quite messy enough.

He didn't puke, thank God, but when he pulled his head back into the carriage he looked ghastly. His knees were buckling, and I thought he was about to faint.

"I've never seen... Oh, God... A dead man..."

"Pull yourself together. This is an emergency. We have to get help."

"Help... Yes... Help."

"Stay there. Don't move. Don't look at the…body."

"The body…"

"Just so. Look out the window. Say your prayers. Think of your mother. Anything. Just don't go away, and don't let anyone near the—"

Simmonds groaned and stared at his reflection in the darkened window.

I ran back and banged on the door of the dining car.

"Bertrand! Come here!"

"What is it?"

"Come quickly. It's fine, everyone, nothing to see. The conductor is unwell, that's all. Everyone here okay? Good, good. Come on, Bertrand."

I grabbed him and dragged him through the door. He was complaining, as usual.

"Why should I worry about that pig of a conductor? He is nothing to me. He is—oh, *mon dieu*."

He had seen the blood on the carpet, the horror-stricken face of Simmonds, and guessed the rest. "Someone is dead, *oui*?"

"Exactly so. Now stay with Mr. Simmonds and make sure that nobody touches anything. I'll be right back."

I hoped my instincts were right, and that I could count on Bertrand in a crisis. He had taken to fucking well enough; would he excel in that other sphere of interest, the investigation of crime?

Dickinson was just coming out of the movie stars' compartment. He was still frowning; presumably Miss Athenasy was causing more trouble. I did not envy him his job, however glamorous.

"Just the man I wanted to see," he said, clapping me on the shoulder. "I'm sick to death of that mad bitch. God, whatever did the old man see in her? She's as thick as two short planks. Come on, why don't you and I go and make whoopee somewhere."

"Something's happened."

"You're telling me. This whole journey is a fucking disaster."

"No. Listen. Something serious. Someone's dead."

"What? Dead? Don't be ridiculous."

"Come and see."

"You're seriously telling me that there is a dead body on this train?" He looked amused; he was almost laughing.

"I am. What's so funny, Dickinson?"

"It's incredible."

"Well, you'd better believe it. I'm telling you that there is a dead man in the first-class bathroom—"

"And I have something to tell you that you may find equally hard to believe."

What was he going to confess? That Daisy Athenasy, in a drug-crazed frenzy, had murdered poor David Rhys just to get her hands on that big sparkler?

"And what is that?"

"I'm a policeman."

Dickinson assumed control with extraordinary speed and efficiency. He dispatched Simmonds to the conductor's car, there to recover with a brandy and a cigarette, and sent Bertrand down the train to prevent any approach from that direction. He tore up the ruined carpet, rolled it up, and stashed it in the bathroom with the body, then locked them away with the conductor's key, which Simmonds had left in the lock.

"And now," he said, joining me in the dining car, coolly wiping his bloodstained hands on a napkin, "we must do our best to find out what has happened. Ladies and gentlemen, please return to your carriages. There has been a terrible accident, and until we have taken stock of the situation I need to know exactly where everyone is."

"By what authority, might one ask?" said Lady Antonia, looking at Dickinson through her eyeglasses.

"By the authority, madam, of the Metropolitan Police Service, in which I am a detective superintendent." He fished in his jacket pocket. "Here is my warrant card." He waved it under her nose; she waved it away.

"I do not need to see it. I have every respect for the forces of law and order. You may carry on with your work as you see fit."

"Thank you so much, Lady Antonia. That's very good of you. Now, if you would not mind returning to your carriage…"

"Yes," she said, rising to her feet, "come along everyone. You heard what the superintendent said. Now then, young ladies. Let's look lively."

She took charge rather splendidly, and within moments an orderly line was making its way down the train, dispersing through the carriage doors. They passed the fatal lavatory without a murmur; there was nothing to betray its gruesome cargo.

Dickinson and I remained in the dining car. The steward flitted in and out of the kitchen.

"The time is two-fifteen P.M.," Dickinson observed. "How long has Rhys been dead, Dr. Mitchell?"

"The wound was still bleeding when we discovered it. I estimate that he was killed this side of one-thirty."

"In that case, we must ascertain everyone's whereabouts at the time of the attack."

"We were here, with Lady Antonia and her companion, Chivers. No. Wait. She had been sent down the train to take care of the luggage."

"Ah, when was that?"

"Just after we—oh, come on, Dickinson. You're not seriously suggesting that someone like Chivers—"

"I'm suggesting nothing at this stage, Mitch. I am simply trying to put together the pieces of the jigsaw."

"Okay. First of all we need to write down what happened,

and approximately when. We left Edinburgh at ten o'clock."

Dickinson handed me a pencil, and I wrote on the back of a menu.

"Then we stopped at York station…"

"Yes," said Dickinson, rubbing his crotch, "just as I was preparing to give your little friend the fucking of a lifetime." He put a hand on my knee. "When was that, would you say?"

This was no time for fooling around, I thought. "Well, what time would you say that was?"

"I wasn't looking at my watch, Mitch." His hand ran up my leg.

"And we were there for maybe twenty minutes," I said, shifting my position to dislodge his hand. "I was talking to the soldiers for a while, then Bertrand saw something in the shed—"

Dickinson was not interested in details. "Twenty minutes, as you say. Write that down."

I must have been staring at him, for he suddenly stopped speaking and held my gaze.

"What is it, Mitch?" His hand went to his crotch. "Want some of this?"

"No," I lied. "It's just occurred to me that I know nothing at all about you. Who are you? Why are you on this train? What is your position with Daisy and Hugo?"

"I see. You begin to suspect me. Good. That's exactly how it should be."

"Well?"

"I am, as my warrant card suggests, Detective Superintendent Peter Dickinson of Scotland Yard."

"And that other card? British-American Pictures?"

"That, my dear Mitch, is what's known as working undercover."

"Why?"

"Can I trust you?"

"Yes."

"I suppose I can. I mean, I know enough about you to put you behind bars for a few years, don't I? So you wouldn't want to piss me off, would you?"

"That's one way of looking at it, I suppose." He was still rubbing his crotch, and the outline of his cock was quite visible through his pants. "But then again," I said, "that's a two-way street, isn't it? I don't imagine that our sort of person is exactly welcome in the Metropolitan Police Service."

"Not officially, no. Although I could tell you a few tales about the young recruits, the kind of training we put them through... You'd enjoy it, Mitch. I could show you if you like."

"I don't think this is the time or the place."

"Good. Well done. You'll make a good detective. I can trust you to keep your head in a tight spot, and not be distracted by—" He ran his fingers down the considerable length of his hard cock, which was straining at the fabric of his pants. "This."

In truth, I would have liked nothing better than to kneel before him and start sucking him off, and had it not been for the occasional presence of the steward, I might have done so.

"So, you want to know why I'm on this train in the first place, I suppose," he said.

"I do."

"I'm investigating a drug smuggling operation."

"Ah," I said. "Daisy Athenasy."

"Precisely."

"So she's bringing the stuff in—"

"Her? Don't be ridiculous. Daisy is one of those rare, delightful creatures who really is as stupid as she looks. What little intelligence she may once have had was used up on snaring and marrying Herbert Waits. No: Daisy is just a cover. But if you take a look inside her trunks, in among the swansdown and the sequins you will find a very large quantity of heroin."

"Good God. Who put it there?"

"That's what I'm trying to find out."

"Not Hugo Taylor, surely."

"You wouldn't think so, would you? The clean-cut hero, every mother's son. But Hugo Taylor has his own secrets. Maybe his hands are tied."

"Blackmail?"

"It's possible. Scotland Yard has a file on him this thick. But we don't act against him; what would be the point? Another career ruined, thousands of weeping fans, a lot of pointless prison sentences. I'd prefer to be out there catching the real villains. What does it matter to me whether Hugo Taylor fucks a few pretty chorus boys?"

"That's a very enlightened view."

"I'm a very enlightened man. As you shall find out, if we ever get to London and anywhere near a hotel room."

"You surely don't suspect Francis Laking?"

"Oh, I do."

"Good grief. And what about Joseph?"

"The muscle man? Yes, it's entirely possible. Although I think his main job is to keep Miss Athenasy quiet."

"By fucking her."

"Yes. And I believe she is absolutely addicted to cocksucking. You'd be surprised where those famous bee-stung lips have been."

"So why David Rhys? What's he got to do with anything? A diamond merchant—and a very successful one, by the look of things."

"All that glitters is not gold—often have you heard that told."

"You mean the diamonds were fake?"

"Come on, Mitch. Who travels by rail wearing thousands of pounds' worth of diamond on his finger? Advertising his wealth in that way? Asking to be robbed?"

"You think this was a robbery?"

"No. I think the diamonds were a cover, and a bad cover at that. Rhys was no more a diamond merchant than I am. I suspect—and I intend to prove—that he was the ringleader of the smugglers."

"I saw him in the bathroom with that man—Andrews."

"When?"

"I can't remember... Let me get this straight." I referred to my notes. "We left York—"

"Just after I had finally got rid of those two reporters."

"Ah, so that's where you were. And they really were reporters, were they? Not assassins, or spies?"

Dickinson arched an eyebrow and smiled. "Oh, yes, they were reporters. And I'm afraid they were in very grave danger of ruining the whole operation with their childish curiosity."

"On the scent of a juicy scandal, I suppose."

"Yes—but on the wrong scent. The papers think they're clever if they catch Daisy and Hugo traveling in a private carriage together—as if they're carrying on some outrageous affair under the nose of her poor husband. Well, believe me, if that was the case everyone, not least Herbert Waits, would be relieved and delighted. It would mean that Hugo Taylor wasn't picking up rough trade in East End pubs, it would mean that Daisy Athenasy wasn't taking dope and sucking off her Albanian bodyguard, it would be a rather wholesome situation rather than the disgusting mess that we are currently in."

"So you threw them off the train at York. Is that why we stopped?"

"No. I couldn't have made the train stop without blowing my cover. But it was convenient. It was preferable to tying them up in the conductor's car, which is what I was intending to do."

"I didn't see them get off."

"You weren't meant to. And as I recall, your attentions were elsewhere. On your little friend's bum, to be precise."

"Yes..." And the soldiers, and the engineer, and the stoker, and everyone else I had been planning to seduce. What a hopeless detective I was! I had not even noticed that two of the most suspicious characters on the train had disappeared.

"What happened next, Mitch?"

"Right, let me see..." I could only think of the things that mattered to me: fucking Bertrand, watching Dickinson's fingers sliding in and out of his ass...

"We left our compartment, but the bathroom was locked. That's right. That's when I saw Rhys and Andrews coming out."

"They had been in there together?"

"Yes. I assumed there was some kind of deal going on."

"That's not like you, Mitch. I would expect you to jump to a far more pleasant conclusion."

"Not even I believe that every single man on the train is queer, superintendent."

"The family man, complete with wife and three little girls... The best disguise in the world."

"But he's been so preoccupied. Obviously his nerves are on edge. And when I spoke to Rhys, he was distracted too. I was in the way. He didn't want to be seen."

"By you?"

"Or by you." I remembered how Rhys had disappeared the moment he heard footsteps coming along the corridor— the footsteps, as it turned out, of a police superintendent. "When he saw you coming, he ran."

"That's when I was getting Hugo and Daisy their dinner. Which turned out to be completely wasted. When I walked in, Hugo was lying on the sofa smoking a cigarette, watching her suck Joseph's cock."

"Didn't he join in?"

"I wouldn't be surprised, but he doesn't know me well enough to let his guard down. As far as Hugo's concerned, I'm just another new publicity manager that the studio has foisted on him. And that means that they're spying on him—or so he thinks. He's convinced that I've been assigned to this film purely to keep him out of trouble."

"So he doesn't consider the fact that Daisy Athenasy is a cocksucking drug fiend to be of interest?"

"Daisy isn't his concern. She can go to hell as far as he's concerned. She's a necessary evil. If you want to star in a British-American picture—and who doesn't, with the fees they pay?—then you have to act opposite her. It's part of the deal."

"Is he big, by the way?"

"Enormous."

"Bigger than you?"

"Even bigger than me. By a good inch. That's got you interested."

"Yeah." My own cock was hard again, and I was losing focus. I wanted to kiss Dickinson, to taste his lips, to inhale his scent. I must have leaned forward without meaning to, because I suddenly found myself only inches from him. I could feel his body heat.

"Mitch..."

"Hmmm?"

"Would it help you to concentrate if we... You know..."

"Mmmm..."

He took my hand and guided it down; his crotch was hot as hell. He sighed. "Just suck me."

It was like a dream—sitting in an open carriage, where anyone might enter, about to have sex with a senior policeman.

"Ooh, gentlemen, excuse me." It was the steward,

bustling in from the kitchen with a tray of clean glasses. We came to our senses.

"That's all right. Dr. Mitchell and I are just—"

"I shall see to it that you're not disturbed."

"No." I stood up and opened a window; we could hear the drip, drip of water from the roof of the tunnel. "We're fine, thanks. Some coffee, if you have any, would be good." I needed to wake up from this strange reverie. Dickinson was acting on me like a drug. But there was a dead man down the corridor, his killer still on the train.

"Coffee coming up, sir. Hot and strong." The steward giggled, and retreated to the kitchen.

"Sit down, Mitch."

"No. I prefer to stand. I don't trust myself."

"So I see." My cock was making my pants stick out at the fly. I closed my eyes and breathed deeply, smelling the mold and moss of the tunnel, the sharp, bitter scent of coal and soot. My cock started to subside.

"We finally made it to the bathroom, Bertrand and I."

"And you…?"

"Yes. And that's when the train stopped, right in the tunnel. Right where we are now."

"So that would have been—when?"

"Hard to say. We had been in there for some time."

"It's difficult to judge time when you have your cock up an arse."

"Yes. Where were you when we stopped?"

"I had just left Daisy and Hugo."

"Had he hurt his head?"

"No. That happened when we stopped."

"Did it? Did it really?"

"As far as I'm aware. You clearly think otherwise."

"I don't know what I think. But the injury was not consistent with his description of how it happened."

"Note that down."

"And then we were stuck in the bathroom for a while." I shuddered at the memory. "It was horrible."

"How did you get out?"

"The conductor released us."

"With his key?"

Shit! The key! The key that he said he had lost! Either Simmonds was lying, or he had lost the key much later than he imagined, between letting us out of the bathroom and our discovery of Rhys's dead body.

"We'll ask him," I said, making a note. "We saw Daisy in the corridor, looking very much under the influence. We saw Hugo's head. We went back to third class, and attended to a couple of bumps and sprains."

"Then you returned to the dining car for lunch. What time was that?"

"The steward complained that we had nearly missed lunch." He was hovering, probably listening. "Hey!" I shouted to the steward. "Come in here a moment!"

"Sir?"

"What time did I come up for lunch? When we were stuck the first time."

"Approximately one-thirty, sir. We normally don't take orders after then, but as it was you, sir, and your young friend—"

Dickinson continued, "And did you come straight here from the third-class carriages? Or did you stop off for more fun?"

"We came straight here," I replied. "I was hungry, so we were in a hurry. That's right: the lights came back on, so it was easy to make our way along the train."

"And you noticed nothing unusual along the way?"

"No. That bathroom was in use again—I suppose now that Rhys was already in there, dead or alive—"

"But you heard nothing? Nothing aroused your suspicion?"

"Nothing. It's been occupied for most of the trip, for one reason or another."

"Every reason apart from the one it was intended for, by the sound of it."

This was true. First of all, poor Bertrand had been assaulted by the conductor, then I'd seen Andrews and Rhys emerging after some kind of tête-à-tête, and finally we had used the toilet for our own enjoyment. It was hardly surprising that one of my fellow first-class passengers was in there as soon as the lights went on.

"Who was in the dining car when you and Bertrand returned?"

"Mrs. Andrews and her daughters. Lady Antonia and Chivers, her companion. Frankie Laking. The steward, of course. And all the other tables were occupied as well, with people I had not noticed before and I doubt I could recognize again."

"There are eight tables, is that correct?"

"Yes, sir," answered the steward, polishing glasses and now listening quite blatantly to our conversation.

"Do you have a passenger list?"

"No, sir. I'm afraid we don't carry such things."

"But you have a book of table reservations."

"Yes, sir. Here."

"So," said Dickinson, flicking through the book, "we can, I suppose, eliminate the people who were actually here at the time of the murder..."

"It's hopeless," I said. "There are too many of them."

"And you believe that all of them may have had a motive to bump off poor old Rhys?"

"Not at all. But they had as much reason to do so as, say, Lady Antonia."

Dickinson looked at me. "One knows so little about people one meets on railway journeys," he said.

We drank our coffee in silence, and I pored over my notes.

Where was the truth in this mess of scribbling? What was I missing? My brain was clouded—by alcohol, by shock, and by the physical presence of Dickinson.

There was a tap at the door, and Simmonds came in, looking much more composed.

"What is it?"

"It's Mr. Andrews, sir. He wants to have a word."

"Send him in," said Dickinson, thoughtfully. "There's something about that respectable father of three that I don't quite like."

"Indeed," I said, "he was out of the dining car at the time of the murder. He came in just before we were served. And I saw him coming out of the toilet."

"Well, I hope he washed his hands before eating."

"Oh, I'm sure he did. I'm certain that he—"

And then I remembered. That was it. The soap. When Andrews had returned to the dining car, I had sensed something odd about him. At the time, I couldn't put my finger on it, and it had troubled me ever since. Now it suddenly fell into place. The smell. He did not smell of the floral soap that was used in the first-class bathroom.

This had been a different smell, a sharper, higher scent.

The scent of lemons.

# VII

Andrews had hitherto struck me as the typical British family man, buttoned up, responsible, emotionally distant. The man who walked into the dining car was none of those things. He looked haunted. His pale skin had gone a nasty shade of gray, his eyes were puffy and bloodshot. I suspected that he had recently vomited. His hair was damp around the forehead, and he could not stop his hands from shaking.

"Is it true, then?" he stammered, wavering in the doorway. I pulled out a chair and seated him before he fell.

"What?"

"Is he...dead?"

"If you mean Mr. Rhys," said Dickinson, "the answer is yes."

Andrews looked wildly around, as if searching for a means of escape—not from us, perhaps, but from the news he had just heard. His stomach heaved, and he grabbed a napkin, but there was nothing left to come up.

"He can't be... Oh, God. What happened?"

"We aren't sure of the cause of death yet, sir. But he

was found in the first-class lavatory." Dickinson was cold, without sympathy. What did he know, or suspect, of Mr. Andrews?

"This is like a nightmare."

"We're going to have to ask you some questions, Mr. Andrews," I said, trying to sound a little more sympathetic.

"Anything. Anything at all. It will all come out now anyway. I don't care what happens to me."

"What was your connection to Rhys?" Dickinson interrupted.

"We met professionally."

"I see. And what might your profession be?"

"I work in the city, for a large bank. Rhys was investing some money. We met at a party in London, and we got talking about—"

"What sort of party?"

Andrews wheeled around. "What do you mean, what sort of party?"

"Were ladies present?"

"Of course ladies were present," said Andrews. "Oh. I see what you're getting at. No, there was nothing of that manner involved. It was a party that the bank throws every Christmas for existing and prospective clients. I was there with Christina, my wife, we were introduced to Rhys, and we hit it off. Talking about money, about politics. We were both too young to have seen active service in the war, but we'd both lost older brothers. That sort of thing."

"He had money to invest, you say?" Dickinson continued.

"Yes. He had had a very successful year—"

"Selling diamonds?"

"Diamonds? Good God, no. Insurance. He's an insurance broker."

"Was an insurance broker," said Dickinson, unnecessarily harshly. Andrews put a hand over his eyes and sighed deeply.

"You'd better tell us everything, my friend," I said, shooting daggers at Dickinson, who had the bedside manner of Jack the Ripper. "Don't worry. Nothing you say will be held against you."

Dickinson raised an eyebrow but said nothing.

"I suppose I must," said Andrews. "Well, the truth is that there was more to our friendship than the normal relationship between a banker and his client. He did invest money with us—quite a large amount of money, in fact—and I made sure that he got the best possible service. But we became friends, too. He invited me to play tennis with him, to go riding. Christina is so busy at home with the children, I think she was glad to see me developing some outside interests. Rhys was a good all-rounder, a top-quality tennis player, a good horseman, a good sport, you might say. It did occur to me that it was strange he'd never married, but one doesn't ask questions of that sort, and he did not volunteer any information.

"I found myself looking forward to our meetings, and thinking about him a great deal in between times. At first it seemed innocent enough; I thought about what a jolly good game of tennis we'd had, how powerful his serve was, how much I'd enjoyed galloping his gray mare. He kept horses in a stable out at his place in Richmond. But then I started thinking more about him—about the way he smiled, screwing up his eyes as if the sun was dazzling him, or about the way he looked when he took his shirt off after a hard game. When I was having relations with my wife, I was thinking about him. Oh, God—I didn't know what was happening to me. I'd never encountered anything like that before: I'm not one of those public school types to whom buggery is as familiar as Latin and geography. I've seen them about the West End, of course, painted up like tarts—but that wasn't me, and it certainly wasn't him. But there was no doubt in my mind about my feelings for Rhys. I'm not a fool, and I don't like blinding myself to the truth. I wanted him, and I began to think that maybe he wanted me as well."

"Go on, Andrews," I said. "Nothing you can say will shock us."

"It happened one weekend at his house in Richmond. He'd invited me to bring Christina and the girls; his sister was going to be there with her family, and he thought it would be jolly if we joined them. The women got on like a house on fire, and the children ran around the garden in a big happy gang. David and I took the horses out, and played tennis, and stayed up late drinking whiskey and talking about our lives. We were both a little drunk that first night, I suppose, and we gave away more than we had meant to about our feelings for each other—and before I knew what was happening, we had our arms around each other and we were kissing like sweethearts. He broke it off, not me. He stood up and walked to the other side of the room, muttering something about an early start in the morning, and we said good night as if nothing had happened. I lay awake till dawn thinking about him, unable to extinguish the fire that he'd lit.

"I must have looked like death warmed over at breakfast, and to tell the truth, so did he; the ladies made all sorts of comic remarks about smelling whiskey on our breath, and so on. We went along with it, but we couldn't catch each other's eyes. He went out for the rest of the morning, seeing his land agent, he said. But we had an agreement to play tennis that afternoon, while the women and children went for a walk in Richmond Park, and, as he hadn't positively canceled it, I assumed we were still on."

"And that's when it happened?"

"Yes. We both played appallingly, hitting the ball out of the court, not bothering to keep score, both of us pretending that it was the whiskey that had spoiled our concentration. Finally we gave it up as a bad job after about half an hour, and headed back indoors. The house was empty. He said he felt sweaty, and that he was going to have a bath, and that I was welcome to join him if I felt that it would do me good.

"We took those stairs three at a time, and reached the bathroom in seconds flat. As soon as the door was bolted, we started tearing each other's clothes off, kissing as we'd kissed the night before—but this time there was no pulling away. Soon we were both naked, pressing ourselves together, allowing our hands to roam everywhere. I had never been with a man in that way before, but I knew exactly what to do. It was like one of those dreams where one imagines one is a concert pianist, or a ballet dancer: the moves just come naturally, without thinking."

"And so you and he had sexual intercourse," said Dickinson, in that cold, forensic voice, as if it were an accusation made in a court of law.

"What?" Andrews looked like he had been awoken from that dream, and was none too pleased to find himself in the dining car of a train stuck in a tunnel with two inquisitive strangers. "Yes. What else do you think I'm trying to tell you?"

"What exactly did you do?"

"Does it matter?"

"It most certainly does." Dickinson winked at me behind Andrews's back.

"I don't know how to put it into words, except I suppose we did what…that sort of person normally does. Normally! It sounds terribly matter-of-fact. But at the time it seemed like I was flying through the sky. We took each other in every way we could think of. Thank God there was no one in the house. They'd have heard us shouting, and wondered what was going on."

"Did you perform anal intercourse?"

Andrews was starting to get annoyed; the upright family

118

man was back at the controls. "Yes, we did. I suppose you will arrest me now."

"Oh no, there's no need for that kind of unpleasantness." Dickinson licked his lips, rather as I imagine a wolf might before devouring a lamb. "I'm sure we can—"

I never found out what he was going to propose, because at that moment the train started moving again. Forward, this time, thank God, south, toward London, and most importantly out of the tunnel. There were no bumps and jolts, just a little rocking and swaying, but what did that matter compared to the blessed welcome daylight? It was fading fast, and had indeed never really got light, but what little illumination there was reflected back off the snow. Out of the dark, Andrews seemed to recover himself. He stood up, cleared his throat, and faced Dickinson, man to man.

"From that time on," he said, "David and I were inseparable. We met on the pretext of business or sport, but we were lovers. I loved him, he loved me. There. Write that in your notebook. I don't care."

"I wonder what your wife would say?"

"You cad."

"I think, sir, that most people would regard you as the cad in this situation."

"Words, words, words. What I want to know is, how are you going to find the killer?"

"I was rather hoping you might able to help us there, Mr. Andrews."

"You are not suggesting for one moment that I had anything to do with it?"

"Did you?"

"Of course not. I told you. I love him."

"And you would not be the first person to kill the one they say they love, in order to protect themselves. Was he threatening to tell your wife? Your employer?"

"Don't be ridiculous."

"Why were you in the lavatory together?"

"What?"

"This gentleman saw you."

"Why do you think? We were...together."

"On a train? Isn't that rather dangerous?"

"We had not been able to see each other for some time. Business had taken him away from London."

"And so you followed him to Edinburgh, did you?"

"I found a reason to be there, yes."

"To silence him?"

"No!"

"Then why?"

"Because I loved him, damn it! How many more times do you want to hear it? I loved him!"

"I suggest that you and he had a fight, that you made demands to which he objected, you fought, and then, when he got the better of you, you decided to kill him."

"Ridiculous!"

"Dickinson," I said, "for Christ's sake, can't you see the man's in agony?"

"And when the train was stuck in the tunnel, and everyone else was running around like a headless chicken, you got him in the lavatory and killed him and cut off his finger to make it look like robbery. Where is that finger?"

"How the hell should I know?"

"We'll find it, you know. And we'll find the knife you used to cut it off with. Be certain of that, Mr. Andrews."

They confronted each other across the carriage.

"Are you arresting me, Mr. Dickinson?"

"Not yet."

"In that case," said Andrews, his composure completely regained, "I shall rejoin my family."

"Isn't it a little late to be thinking of them?"

Andrews opened his mouth to speak, but thought better of it, and left the carriage. Dickinson smiled that horrible, wolfish smile, and lit a cigarette, blowing smoke out in a long, cool line.

"What was that all about?"

"You don't like my style of investigation, do you, Mitch?"

"It was cruel and unnecessary."

"And very efficient."

"You don't seriously think that Andrews had anything to do with Rhys's murder, do you?"

"Do you?"

"Of course not."

"Why not?"

"Because he loved him! Weren't you listening?"

"I was listening, Mitch. Were you?"

"What do you mean?"

"You heard what he said, I grant you. You lapped it up. I saw the look in your eyes. Poor Andrews, you thought, in love with another man just as you have been, trapped, desperate, at last he finds a friend, it's beautiful, how could he possibly kill him? But did it never occur to you that he was lying? Or do you think that all men of your persuasion are intrinsically honest?"

He had a point, but it was one I was unwilling to concede. "What do you mean, 'my' persuasion? Aren't you the same as me?"

"I'm a policeman, Mitch."

"Meaning?"

"Meaning I can't afford the luxury of being like you and your friends. Yes, I enjoy a bit of bum when it's on offer, I don't deny. I've got a big cock, and I like it to be appreciated. I very much want you down on your knees sucking it, then taking it up your arse. But I don't love you, Mitch."

"You don't love anyone, I suppose."

"Not on duty."

"I see."

I was torn between revulsion at his cold, misanthropic nature and excitement at the idea of submitting to his selfish desires. I took a step toward him, and was about to sink to my knees and worship his authority when it struck me.

The scent.

Lemons, maybe oranges, limes.

It was on the tip of my tongue to ask "Why did Andrews smell the same as you when we were in the tunnel for the first time?"—but for some reason the words died on my tongue. I stopped, stepped back. Dickinson must have seen something in my eyes.

"Don't judge me, Mitch. I'm just doing my job."

"Of course you are. And the last thing you need is a would-be Sherlock Holmes telling you how to do it. I'm sorry if I sounded harsh."

"That's fine. We're friends, aren't we?"

"Friends and more, I hope," I lied.

He sensed my unease. "Do you need to go somewhere, Mitch?"

"I should find Bertrand…"

"Go on, then. I won't keep you." He stood with his feet apart, his hands behind his back, thrusting his hips slightly forward. God, he was a powerfully attractive man! I wanted him to fuck me, I wanted to give in to him, to succumb to whatever threat he represented, to stop thinking for myself and let him take control…

"Thanks. I'll be back if you…need me."

"To help with the investigation, you mean?"

"Yes. Of course. I won't be long."

"Oh, and Mitch?"

"Yes?"

"Just one thing. Don't try to use the first-class bathroom."

I heard him laughing as I hurried down the corridor.

By now we were picking up speed, the countryside flashing past the windows, blurred lines of white and gray as we headed south through driving snow. The nightmare of the tunnel was receding, and it felt good to be on the move again, toward London, toward Boy Morgan. I hadn't thought of him for hours.

The corridors were quiet and empty; nobody wanted to move around much, I suppose, on a train where a man had been murdered. By now the news must have reached every single passenger. Someone on the train knew what had happened to David Rhys—perhaps more than one person. In any case, they would not wish to draw attention to themselves.

I walked past the bathroom, the door still locked, the floor bare where Dickinson had ripped up the sodden carpet. Past Daisy and Hugo's carriage—God knows what was going on in there. I had half a mind to pry, in the hope of catching a sight of Joseph's allegedly huge prick violating Daisy's famous mouth, but I hurried past. It was Bertrand who concerned me now. The poor boy had been thrown into the deep end, and he would need my help.

As I neared the third-class carriages, my way was blocked by two of the soldiers I had first spotted at York station, the dark, quiet one and the snub-nosed redhead. They leaned against opposite sides of the corridor, their legs extended, both of them smoking. There was no way of getting past without climbing over them.

"Gentlemen."

"Ah. Yankee Boy."

"How's it going?"

"Not bad." The redhead did all the talking; his friend looked at me through narrowed eyes, blowing smoke at me.

"Have you seen my friend?"

"The little frog?"

"Belgian, actually, but that's the man."

"I'd say we've seen him, haven't we, Ken?"

"Aye."

"Where is he?"

"In the conductor's car." He jerked a thumb over this shoulder, to the rear of the train.

"What's he doing there?"

The redhead grinned—he had a couple of teeth missing, which made him look like a boxer—and made an obscene gesture, thrusting two fingers of one hand into the other fist. It needed no interpretation.

"With…"

"Yeah. The sergeant, and McDonald."

I could picture the sergeant easily enough—and I vaguely remembered the fourth member of the party, a short, squat soldier with a prematurely receding hairline and a broken nose.

"Both of them?"

"Yeah. It's their turn."

"You mean…"

"Aye," said the taciturn Ken, "we've already had him."

"You haven't!"

"Don't believe me?" asked the redhead. "Then take a look." He faced the engine, and lifted up his kilt. His cock was still engorged from recent sexual activity, and from the tip of his long foreskin hung a milky drop of semen. He rubbed it between thumb and forefinger. "The rest went up his arse."

"I see." It was a nice cock, rosy red against the white of this thighs, clashing with the violent orange of his pubic hair. "And you, too?"

"Go on, Ken, show him."

Ken in turn lifted his skirt, and showed a bigger, thicker, darker piece of meat, again still swollen.

"That made him squeal, didn't it, Ken?"

"Aye. When you weren't keeping him quiet with your cock in his mouth."

This was exactly the kind of encounter that I'd been hoping for—two randy soldiers waving their half-hard, sticky dicks at me—but I was worried about Bertrand. Was he a willing victim of this four-man assault? I certainly would have been, but he was less hardened in vice than me.

"Let me past."

"Ain't you going to show us yours?"

"Not yet."

"Aw, come on," said the redhead, waggling his prick at me. "I'm getting hard again." And he was: his prick was getting fat around the middle, and it was climbing toward the horizontal. "Who knows? Maybe you can suck another load out of me, Yankee Boy."

I was quite sure I could: and I could fuck his rosy red ass as well, to pay him back for his impudence. But I had neither the opportunity nor the desire, at that moment, to do anything of the kind. Somehow I had exposed my poor assistant—as I now thought of Bertrand—to unspeakable degradation in the conductor's car.

"Another time, Red," I said. "I'll make it worth your while. And here's something while you're waiting." I held out a handful of coins, and he dropped his kilt.

"Pop it in my sporran, if you please, sir."

I believe that one of the functions of the sporran, that strange furry purse worn at the front of the kilt, is to weigh the skirt down in high winds or, presumably, in case of spontaneous erections. In any case, I enjoyed fumbling with the buckle, and gave Red's prick a good squeeze before I dropped the coins.

The soldiers stood aside and let me pass. I knew they would. They'd do anything for money.

The conductor's car was located at the rear of the train, and I passed through several third-class carriages as I went, scanning the faces for any obvious signs of homicidal mania. There was nothing unusual—just pale, frightened people who were glad to be on the move again, eager to get to London, the end of this horrible trip.

Access to the conductor's car was not easy. There was a door at the end of the third-class carriage, and beyond that, just the couplers, the track visible beneath them. To get into the car, one had to step carefully over the gap and through a wooden door—which, of course, was securely closed.

"There's nothing through there, pal," said one man, a laborer by the look of him, perhaps traveling to London to look for work. "Just a load of boxes and trunks, and a couple of soldiers. On guard duty, they said."

"Thank you, sir. I need to speak to them." I opened the carriage door, and thumped on the wooden end of the car. "Open up! Let me in!"

I could hear nothing above the roar and clatter of the wheels on the track, but if there was anyone in there, they would certainly have heard me knocking. I banged again, harder this time.

There was no particular reason why they should let me in—but, to my surprise, the door opened an inch and I saw the sergeant's face in the crack. I forged ahead, taking my life in my hands: if he'd slammed the door and I'd missed my footing, I might have fallen down between the cars and lost a leg, at the very least. Fortunately, the sergeant was well disposed to me, and he opened the door fully, extending a strong hand to pull me in.

The car was lit by storm lanterns, swaying around from hooks in the ceiling, casting crazy shadows from the luggage piled up and roped in place. One trunk had been placed in the middle of the floor, in the brightest pool of light. Over that trunk, lying on his stomach, his clothes pulled up and down to reveal the midsection of his body, from chest to knees, was Bertrand. He was facing away from me—the first thing that struck me was his widespread ass, the hole wet and open. I guessed that I had just disturbed the sergeant, who had pulled out, leaving Bertrand gaping. Just beyond the main circle of light stood the other soldier, the one they had called McDonald, his hands clasped around the back of Bertrand's head. He was completely naked, apart from his black leather shoes and long wool socks. His body, as it moved in and out of the light, was thickset and hairy. The sergeant wore his kilt, shoes, and socks, but no shirt.

"Come to join the party?" he asked, his voice low and gruff. He bolted the door behind me.

"Bertrand! Are you okay?"

"He's doing fine, I'd say. Wouldn't you?"

"Have you hurt him?"

The sergeant laughed. "I don't hear him complaining, do you?"

Bertrand was wriggling now, trying to move his head away from the cock that filled his mouth—he must have heard my voice.

"Now," said the sergeant, slowly unbuckling his kilt, never taking his eyes off me, "where was I? Ah, yes." He dropped his kilt to the floor, and his cock sprang up. "I remember." He spat in his hand and wiped it over the head. "Fucking the French boy."

Bertrand made a sort of grunting noise as McDonald's prick thrust into his mouth; surely he wasn't still trying to assert his Belgian nationality at this critical moment?

The sergeant turned and positioned himself between Bertrand's spread legs, aiming his thick, long dick at the target. Then, with one slow, firm thrust, the whole thing disappeared into the warm tightness that I knew so well. The sergeant sighed, closed his eyes, and started fucking. From the way Bertrand's hips were moving, I could tell that he was enjoying himself. He raised his ass to meet the sergeant's thrusts, bracing himself on the trunk with his elbows. Soon the sergeant, McDonald, and Bertrand had established a rhythm; each shove from the rear pushed Bertrand down onto McDonald's dick, each thrust from the front rammed his buttocks against the sergeant's hairy thighs.

I stood for a while watching in stunned silence, but that couldn't last long; my dick was eager to join in. Bertrand had no holes left to fuck; I would have to wait my turn. Judging by the way the pace was accelerating, I would not have to wait long. In order to waste no time, I started undressing. It was cold in that car, I suppose, but three naked men were warming it up nicely, and I was ready to add my body heat to theirs. I slipped off my shoes and jacket, pulled my shirt over my head, and started unbuttoning my pants.

"Come here," ordered the sergeant, never breaking the rhythm he was beating into Bertrand's ass. "Let me."

His hands were huge, his fingers thick but surprisingly deft as he opened my fly and started feeling the bulge in my underpants. Then, to my surprise, he started kissing me full on the mouth. I must have made a very good impression at York station, I thought, rather smugly.

The sergeant drew my cock out—it was, of course, fully erect—and started squeezing and stroking it while never breaking the kiss. His mouth tasted of tobacco and whiskey and—yes, I was certain—cock and ass. He must have prepared Bertrand for fucking just as a gentleman should.

My pants dropped around my ankles and I stepped out of them. I heard McDonald groan, and out of the corner of my eye saw him pumping hard into Bertrand's face, groaning as he shot his load. His cock withdrew from Bertrand's mouth with a plop, and before I knew it McDonald was on his knees sucking me. Bertrand raised himself on his elbows and craned his neck to watch.

"Oh, Mitch..."

"I can't wait to hear... Oh, yeah... How you got yourself into this mess."

"They... They made me... I'm sorry."

"Don't apologize." I could say no more, as the sergeant

pulled me back into a kiss. His stubbly face was setting my skin on fire. From the ardor of his kisses, I guessed he wasn't far off either.

But before he reached the point of no return, he broke the kiss and pulled out of Bertrand's ass. "Turn over," he commanded. "I want to see your face when I fuck you."

Bertrand obeyed, and in the light of the lantern I could see how the rough wood of the trunk had pressed into his hairy belly. But his cock was as hard as could be, and had already oozed a sticky load of precum. He'd obviously not yet been allowed to come, despite the fact that the other two soldiers had already taken their turns with him.

The sergeant slid his big dick back into him, and Bertrand sighed and closed his eyes. I watched the big man's muscular buttocks rippling as he pumped away, holding Bertrand's ankles in his strong, hairy hands. McDonald was still slurping on my cock; he was obviously not the type to give up just after coming. I looked down on the top of his head, which was remarkably bald for one so young, and grabbed his ears.

The sergeant grunted, pulled out of Bertrand's ass and shot one huge load of semen right over his body; it landed with a splat on the floor behind Bertrand's head. The rest—and there was a great deal—was soon glistening on his belly, running down his sides, matting the hair. The sergeant buckled at the knees, and put an arm around my shoulders for support.

"Just you two to go now, then," he said. "How are you going to do it?"

I was ready to pump a load down McDonald's throat, but I could not bear to see poor Bertrand left unattended, so I disengaged my dick and took the sergeant's place. Bertrand was not quite as tight as he had been the first time I fucked him, and he was well lubricated. I slipped in easily, and set about fucking him as hard as I could. The two soldiers watched and offered crude encouragement, smacking

Bertrand around the face with their sticky, half-hard cocks. Bertrand started jerking himself, hard and fast. I felt his ass ring tighten around me, and soon he was adding his own load to the sergeant's. I kept fucking him as he squirmed and moaned on his uncomfortable bed, then I leaned forward, pressing my belly against his, lifting his ass into the air and pumping another load inside him. The soldiers applauded.

It was a rather quiet procession that made its way through the third-class carriages toward the front of the train. The sergeant went first, then me, then Bertrand, then McDonald. It must have looked as if we were under arrest. I hope nobody had a keen sense of smell: the aroma of sex must have been strong on us, but fortunately a good many of the passengers were smoking. The sergeant and McDonald rejoined their brothers in arms, and started passing around a bottle of whiskey. I would have liked to join them, but there was a small matter of a murder to solve.

"What have you found, Mitch?" asked Bertrand in a half-whisper, as we walked forward.

"Plenty," I said, thinking of the interviews that Dickinson and I had conducted. "Plenty."

"But what, exactly?"

We had reached our compartment, and sat down, closing the door.

"Well…" I began. And then I realized that I did not have the slightest idea who had killed David Rhys. I was still in the dark.

# VIII

OUR RECENT EXERCISE IN THE CONDUCTOR'S CAR, AND THE steady jogging of the train, made both Bertrand and me very comfortable when we finally reached the safe haven of our carriage. He was complaining of a headache—the soldiers had plied him with whiskey, he said, but he would say no more (for now) of his "ordeal"—and my head was splitting for different reasons. I couldn't understand what was happening here, under my very nose, on this train. I was confused and in shock, I suppose. The discovery of the body, the distress of Andrews, the muddle of assumed identities, and, above all, the brutal methods of Superintendent Dickinson, had been too much for me. We exchanged a little desultory conversation, and then, I'm ashamed to say, we both fell asleep.

The next thing I knew, Bertrand was tugging on my sleeve.

"We've stopped again, Mitch!"

My eyes were dry and my tongue was stuck to the roof of my mouth; I don't like sleeping in the afternoon. I had had strange, vivid dreams, and for a moment or two I couldn't remember what was real and what was fantasy. But there was Bertrand—very much flesh and blood—and outside the window were the lights of Peterborough station. It was dark outside. The snow had given way, as we traveled south, to a nasty, wet sleet, making the platforms glisten.

I heard the slam of carriage doors and the tramp of feet, and saw the unmistakable dark blue of a British policeman's uniform. Looking up and down the platform, I could see that the station was crawling with cops. How they had got there I did not have time to figure out—but their purpose was all too clear. They swarmed aboard the train at each end, while each door was guarded. We were surrounded.

I heard the sound of running feet and quickly stepped out into the corridor, where I almost collided with Mr. Andrews. His eyes were wide, his brow damp with sweat. He almost screamed when he ran into me, but then a look of wild hope crossed his face.

"Can you hide me?"

"I don't know—"

"You must believe me, I didn't kill him. I loved him. You understand. Please, help me. I did not kill him."

Tramp, tramp, tramp came the heavy police boots along the corridor.

Andrews's eyes scanned our compartment for hiding places—under the seats, up on the luggage racks.

"Please..."

"There is nothing I can do. What can I do?"

I wanted to help him, but I was neither willing nor able to pit myself against the full weight of the law.

They were nearly upon us. Andrews took one last desperate look at the window, calculated his chances of escape at zero, and suddenly relaxed.

"It's quite all right," he said, more himself again. "I understand." He rummaged in his jacket pocket and pulled out a small slip of paper. The police were at the compartment door, and Andrews had no time for explanations. He dropped the paper behind him and held out his hands.

"William Andrews?"

"Yes."

"I am arresting you on suspicion of the murder of David Rhys."

Andrews was handcuffed and led away. The tramp, tramp, tramp of boots receded, doors slammed again, the train was quiet.

Bertrand and I looked at each other and ran to the window, just in time to see Andrews's blond head being pushed into a waiting police car. I saw Peter Dickinson, immaculate as ever, shake hands with a uniformed colleague, before the bells rang and the car pulled away.

The engine puffed and hissed, and we were on the move again. Dickinson remained on the platform. I watched his figure recede as we moved onward to London.

Bertrand was poring over the scrap of paper that Andrews had left behind him.

"What does it say?"

"It is an address in London."

"Where?"

Bertrand handed me the paper—torn from the top of a letter, a printed address in curly type.

"The Rookery Club, 43 Russell Square," I read. "Why do you suppose he dropped that?"

"An accident?"

"That was no accident. That was a message. When we get to London, we'll go to the Rookery Club, 43 Russell Square."

"You do not believe that he is the killer?"

"No."

"But why? The police believe he is."

"There is something wrong."

"What?"

133

"The smell."

Bertrand looked confused, as well he might; I barely knew what I was thinking. "Something does not stack up. Why would Andrews kill Rhys, the man he loved?"

"*Quoi?*"

I explained, briefly, what Andrews had confessed in the dining car; Bertrand was wide-eyed. "Perhaps, after all, you are right—all British men really are this way."

"Certainly on this train that seems to be the case."

"But, after all, this Monsieur Dickinson, he is a detective, no? And he has his reasons for believing the Andrews is the killer."

"You said yourself that you didn't like Dickinson."

"*Pff.* I do not like the police. That does not mean to say that I think they are necessarily wrong."

"But in this case I think they are. I think there is something going on that we don't know about. The smell..."

"Always this smell. What are you talking about?"

"When Andrews came back into the dining car after the blackout, he smelled of lemons, limes, something like that. A very distinctive citrus perfume. Only one other person on this train smells the same."

"Dickinson."

"Ah! You noticed it too. And for Andrews to smell that way, he must have had some close contact with Dickinson before the murder. That, to me, seems suspicious."

"*Bien*, if that is all, I think there are others on this train who have had what you call close contact with Dickinson. Perhaps they, too, had *une liaison*."

"I don't think so. Andrews was desperately in love with Rhys. He had traveled all the way to Scotland to be near him—and I think he had even brought his family on this train just so they could be together. Why would a man who is so much in love risk everything for a few moments of fun with Peter Dickinson?"

Bertrand looked sulky. "He interested you."

I was stung. Bertrand was right: I'd been eager enough to rush into *une liaison* with Dickinson.

He put an arm around my shoulder. "Come. Let us consider the aspects of the story. We shall find the truth, shall we?"

I doubted that we would: I had proved myself to be a wholly unworthy detective, fucking and napping on the job while an innocent man was framed for a murder that someone else on the train had committed.

"First of all," I began, "there is Hugo Taylor, who received a blow to the head and was reluctant to tell me the truth about how it happened. I don't buy his story about the cocktail cabinet, or whatever it was. Second, there's Daisy Athenasy, whose dope habit has probably involved her in some kind of drug smuggling operation. She's costing the studio thousands of pounds, she is unfaithful to her rich, older husband, who is also her employer, and she loves diamonds, which links her to David Rhys."

"If he was, in fact, a diamond merchant," Bertrand observed.

"Good point. Andrews says he wasn't. Also in Hugo Taylor's party is Francis Laking, aristocratic but impoverished, desperate for money, possibly to pay off blackmailers; he's such a screaming queen that he's almost certainly attracted that kind of attention. He's charming, he's witty, he knows everyone, but does anyone really know him? Is he who he says he is?"

"In short, you suspect everyone."

"Look at Peter Dickinson. Posing as an employee of the British-American Film Company, but in fact a superintendent from Scotland Yard. Lady Antonia Petherbridge—to all appearances the epitome of the English upper classes, but in fact, according to Francis Laking, a dangerous political radical, probably with dubious foreign connections."

"And me?"

"What?"

"What about me?" Bertrand said skeptically. "Surely, as a foreigner, I come under suspicion. Traveling without a ticket, my clothes—*comment dire, débraillé?*—poor, and old, and dirty. Perhaps an anarchist, with a bomb in my suitcase."

"You don't have a suitcase."

"And look how easily I befriended you. And what was Simmonds really saying to me in the *toilette*? And why did I entertain the soldiers? *Hein?*"

This gave me pause. What did I know about Bertrand, apart from the fact that his ass fit my dick like a glove?

"What are you trying to tell me?"

"Simply this. We are all strange, to those who look hard enough."

"Then we must continue to look."

"*Bien.* And my soldiers?"

"I hadn't thought of them. But yes, what about 'your' soldiers? Why did they find it so desirable to keep us out of the way at the rear of the train while we were stuck in the tunnel for the second time?"

"Because, perhaps, they realized what a good fuck I am," said Bertrand, looking very pleased with himself.

"Yes. But perhaps, also, they were following orders."

Bertrand shrugged. "*Je ne sais pas.* For me it is too much."

There was nothing we could do for the rest of the trip other than stare out the window, stare at my notes, and stare at each other. You might be forgiven for expecting me to beguile the time by fucking Bertrand again, or at least getting him to suck my dick. But, for once in my life, I was not in the mood. I felt defeated and dismayed. I trusted nobody, and I felt impotent—not only in the sexual sense. There was nothing I could do to help Andrews, and I was certain, for reasons that had not yet struggled above the level of intuition, that he was innocent.

Also, of course, there was the fact that I had already come three times in the last 12 hours, once up Vince's ass and twice up Bertrand's.

The rhythm of the train soothed me. Ter-ticky-ti-tum-tum. Ter-ticky-ti-tum-tum. Ter-ticky-ti-tum-tum. There's nothing I can do. There's nothing I can do...

I slept again, and woke, cold and miserable, as the train pulled into Kings Cross Station, journey's end. It was eight o'clock in the evening. We were nearly two hours late. The passengers were already alighting from the train with boxes and bags, hailing porters, disappearing into the crowd. What chance had I of piecing together the events of the day, now that all the witnesses had disappeared? Who was I fooling? I wasn't a detective—not even an amateur. I'd been involved in one freak crime a few years ago, and I'd fed that fantasy with a lot of random reading and daydreaming—but when it came down to it, I'd been led by my dick, blinded by lust, and hoodwinked by a crafty copper. For all I knew, I had helped the killer to strike.

Nothing but a lingering smell of lemons, and that scrap of paper that Andrews had dropped in the compartment before his arrest. I stared at it, as if it might somehow rescue my shattered self-respect.

There was a discreet cough at the compartment door. I looked up, and there stood Simmonds.

"Excuse me, sir."

"Yes?"

"I wanted to apologize to the young gentleman for the... er...the way I behaved earlier. It was unforgivable."

I was in no mood to be charitable, and interrupted Bertrand before he had a chance to accept the no doubt sincere apology. "It's rather late for fine words, Simmonds. You should have thought of that before you beat him up. If you think you can stop us from complaining to the authorities, you're—"

"*Tais-toi*, Mitch. It is quite all right, *monsieur*. I forgive you. You were only doing your job."

"No, sir. I was not."

"Excuse me?"

"I was acting beyond my authority."

"What do you mean?" I asked.

"I had been told... Oh, God, what have I done?" He sat down, and gripped his hair in his hands.

"Pull yourself together, Simmonds," I said, feeling perhaps that some vital piece of information was about to drop into my lap, "and tell us what's on your mind."

"That Mr. Dickinson..."

Dickinson again. Always Dickinson.

"Yes? What about him?"

"He told me that there were reporters on the train, and he told me to deal with them harshly. I was not to let them anywhere near Mr. Taylor's carriage. I was to use...force, if necessary."

"But why Bertrand? He doesn't look like a reporter. Does he?"

"Dickinson told me he was."

"*Moi? Journaliste? Mon dieu*," said Bertrand, as if the very thought disgusted him.

"So you dragged him into the bathroom, beat him up, and attempted to have sex with him."

"Ah, that."

"Yes, ah that, Simmonds. You didn't think that Bertrand would have kept that quiet, did you?"

"I am sorry. I don't know what came over me."

"The point is that you nearly came over Bertrand. He said you tried to stick your cock in his mouth."

"I... Well, I... It had been a long time, and..."

"I see. And how much money did Dickinson give you? I presume there was money involved."

"No, sir. But he said that he'd overlook certain matters."

"Arthur."

"Among others."

"Did Arthur squeal?"

"I don't know. Someone did, I suppose. Dickinson said he knew all about me. He said he knew every queer in Edinburgh."

I gulped. My happy home life with Vince suddenly seemed terribly vulnerable.

"And did he threaten to expose you?"

"Yes. I have a wife and children, sir. I have an elderly mother who lives with us. I'm a church warden. Oh, God forgive me…"

Bertrand's eyes were wet, and even I was starting to feel sorry for the man, who, after all, had only taken advantage of a situation, as I had done on many occasions. Admittedly I had never hit anyone (at least, not without being invited to first), but then I was not living under the dreadful conditions that Simmonds endured.

"You have to make up for what you have done, Simmonds."

"Yes, sir. I see that."

"Are you willing to help us?"

"How can I help you, sir?" He looked up at me, the very picture of grief and remorse.

"Help us find the killer of David Rhys."

"But… You don't mean… The man they arrested at Peterborough…"

"Andrews. Exactly. He no more killed Rhys than you or I did. Assuming, that is, that you didn't."

"For God's sake—"

"Exactly. You may be a bad man, Simmonds, but I don't think you're that bad."

"But Superintendent Dickinson said that he had proof."

"Oh, and I'm sure he does. Proof that will stand up very nicely in court, watertight and tailor-made. But I don't like that kind of proof. It is based on facts, rather than human nature." I was paraphrasing Hercule Poirot here, but as neither Bertrand nor Simmonds was a reader of detective fiction I felt I was on safe ground. They looked full of admiration, hanging on my words. I rather liked that.

"So," I continued, rapidly improvising, "the question is, who had the motive for killing Rhys? Who would want him dead? What does our knowledge of the people on board this train tell us?"

"According to you, Mitch, everyone on this train is either homicidal or homosexual," Bertrand piped up.

"That may be true..."

"So," said Simmonds, "what should we do?"

"We? So you are with us, then?"

"Yes. I don't have to return to Edinburgh for a couple of days. The wife and kids are with her mother. I'm supposed to be visiting my family, but I'd be very happy to come with you." I noticed that he was casting sidelong glances at Bertrand, who was blushing and staring at his feet. Ah! So that was the way the wind was blowing, was it? Bertrand's "disgust" for Simmonds was not quite as profound as he had originally suggested.

"Good. Between us, we will solve the mystery. I am staying with my friend Boy Morgan, who lives off the Kings Road in Chelsea. I suggest that we find you a cheap hotel somewhere."

"I know the very place, sir," said Simmonds. "The Regal Hotel in Bloomsbury. It's where I tend to stay when I'm... not staying with my relations."

"I see. A sympathetic establishment."

"Very."

"Is it clean?" asked Bertrand, assuming his coffee-drinking expression.

"It's clean and it's quiet," said Simmonds. "It is also affordable."

That hit home.

"As for that," I said, "I will cover any expenses, within reason. I assume that the two of you would not object to sharing a room?"

Bertrand blushed deeper, and Simmonds stared out the window.

"I thought as much. Good." I gave Bertrand a few bills. "That should cover your immediate needs. Oh, and Bertrand, for God's sake, get yourself some new clothes."

I was still puzzling over the mystery of the Flying Scotsman as I left Kings Cross in search of a taxi that would take me to Chelsea. Boy Morgan had expected me hours ago and would be worried by now. Perhaps he had telephoned Kings Cross and learned of the delay. Perhaps he had heard that someone had died on the train, and was fretting over me. Yes, surely he still cared enough for that. Surely the closeness we had enjoyed at Cambridge and after meant something to him still, as it did to me...

The cab trundled south, but I was oblivious to the sights and sounds of the town. I could only think of Morgan, and the welcome that I hoped he had prepared for me. God forgive me, I had even stopped worrying about David Rhys.

"I'd given you up for lost."

Boy Morgan stood in the doorway in a white shirt, unbuttoned at the throat, the sleeves rolled halfway up his long, muscular arms, lights from the hall blazing behind him.

Well, that answered one question: he had not lost his looks in the months since I had seen him.

"We had a little trouble on the line," I said, struggling up the steps with my cases. "You'll never believe what happened. We got stuck in this tunnel south of York, and while we were in there—"

I got no further than that. Morgan threw his arms around

me, hugging me tight against his chest, and then, before I had time to catch my breath, kissed me on the mouth. There was not much I could do—my hands were weighed down with luggage—but I opened my lips and allowed his tongue to enter.

That answered another question: he was just as eager as me to resume our relations where they had left off.

"So," he said, eyes shining and cheeks flushed, "Vince couldn't make it this time?"

"No, he's—"

"And Belinda has gone to bed already. She gets so tired, looking after the baby, you know—"

"Boy."

"Yes, Mitch?"

"Could I possibly come in?"

"Oh! God! Sorry!" He suddenly realized that we were embracing in an open doorway, that I was holding my luggage and was travel-weary. "Yes, of course. Let me help you. We don't run to a butler and a footman in this establishment, I'm afraid. You'll have to make do with me." He took my luggage, and I followed him up the stairs.

"The nursery is on the top floor; that's where Belinda sleeps most nights, so as not to disturb me if she has to get up."

"I see. And where am I?"

"Down here." He led me along the landing. "It's not too bad. You've got your own bathroom and everything."

"Sounds ideal."

"Speaking of which, I bet you could do with a bath, couldn't you? We've got running hot water, you know."

"Even in Edinburgh, we don't have to boil kettles."

"I could start running it for you, if you like."

"That would be—mmmmmffff!" The moment we were inside the guest room, he dropped the cases and started kissing me again. This time my hands were free, and I was able to feel the familiar rower's muscles, the narrow waist, the high, firm buttocks, and that ever-present bulge in his pants. God, he was even more eager than I was—but then, I reflected, he probably hadn't shot three loads already today. Given his wife's nursery duties, I wondered if he had sex more than once or twice a week. Well, I'd soon make up any shortfall in that department.

"Take your clothes off."

"Boy—"

"Please. I want to see you again." He was tugging at my shirt, pulling it out of my waistband.

"Come on, then. Help yourself." I stood still and allowed him to undress me. It reminded me of nights at Cambridge, when we'd helped each other to dress for the May Ball, or formal dinners—but in reverse. This time, instead of putting in collar studs, tying ties, and buttoning buttons, he was removing everything as fast as possible—and not with the greatest finesse. Buttons and studs were pinging across the floor, and when he encountered some difficulty with my fly, he simply tugged until the offending button tore off.

"Easy, Boy! I don't have that many pairs of pants!"

He was kneeling in front of me now, and looked up with those adoring puppy-dog eyes that I'd long ago fallen in love with.

"It's been ages, Mitch."

"Yeah. So a few seconds won't make much difference."

"I can't wait."

"You always were impatient," I said. "Here." I hoisted the leg of my underpants aside and pulled my cock out, thinking that I'd better give him what he wanted before he shredded my entire wardrobe. He looked very grateful.

"It's bigger than ever."

"Your mind's playing tricks, Boy."

"Can I suck it?"

I wanted him to, of course, but it occurred to me that it

needed a good wash before it went anywhere.

"Hold your horses. Where's this bath I was promised?"

"Coming right up."

He disappeared into the en suite bathroom, giving me leisure to remove the clothes that he'd left in such a state of disarray. It was difficult to untie my shoelaces, hobbled as I was by my pants, but I managed somehow. When Morgan came back into the room, I was stark naked.

"You've got hairier," he said.

"Must be that cold Scottish weather."

"Come here, Mitch." He held his arms open. "Let me hold you."

There's always been something about the juxtaposition of a fully clothed man with a naked man that has stimulated my interest. I let him hold me, feel me, kiss me from the neck downward. When his mouth traveled south of my navel, I pulled him back to his feet.

"Your turn," I said. "Show me what two years of married life has done to you."

"I'm still in good shape," he said, whacking himself in the gut. "I keep myself fit."

"I don't know... You look a little bit thick around the middle." He looked nothing of the sort, but I loved teasing him. He didn't bother to unbutton his shirt, but pulled it right over his head. He was as lean and muscular as ever.

"There. What do you think?"

"Not too bad, Morgan, for a sedentary city boy. But I bet you've got a big fat ass from sitting in that bank all day."

"Bollocks." He undid his belt and was soon stepping out of his pants and underpants. All that was left was his black wool socks.

"Turn around." He obeyed. "Hmmm. Not bad." I smacked him hard on the ass, as we used to in the changing rooms after rowing practice, and grabbed his dick, long and lean and as stiff as a broom handle. "Not bad at all."

"Come on. Your bath's ready."

"Is there room for two?"

"All in good time. First of all, I'm going to wash away the cares of the day."

I stepped into the steaming water and sat down—it felt good. Morgan knelt on the bathmat, rubbing soap onto a sponge.

"Right. Let's get you nice and clean." He started washing the back of my neck, my shoulders. I lifted my arms and he worked the soapy sponge around my armpits, pushing the dense black hair into whorls.

"Now lie back."

My cock broke the surface like a periscope as Morgan washed my chest, my stomach, skirting down my hips and on to my thighs. He pulled my feet up one at a time and washed them by hand, working the soap between the toes, massaging and caressing me until I was almost falling asleep. Even my dick was relaxing, and had fallen from the upright to the horizontal, lying across one thigh. It wouldn't be allowed to rest for long.

"It's been so long, Mitch..."

"Mmmm..."

"I wasn't sure if you would still...you know...want to."

"Mmmm..."

"What with me being married, and you being with Vince."

"Morgan?"

"Yes, Mitch?"

"Can we talk about this later? Right now I just want to make up for lost time."

"Right. Yes, of course." He was blushing; Morgan always blushed easily, either from embarrassment or arousal, and this time it was a combination of the two. He stood up; his dick was still as stiff as before, and there was a tasty-looking droplet oozing out of his pisshole.

"Looks like you're ready to explode."

"Yeah..." He slapped his cock a few times with the palm of his hand—it bounced crazily in the air. "I just need somewhere to stick it."

This was the Morgan I knew—direct and to the point. And, all things considered, it was probably better if he played the man this time around. I'd done so much fucking in the last few hours that I was by no means confident of being up to the job. I raised my knees.

"You haven't washed my ass yet."

He took the hint, soaped up his hands, and started rubbing vigorously around my wet hole. The water sloshed around the tub, lapping over my cock and balls. His middle finger found its way inside me, giving me a taste of what was to come. I hauled myself into a seated position and tried to get my mouth onto his cock, but it was too awkward; I slipped forward, taking a great deal more of his finger inside me and, I fear, almost spraining his wrist in the process.

"I'd better get out. You can fuck me on the floor."

Without bothering to towel myself dry, I knelt on the bathmat and offered my dripping ass.

"Oh, Mitch..."

It didn't take long. He lubricated his cock from a tub of Brylcreem in the bathroom cabinet, knelt between my feet, and pushed. I took him all the way, pressing my face into my forearms. It hurt, but it felt so good.

We knew each other well enough to fall quickly into a rhythm—and Morgan was so horny that he needed to come, and soon. I surrendered to the feeling in my ass—I didn't have a lot of choice—and to my surprise I felt my own orgasm building up inside me. It's just as well the bathroom was below the nursery; if we had been above, Belinda surely would have heard a strange rhythmic banging as her husband fucked me. His hands gripped my hips, pulling me into him. The momentum increased, and Morgan started to huff and grunt, a sure sign that he was about to come. When he did, he collapsed on top of me, and I felt his hard stomach, his erect nipples, make contact with my back. Those last few merciless thrusts sent me over the edge, and I squirted onto the bathmat.

Morgan, thankfully, is always in a good mood after sex; other men might have been overcome by remorse at what he had just done. He pulled out of me and jumped in the bath, splashing water over his athletic limbs, washing his cock, squeezing out the last few drops of spunk. When he was done, I jumped in and did likewise. We toweled down, drying each other's backs, and crept out of the bathroom with our clothes bundled under our arms.

We parted on the landing.

"This is your room, Mitch. You'll find everything you need for the night. Sort your cases out in the morning. Sleep tight." He looked left and right, up and down, and kissed me on the lips, ruffling my hair. "It's good to have you back, old chap."

We went to our separate beds and I, for one, slept like a log.

# IX

Morgan put a cup of tea on my bedside table and drew back the curtains.

"Come on, lazybones! Belinda's dying to see you, cook is getting impatient about breakfast, and I'm bloody starving." He pulled back the covers; I was naked under them, and hard, as usual upon waking. "Oof! Bit too early in the morning for that." He turned away. "Oh, by the way. Telegram for you. Just arrived. Hurry up and get dressed. I'll see you downstairs."

I tore the telegram open; it was from Vince, of course.

ENJOY LONDON STOP BEST TO MORGAN AND BELINDA STOP LOVE YOU STOP VINCE

My heart somersaulted in my chest, and I felt a rush of confused emotion—love, shame, pride in Vince for having sent such a message, guilt at my own almost nonstop betrayal, interrupted only by sleep. I put the telegram in my wallet, splashed water on my face, and dressed quickly.

Clean clothes had been laid out for me—presumably while I snored. Perhaps by Belinda.

She stood when I came into the dining room, and held the baby out to me. It crowed, and extended its arms, and I was obliged to take it. Morgan beamed.

"Mitch, darling," said Belinda, kissing me on both cheeks. "How good to see you again. I hope the journey wasn't too awful. We heard that you'd been stuck in the tunnel." She shuddered. "What a nightmare."

Was that all they had heard? Perhaps the news of Rhys's death, and the arrest at Peterborough station, had been suppressed—for now, at least.

"Oh, it wasn't too bad. I found ways to pass the time."

"I don't doubt it," said Morgan, who knew me too well. "Come on, old chap. Breakfast. We've been waiting hours for you and the toast has gone all soft. Cook!" He shouted.

"Harry, darling, please use the bell."

"Oh, sorry, old girl. Can't get used to it." He tugged on the tapestry bell pull.

The baby was blowing bubbles, grabbing handfuls of my face with its clammy hands.

"So, Mitch," said Belinda, "what do you think of your goddaughter?"

Of course! That's why I was here. "Oh, she's absolutely splendid. What a little beauty." I held her up in the air, bounced her a few times, and was showered with spit for my troubles.

"Here, hand her back," said Belinda. "I can see you're not used to little children."

I wiped my eye with a napkin. The baby started squalling.

"What have I done?"

"Good lord, Mitch, you don't have to do anything to set a little one off," said Morgan. "Don't look for rhyme and reason where children are concerned. I'll take her, darling."

He scooped the baby up and soon had her gurgling and laughing again. He looked perfectly at ease with the child, who clearly adored him.

Belinda smiled fondly. "I think Harry's met his intellectual match at last, don't you, Mitch?"

"Certainly looks that way."

The cook, who looked exactly like the many aunts I'd left behind in Boston, appeared in the door, arms folded.

"Ah, cook," said Belinda. "Mr. Mitchell is up, and we are ready for breakfast."

"So I see."

"Complete works, Mitch? Egg, bacon, sausage, fried bread, grilled tomatoes, mushrooms, eh?"

"Oh, I, well..." I was hungry enough to eat whatever cook could give me, but the look on her face was making me nervous.

"Don't worry about cook. Her bark's worse than her bite. Eh, Mrs. Sleightholme?"

"I don't know why I put up with your sense of humor, sir, I really don't," said the formidable Mrs. Sleightholme, but I could see that she was melted by Morgan's cheerful manner—as was everyone. "I suppose I'll manage to rustle up something, even at this late hour." It was barely half past eight, but she was making me feel as if I'd slept till noon.

"Good show. Two full fry-ups then. Belinda will nibble on a piece of dry toast, as usual."

"Some of us are trying to regain our figure after you-know-what," said Belinda. "It's all right for you." She prodded Morgan in the stomach. "You get plenty of exercise. All I do is change nappies."

Morgan grabbed her hand, brought it to his face, and kissed it. The baby, sandwiched between its parents, chuckled in delight. Husband and wife were obviously very much in love. Any evil thoughts I may have harbored—how Morgan would break down and confess that it had all been a horrible mistake, that he wanted me after all—were crushed. I remembered the telegram from Vince and felt like even more of a heel.

Breakfast came and went, the baby was charming, and Belinda was every bit as nice as I remembered. The perfect match for my best friend. A wonderful mother and a beautiful woman. C'est la vie.

Dishes cleared and baby taken out for its walk, I told Morgan all about the adventure of the Flying Scotsman, of Rhys's death, and the suspicious cast of characters that had dispersed at Kings Cross Station. I left out a few irrelevant details—but there was enough fucking and sucking in the narrative to keep him interested.

"I knew there would be some kind of excitement when you arrived! And here we have it—a ready-made murder mystery. Gosh, won't that be fun!"

"Boy, you talk about it as if it's a game. A man died."

"I know, old chap. But come on, admit it. It's thrilling."

"Yes," I said, trying not to sound too gung-ho—but Boy's enthusiasm was hard to resist. "And what would you suggest we do about it?"

"Pay a few calls. Ask a few questions. Track people down. Come on, Mitch, this stinks to high heavens. You know you're not going to go back to Edinburgh without getting to the bottom of it." He paused for a moment, thoughtful, then added "and you're not going back to Edinburgh without getting to the bottom of me, either. My poor arse hasn't been fucked for so long I've practically forgotten what it feels like."

"Come on. All those guys at the rowing club…"

"You must be joking. They'd tar and feather a fellow sooner than admit they like a bit of bum fun."

"I'll come to that in good time," I said, letting my hand brush over one tight buttock.

"Come up it, you mean."

151

"But you're going to have to earn it."

"I see. The old Holmes and Watson act, is it?"

"Something like that. So where do we start?"

"That's easy, guv. Your new friend Hugo Taylor opens in a play tonight."

"You're right. With Tallulah Bankhead."

"Oh, God. Ghastly woman," said Morgan, "but the wife likes her. Want to go?"

"Yes, but how on earth can we get tickets to a Hugo Taylor first night?"

"Come on, Mitch, you're the friend of the stars. Pull strings."

I telephoned the Regal Hotel, and was told that the gentlemen in Room 23 had not yet got up—that didn't surprise me—and I left a message, arranging to meet at the Garrick Theatre.


There was no sign of Bertrand and Simmonds when we turned up at the Garrick—already, at midday, the scene of a minor riot. Fans of both sexes were milling around the front of the building, hoping to catch a glimpse of the stars. Office girls mixed with slim young men in belted raincoats and soft felt hats; both Taylor and Bankhead attracted the ardent admiration of what the newspapers referred to as "the lavender league." The opening of *La Dame aux Camélias*, with Tallulah as Marguerite Gautier, Hugo as her lover Armand, was a gala day in the West End. The "Tonight at 8.00" signs were pasted over with SOLD OUT notices.

It was time, as Morgan said, to pull strings.

We elbowed our way through the crowd—and I felt a few hands "accidentally" touching me fore and aft along the way. Finally we made it to the door, where a splendid uniformed attendant was keeping the crowd at bay.

"I have an appointment with Mr. Hugo Taylor."

This kind of lie might well have earned me a kick in the

pants, but I was in luck. Perhaps the attendant had been told that Mr. Taylor was in the habit of receiving strange young men at the theater; perhaps he simply liked the sound of my American accent. In any case, he let us in.

And there, standing in the lobby surrounded by a throng of pressmen, was Francis Laking. He saw me, wiggled his fingers, and eventually tore himself away.

"Please, gentlemen, that's enough! Honestly! They would rip you to shreds, those reporters. Mitch, darling." He kissed me on the cheek; Morgan looked uncomfortable. "And who is your new friend? I say, you don't waste any time, do you? Only in London a few hours."

"Harry Morgan. Sir Francis Laking, baronet."

They shook hands.

"And if I might say so, Frankie, you don't waste much time either. I thought you were attached to Miss Athenasy.

"So I was. But really, I've had enough of her. And besides, with her being taken into custody, there's not much to do."

"What?"

"Didn't you hear? My dear, I don't suppose you did. They will have hushed it up. She was picked up at Kings Cross, you know, and probably not for the first time. Bags full of swag, apparently."

"What? Drugs?" Dickinson had told me about suitcases full of heroin—but Dickinson could be lying.

"No, jewelry."

"Good God. So the diamond ring…"

"No comment." He put his finger to his lips. "We can't talk here. Come through to the green room."

Inside, Frankie threw himself down on a battered leather couch—scene, I imagined, of many an amorous backstage encounter. The green room was a shabby sort of place, considering the kind of people who used it—but then, theaters always seemed like shabby places to me.

"Oh, I thought they were going to tear me limb from

153

limb, Mitch! A poor defenseless creature like me. Where were you when I—"—he batted his lashes, pouted his lips like Daisy Athenasy—"when I needed you?"

"Come on, Frankie. Spill the beans."

"Well, my dear, the fact is that they found the ring in her luggage."

"The ring? Rhys's ring?"

"The very same. Hacked off his hand."

"Not still...on his finger?"

"Oh, God, no. Please. How disgusting. No—of the finger there is no trace. I believe they are searching the track."

"But how on earth did the ring end up in Daisy's luggage?"

"That's what she's wondering."

"So you don't believe that she had anything to do with it?"

"Daisy? Come off it. She's not bright enough to be a criminal mastermind. Someone's set her up."

"Dickinson."

"It does ever so slightly point at him," sighed Frankie. "Oh, and when I think of all the times I tried to make myself available to him... Well, one lives and learns. Or in my case, doesn't learn."

"So who are you working for now, Frankie?"

"Officially, Hugo Taylor. He likes having me around. 'You seem to know the most fascinating people, Francis.' " His impression of Taylor was perfect. "He thinks I'm going to be a sort of upper-class procuress, my dear, ushering lines of handsome young men and rich old widows into his dressing room. He really is disgustingly self-interested."

"And unofficially?"

Frankie's hand fluttered around his collar. "Miss Bankhead. Tallulah."

"Of course."

"Isn't she divine?"

"If you say so."

"Oh, but she's camp! Why, last night, we stayed up till four dancing the Black Bottom and drinking whiskey sours."

"You look very well on it, I must say."

"Well, I took the precaution of helping myself to a little bit of Daisy's stash. She'll thank me for it, now she's in police custody. As a result, I feel marvelous."

Morgan sat throughout this with a face like thunder; he did not like men of Frankie's stamp, and was not much good at hiding it.

"But I can see that I'm upsetting your charming friend," said Frankie. "I presume you came here for a reason, Mitch, and it wasn't to ask me to dinner."

"I'll be honest with you: we were hoping to get some tickets for tonight's show."

"I see." Frankie sighed. "They never want me for myself... Very well. How many do you want? A pair? Two pairs? A box?"

"Are you kidding?"

"I'll get you a box if you want one. I can put ghastly old Lady Crawley in with the Prime Minister. She'll sleep through the whole thing anyway, and he'll be thrilled to bits at sharing with someone so dreadfully rich. Silly man."

"Well, if you're sure..."

"That's awfully decent," said Morgan, making a big effort to be polite.

"If I can't help a sister... Oops, sorry, there I go again. And I suppose you can come to the party afterward, at the Royal?"

"You bet."

"Oh good. It'll be ghastly, of course, but they'll all be there. You know. Everyone." He winked.

"Who?"

"Oh, come on. Don't pretend you haven't heard! A certain personage?"

"Frankie, I don't know what you're talking about."

"Well, then, wait and see. Oh, my, what a night. Now stop trying to seduce me, and let me get on with my job. Really! It's a burden being so irresistible to men..."

We left the theater with a spring in our step, and, more to the point, five tickets for the opening night in my pocket. Bertrand and Simmonds were outside, keeping clear of the crowd. They looked entirely wrapped up in each other.

When the necessary introductions had been made, I asked Bertrand what, if anything, he had managed to find out about the case. It was quite clear to me that he had spent most of the last 12 hours with his legs wrapped around Simmonds's back.

"So—what's new?" I asked him.

"Thomas has told me something."

"Thomas?"

"Me, sir," said Simmonds. "Thomas."

We shook hands again. Out of his uniform, Simmonds looked a great deal more presentable.

"Come on, then. Out with it."

Bertrand and Thomas glanced at each other and smiled shyly at some private joke, and then Thomas began.

"Well, it started last week. The police were sniffing around Waverley Station, which isn't unusual, because we get a lot of funny characters passing through on the way to and from London. But this time they were in the office asking a lot of nosy questions about the running of the trains, the staff, the passengers. Eventually Superintendent Dickinson was brought in, and he told us that he was working undercover to bust a drug smuggling ring. He told us that we'd be carrying Hugo Taylor and Daisy Athenasy down to London, private compartments and all that, and that we were to follow his orders for the duration of the journey."

"And what were those orders?"

"Ah," said Bertrand, "now you hear it."

"He said that there would be a dangerous gang of criminals traveling on the same train, and that if we found anyone acting suspiciously we were to use all necessary force to apprehend them."

"On Dickinson's authority?"

"Yes."

"And nobody thought this was unusual?"

"No. It was done with the full cooperation of the station management."

"So that's why you were so hard on poor little Bertrand here."

"Yes. I will never forgive myself for what I did."

"Looks like you've made friends now, though," said Morgan, who was always good at lightening the mood. He'd been looking at Bertrand with a little more interest than I altogether liked.

"Isn't it time that you got off to work, old chap?" I prodded.

"Yes, I suppose I should put in an appearance. I'll see you tonight." He shook hands all around and jumped onto a passing bus.

"And I must be off as well," said Thomas. "I'd better go and say hello to my relatives, tell them I won't be seeing too much of them on this trip." He squeezed Bertrand's shoulder. "Or on any trips in the foreseeable future."

When we were alone, I took Bertrand to a café in Soho for some lunch.

"All right. I want to hear all about it," I said expectantly.

"He is married. What can I say? There is no future."

"That's a thoroughly defeatist attitude, Bertrand, if I may say so."

"What can we do? He has a wife and children, he has a job that he cannot afford to leave."

"But do you like him?"

"Ah, for that." He shrugged his shoulders. "I like him

well. Perhaps I even love him. But what does it matter?"

I wanted to shake him out of this ridiculous Continental gloom. "So tell me, is he a good lover?"

"Oh, yes."

"What did you do?"

"*Tout.*"

"He fucked you?"

"Yes. He fuck me." He shifted in his seat rather uncomfortably, which was hardly surprising considering the abuse that his ass had taken. "He is very big, Mitch."

"Bigger than me?"

"Maybe. I would have to see you both at the same time to be sure."

"That can be arranged." I was getting stiff again, and I rearranged my napkin so as not to terrify the waiters. "So, you fucked all night, then?"

"Some of the night. For many hours, we talked. And then for maybe two hours we slept."

"And then you woke up this morning..."

"Yes. We fucked again."

"*Mon pauvre petit.* You must be sore."

"It is a pain that I can endure."

"I bet you can, you horny little—"

The waiter brought our lunch, and we were obliged to change the subject.

"So today, my friend, we must give you some time to recover before, no doubt, you spend another night with your legs in the air in the Regal Hotel."

"Not always. He likes me to sit on it and slide down—"

"And we must pay some visits. Let us try, Bertrand, to keep our minds off sex, at least for the next few hours."

Our first port of call was the Rookery Club in Russell Square. We rang the bell several times before we finally heard footsteps.

A little hatch slid back in the doorway.

"Who is it?"

"My name is Mitchell."

"Don't know you." The hatch slid back. I hammered the door.

"Wait! I have information for you!"

The hatch opened again. "Are you the police?"

"Of course not. Are you going to let me in?"

"What's the password?"

The password? This was ridiculous, like something out of the corny crime stories my kid brother read back in Boston.

"I don't know. But I have this." I unfolded the scrap of letterhead that Andrews had dropped and pushed it through the hatch. It had the desired effect; bolts were drawn, chains rattled, and the door opened.

"Come in quick, then," said an old gentleman in carpet slippers and a long, shapeless knitted garment. "We don't want the whole world and his wife seeing you."

We followed him up two flights of stairs. The carpet was worn, the runners loose, and the banisters wobbled as we gripped them. It looked as if the house had not been decorated, or even cleaned, since the 19th century. The old man himself looked Dickensian, or Thackeravian, or whatever the correct adjective might be. The ghost of queerness past...

"In 'ere..."

He pushed open a heavy, dark wooden door, the brass doorknob so corroded that it looked like an archaeological find.

And there, on the other side of the door, was a kind of Wonderland.

Crimson sofas in various stages of disrepair were arranged in a rough circle, covered in a crazy assortment of furs, rugs, and throws which spilled down onto the floor. The parquet was worn, uneven, and black, the crystals on the chandelier were thick with dust, and the heavy black velvet drapes so worn and frayed that if they were ever opened, they would surely disintegrate.

"Welcome to the Rookery," the old gentleman said. "To whom do I owe the pleasure of your acquaintance?" His cracked old voice veered crazily between a sort of theatrical diction and its (presumably) native Cockney.

"William Andrews sent us."

His mouth went into a tight little circle, and he paced up and down for a while, his slippers slapping against his stockinged heels. "And what did Mr. Andrews suggest you might find here?"

The true answer was "nothing"; I wasn't even certain whether Andrews had dropped the paper on purpose. "I was hoping you might be able to answer a few questions."

"Oh, yes. I 'ope you're not the long arm of the law."

"On the contrary. In fact, I hope to rescue Mr. Andrews from its clutches."

"Hmmmm..."

"You don't seem surprised to learn that he's in trouble."

"Me, dear? I'm never surprised by anything. But that Andrews... He's been riding for a fall for some time."

"In what way?"

"The usual way. Wanting more than he can reasonably expect. Breaking the rules. Getting greedy."

"Greedy? You mean he was involved in some kind of racket?"

"Oh, no, dear. Very upright gentleman, indeed, from what I could make out. Always turned 'is nose up at some of our more...colorful members. No, 'e's one of them as wants to 'ave 'is cake and eat it."

Bertrand was finding this hard to follow.

"Please explain yourself," I said.

"Let's have a little drink." He poured neat gin into three glasses, took a swig, and smacked his lips. "There. That's better. I always find a nip of something around this time of day stimulates the memory. Now, where were we? Your Mr. Andrews. Well, yes, a very proper gentleman, indeed. Not the sort we're used to at the Rookery. It's all a bit rough and ready here, you see." He pursed his lips. "Some very troublesome sorts we get. Theatricals, a lot of them, and quite honestly they've got the manners of a pigsty. They treat the place like some kind of knocking shop—"

"Knocking shop?" Bertrand frowned. "A shop where you sell... *Quoi*?"

"Oh, come on, dear, you have plenty of 'em in France."

Bertrand rolled his eyes, but was obviously tired of explaining himself. "Ah, I see. That sort of shop."

"And is the Rookery a knocking shop, by any chance?"

"Certainly not." The old man gathered his moth-eaten cardigan around him. "The very idea. It is a gentleman's club. I do not like to pry on what goes on in the privacy of the upper rooms, but there is certainly nothing as common as prostitution under my roof. Really. The very thought. 'Ave another gin."

"No, I'm—" I protested, but he filled our glasses to the brim. I took a sip and continued. "So. Tell me all about William Andrews."

"What's in it for me, dear? And why should I trust you? Couple of foreigners, that's all I know about you, coming in here without any enquiry about membership..."

He wanted money. I laid five pounds on the table.

"That should cover it, I imagine."

"For now, dear, that will do nicely." He screwed the money up and put it into a pocket. "Well, now. Mr. Andrews. Oh, dear, oh, dear. Where shall I begin?"

"Why did you call him greedy?"

"He got the idea, dear, that he and his friend were going to start a new life together, and live happily every after."

"And why shouldn't they?"

"Well, for one thing, Mr. Andrews was married."

"Pah. They are all married," said Bertrand.

"True enough, dear, but we learn not to look too closely at ring fingers at the Rookery. What they do in their home life is no concern of mine. But what I will not have is people rocking the boat."

"Meaning?"

"Saying things that are better left unsaid. Things that would be of interest in a court of law. Upsetting the other members."

"Had Andrews upset anyone in particular?"

"Yes, 'e 'ad. 'E got into some right barneys, especially after a few drinks. Standing up like 'e was at Speakers' Corner, telling anyone who would listen that 'e should have the right to live as 'e chose, that society 'ad no right to condemn, and so on and so forth. I've 'eard it all me life, dear, and all I can say is, fine words butter no parsnips."

Bertrand looked puzzled again.

"Who did he argue with, in particular?"

"There was one night, just before Christmas it was, when he was in here with that friend of 'is, nice-looking piece—"

"Dark hair? Deep-set eyes? Welsh?"

"That's the one, dear. Well, they'd been staying for a couple of nights, then off 'e goes, the friend, always disappearing, up to no good, if you ask me, very secretive in 'is ways… And there's your Mr. Andrews in 'ere, knocking back the firewater, going on about how unfair 'is life was, 'ow 'e wished 'e'd never married, bla, bla, bla. So one of my gentlemen ups and says, 'Well, if you're so bloody sorry that you got married why don't you 'ave the courage of your convictions and leave 'er?' Oh, 'e didn't like that, your Mr. Andrews. 'I can't just walk out on me kids,' 'e says. 'I've got responsibilities. It's not that simple.' On and on they go, and it almost came to blows. Imagine! Here! In a respectable establishment! Fighting like cats."

"So he had enemies?"

"I wouldn't go that far. It was just a silly bitch fight. I'm used to them. I only mean to say that Andrews was a liability, and I'm not surprised if he's in some kind of trouble."

"But if you could just tell me who—"

"Now, if you gentlemen have quite finished helping yourself to my gin, we have a party here tonight and I haven't even started getting ready."

"Any particular occasion?" His eyes followed my hand as it went once more toward my wallet.

"Well, it ain't the king's birthday…"

I got my wallet out.

"It's a theatrical affair, really…"

"Yes?"

"Invitations are practically impossible to secure."

"I'm sure you could do something, Mr.…"

"Marchmont."

"Mr. Marchmont. My friend and I are eager to come."

"Well, then." He snatched two pound notes out of my hand. "I'll see what I can do. The revels commence at midnight."

This was proving to be an expensive case, I reflected, as Marchmont pushed us out the door and onto the street. My wallet was almost empty, and I knew it was no good applying to Bertrand for a loan.

"Perhaps," he said, "it is time for me to launch myself at my uncle."

Alone in London, my first instinct was to go looking for adventure—and here was Soho, famed haunt of vice, at my very feet.

Soho—that reminded me. I still had Dickinson's card in my pocket, and an address for the British-American Film Company, not five minutes' walk away. That would be my next port of call—to find out more about Daisy Athenasy and her long-suffering husband, Herbert Waits.

British-American was situated on the top two floors of a dingy Victorian building at the northern end of Wardour Street; it must once have looked splendid, with its decorative stone flourishes and leaded windows, but now it was dirty and decayed, split up into half a dozen offices, covered in soot and pigeon shit.

"Fourth floor," said the bored receptionist, without even looking me in the eye.

The waiting room was full, both of people and of smoke. Three young women and four young men were reading magazines and sharing cigarettes; as soon as I appeared in the doorway, the stream of gossip stopped, and seven pairs of eyes were fixed on me. Four of those pairs were heavily outlined in kohl, at least three heads of hair had been bleached and one hennaed, and it was impossible to discern who was wearing which scent, as the room was heavy with the stuff. They were unmistakably actors, all of them several rungs down the ladder from the Bankheads and Taylors of the profession. Why, some of the girls even made Daisy Athenasy look high class.

"Oh, God," sighed one of the young men, a fey little creature with beautiful green eyes, his brown, wavy locks held back off his face with bobby pins. "Now I'll never have a chance. I might as well leave right now."

"You'd better make yourself known, dear," said the redhead, who had possibly modeled herself on Clara Bow. "Oi, Gladys!" she screamed, in a voice more suited to a fish market than a theater. "More meat for the mincer!"

A frosted glass hatch shot open, and yet more smoke poured into the already stuffy room. "Name," demanded an amphibious voice from beyond.

"I'm actually here to ask a few questions—"

"Name, dear. I haven't got all day," came the croaked reply.

"Mitchell."

"First name?"

"Mitch."

"Oooh! American!" trilled the boys and girls in the waiting room. "How thrilling!"

"Sit down, Mitchell." I could only see the top of Gladys's head, which was crowned with a dense gray bun. "You'll be called." A mottled hand shot up, and the hatch was closed.

"Not seen you before," said Bobby Pins, winding his legs around each other. "You're new." It sounded like an accusation.

"Well, actually I—"

"You done any pictures in America? Do you know D. W. Griffith? Lillian Gish?"

"No, I'm not a—"

"Fancy a bit of rehearsal? I could go over your…lines."

"He don't need your help," said Clara Bow. "He looks like a lady-killer to me."

"Oooh! Dream on, Betty! If anyone's going to get killed round here, it's not you."

"That's enough talk about killing," said the only possibly straight-looking man in the room, a handsome lad with dark hair and a pronounced dimple in his chin. "Under the circumstances, and all…"

"What circumstances?" I asked.

"Ooh, don't you know?" screeched Bobby Pins. "Daisy's muddled up in a murder. Too shameful!" He lowered his voice. "Mind you, I wouldn't be at all surprised if Bertie framed her for it, to get her out of his way. I mean it stands to reason—"

"You'd better shut your mouth," said Dimples. "You don't know anything about it."

"I know plenty," said Bobby Pins. "And what I don't know, I'm prepared to guess."

The hatch shot open. "Billy Vain and Betty LaMarre!"

"Ooh, that's us dear," said Bobby Pins, grabbing one

of the blonde girls who had been deeply absorbed in a fan magazine. "Wish us luck!"

"Break a leg," said Clara Bow.

"Break both," muttered Dimples.

Amid much flapping of wrists, Billy and Betty departed. This left six of us in the waiting room: Clara Bow, Dimples, another dark-eyed blonde girl almost indistinguishable from Betty LaMarre, and a couple of other young men. One was another obvious queen, licking his fingers as he flicked through a magazine, occasionally repositioning one of his peroxide spit curls, watching the world through dead eyes. The other was of much more interest to me, a short, freckle-faced redhead who looked as if he'd stepped straight off a building site. He was nervous, smoking heavily, and looked almost as out of place as I felt.

"So what are you up for, Buddy Rogers?" asked Clara Bow, exhaling a long stream of smoke at me, in that way that looks seductive on screen but is disgusting in real life.

"Me? Same as you, I guess," I replied.

The two magazine-reading blondes snickered.

"Funny," said Clara, "you don't look the type. But then you really can't tell these days, can you?"

"What's the...er...name of the picture?" I gathered that we were all auditioning for something. My question elicited more shrieks and snorts from the blond corner.

"Oh, darling," husked Clara, "I'm not sure if these pictures ever have titles. Do they, Clive? You'd done enough of them to know."

Dimples blushed and nervously pushed back his hair. "I really couldn't say."

"Now take Clive, here," continued Clara. "To look at him you'd think he was, I don't know, a bank clerk, or a schoolteacher, or a soldier, or something, wouldn't you? Something normal, at any rate."

"Shut up, Vicky."

"A family man, with a wife and a baby tucked away in the suburbs. Reads the paper on the train to work every morning, does an honest day's labor, then hurries home to a nice plate of stew every evening."

"For Christ's sake." Clive stood up and went to the door.

"But not our Clive. He's found other ways to make a living, haven't you, darling? Much more interesting than pushing paper in a bank. Well, it takes all sorts, that's what I say. I don't judge."

"Just as well," said the blond boy, not looking up from his magazine. His girlfriend nodded in agreement.

"What about you?" I turned to the redheaded boy, who sat silent throughout, bunching up his fists until the knuckles were pale.

"Yeah, you know... Just lookin' for a bit of extra pocket money."

"That's what they all say, to start with," said Clara Bow—or Vicky.

"I suppose so..." Ginger rubbed his fists up and down his sturdy thighs. He was wearing an old, ill-fitting suit for the occasion; the pants were shiny with wear. "Beats laying bricks for a living."

The hatch flew open again, and the oracular Gladys croaked once more. "Clive Elliott. Sean Hanrahan. Mitch Mitchell." Shooof! The hatch closed again.

"That's not fair!" said the blonde girl in a grating whine. "We've been here for hours."

"Patience, my sweet," said Clive. "Your talents will be recognized one day."

"Bitch," spat the blonde, and returned to her reading.

A door was opened, and the three of us stepped into the inner sanctum—a cluttered office, jammed with desks and chairs and typewriters, into which the bright winter sunshine filtered through dirty windows. Gladys, now visible in full for the first time, sat, vast and squat, at the communicating window. Other desks were staffed by a strange array of creatures, all bent over typewriters or in danger of being buried under piles of paper. A phone rang, unanswered.

"What do we do now?" I whispered to Clive.

"He'll be down in a minute."

"Who?"

"Well, not Cecil B. DeMille, I can tell you that much."

Sean, the redhead, was shifting nervously from foot to foot; I felt like putting an arm around him.

Another door opened, and there stood a rotund, well-dressed man in his 60s, bald-headed, bespectacled, exuding an air of slightly seedy geniality. It could be none other than Herbert Waits, the owner of the British-American Film Company, the hapless husband of Daisy Athenasy, the man I'd heard referred to in the waiting room as "Bertie."

He was holding a cigar—more as a prop than anything else, I suspected—and waved it toward us. "Gentlemen, gentlemen! Don't stand there as if you're waiting for a bus! Come on up!"

True to the company name, he spoke with an unplaceable mid-Atlantic accent.

Clive, Sean, and I followed him up the dark staircase. Two doors opened on to the landing. One was slightly ajar, and through it I had a brief glimpse of entwined naked limbs. I heard the click of the shutter, saw the dazzle of lights, before Waits blocked my view with his considerable bulk, softly pulling the door closed.

"This way to stardom, folks." He gestured to the door across the landing, through which we obediently filed.

"Good to see you again, Clive." Waits shook Clive's hand, for all the world like businessmen at a conference. He referred to a clipboard. "And our two newcomers, Mr. Hanrahan and Mr. Mitchell. Welcome to fairyland."

We shook hands in turn, and sat, the three of us in a row.

Waits paced up and down, gesticulating with his cigar, rarely smoking it.

"Now, gentlemen, I suppose you know why you're here. We're casting today for a variety of films, hence the open audition, and I guess you're all aware of the nature of the material that you may be required to shoot. Have you filled them in, Clive?"

"Not yet, sir."

"The first question I have to ask you is, do you want to be famous?"

"Yes!" answered Sean, as eager as a puppy. "I do!"

"Good boy. And you, Mitchell? They tell me you're an American."

"Yes, sir. From Boston."

"Got any picture experience?"

"No, sir."

"Good, good. You're just the type we're looking for. Handsome. Outdoorsy. The athletic kind. You play football?"

"Sometimes. I rowed at...er...college." I didn't think he needed details of my postgraduate medical studies at Cambridge.

"A rower, huh? Good. Builds up the shoulders. Audiences like strong shoulders, don't they, Clive?"

"I suppose so."

"Take Clive, here. Very much a man's man, to look at him. Every inch a man's man, you might say. Look at the shoulders on him. Stand up, Clive."

Clive stood; he was a good six feet tall, and built like a swimmer.

"That's what we want," said Waits, holding the cigar between his lips and squeezing Clive's shoulders with both hands. "A bit of muscle. You boys think you can match up?"

"Sure," said Sean, jumping to his feet. By now, I was aware

of the kind of "acting" that was required of us; I'm not sure that Sean was. He still seemed to think he was auditioning for some kind of action caper. Well, there would be action, of that I was confident. "I built these muscles working on building sites. Lugging around bricks, putting up scaffolding."

"Impressive, son, very impressive." Sean bunched up a bicep, and Waits squeezed it appreciatively, his lips working around the cigar. I began to see that, perhaps, Daisy Athenasy's infidelities might not have caused her husband too many sleepless nights.

"So, let's get down to business." Waits picked up his clipboard again. "You first, Hanrahan. Off with your shirt."

"Here? Now?"

"Yes. C'mon. I haven't got all day. People to see. This may be your only chance."

"Yes, sir." Sean unbuttoned his jacket and threw it aside. His shirt, pulled over his head, followed it to the floor.

His physique was impressive, the skin milky white, his back and shoulders dusted with freckles. There was a little patch of reddish hair on his chest, and his nipples were as pink as rosebuds. Waits licked his lips—and so did I.

"Good. Great." He paced around Sean like a connoisseur at an auction room—or a butcher at a meat market. "Very nice indeed. You'll photograph well. Lift your arms above your head." Sean obliged, exposing his underarms, the hair red and slightly damp with sweat. Waits inhaled.

"Okay, Mr. Sean Hanrahan. You'll do."

"I got the job?"

"You passed the first round."

"Wow."

"Now, Mr. Mitchell. Your turn."

I followed suit, and stripped to the waist. Both Waits and Clive eyed me appreciatively.

"Good. Dark. Kind of hairy. You'll make a good contrast. An Arab sheik, perhaps."

"Oh, God, Bertie, not another *Desert Song*—"

"You'd better strip as well, Clive. To make sure you haven't let yourself go."

"I was under the impression that I would not need to audition."

"It's all about teamwork, Clive. I've got to see how you work together. Skin tones, body types. Facial features. Chemistry, boy. That's what audiences want. Chemistry."

Clive sighed and stripped. His body was as beautifully proportioned as a Greek statue, and just as smooth, his skin tanned to a light, even gold. He must have traveled abroad, I thought.

"There we go. Three of the finest specimens of manhood it's been my pleasure to view for a long time." Waits was delighted, scribbling notes on his clipboard. "Now let me see. A young boxer, that's you, Hanrahan, is training for the big title fight. Can you box, by any chance?"

Sean threw a few punches; they looked convincing enough.

"That'll do. His trainer—that'll be you, Clive—puts him through his paces, then gives him a rubdown before the fight. A thief breaks into the changing room..." He was pacing about, his eyes closed, drawing absurd images from the air. "He steals your shorts. We don't need to see that, just the discovery that the shorts are gone. So when you face your opponent in the ring you're only wearing your boots."

Sean looked puzzled, trying to work out the plot.

"And the opponent," I said, "would be me, I presume."

"Yes. We'll bill you as something like "The Great Effendi." I don't know—something exotic. You strip down to your shorts, but then in the interest of a fair fight you lose 'em, bla, bla, bla, and so on in the usual way until the end of the reel. Clive is there to ensure a fair fight, no hitting below the belt. Hey, that's it! Good title! *Below the Belt*. Okay, stay there."

He bustled out of the room, and we heard him yelling in the corridor. "You guys done yet? I need the studio!"

"Surely we're not going to shoot the movie here and now, are we?" I asked.

"Oh, yes," said Clive. "Waits doesn't waste time on rehearsals."

"But I thought British-American was a legitimate film studio."

"So it is. But these pictures don't go out with the British-American name on them. It's all strictly hush-hush."

"But why? Surely he doesn't need to make this kind of stuff."

"Are you kidding? How else do you think he finances those terrible Daisy Athenasy pictures? She's box office poison. If she wasn't blackmailing him, he'd have divorced her years ago. Hell, he'd never even have married her. But there's a girl with an eye for the main chance. She knew there was no future in skin flicks…"

"Gentlemen," said Waits, returning to the room and holding the door open, "if you would be so good as to come through to the studio. There's no need to bring your clothes."

*Below the Belt* will never go down in the annals of film history, and I sincerely hope it will never be screened outside certain small but lucrative circuits, but, if nothing else, it serves as a record of a very enjoyable afternoon. My "costars" were both attractive men whom I would have been happy to have in any combination and under any circumstances—but, having them both together, our encounter spiced with exhibitionism, made this a truly epic fuck, almost worthy of D. W. Griffith himself. Waits and his cameraman—a harassed fellow in shirtsleeves and pegged pants—watched us with a kind of appreciative detachment, never touching us except to rearrange a limb or measure a focal length.

The plot, such as it was, progressed roughly along the lines described by Waits. The entire set was a black back-cloth tacked against the wall, a couple of chairs, and, for the massage scene, a towel-covered table, which wobbled alarmingly when Sean lay on it. Costumes were produced from a couple of enormous wicker baskets bursting with shoes, boots, shirts, and various bits of uniform. Women's garments mingled promiscuously with men's. Waits catered to all tastes.

I watched the first scene from behind the camera. Sean warmed himself up with an impressive display of shadow boxing, until the sweat was dripping from his brow and chest. He had still not, perhaps, grasped the exact nature of what was to follow—and I greatly enjoyed the look of surprise on his face when Clive took control of the action, peeling down Sean's shorts. For a moment, it looked as if the startled young redhead was going to bolt—but Clive's experienced hands put him at ease, and soon he had developed an impressive erection, as rosy red as his nipples, standing out in an elegant curve from his ginger bush. He stepped out of the shorts, never removing his boots, and allowed himself to be led to the massage table.

"Cut!" yelled Waits. "Reset."

The cameraman did his measuring and repositioned his camera while Sean got comfortable on the table.

"I hope this never gets shown in Ireland," he said, before succumbing to Clive's caresses. The camera was running again, and soon the massage had turned into a blow job. Sean groaned loudly, burying his fingers in Clive's long chestnut hair; what a shame, I thought, that we were not shooting with sound. Perhaps Waits would cut in suitable intertitles.

Just before Sean came, Waits yelled "Cut!" again. The cameraman shot a few close-ups of Sean's glistening wet cock and beefy ass.

"Now for the discovery. Look, Sean, where are your shorts? You can't find them. You look surprised, then shocked. Someone has stolen them. That's good. Now you hunt around for them, both of you. No, you can't find them. You scratch your heads. Clive, you turn out your pockets. Maybe he's got them hidden down his pants, Sean. Have a feel. What's that? Wow! That's a big one! Look surprised! You've never felt one that big! Good boy, you're a natural. Okay, Mitch, get ready for your scene."

I changed into my shorts and boots, making no effort to disguise the erection that had sprouted sometime during Act One. Any misgivings I may have had about committing my indiscretions to film had been blotted out by lust. I bounded into the ring, threw off the robe that Waits had wrapped me in (I think he was hoping to summon up some flavor of the exotic) and bounced around on the balls of my feet, as I'd seen boxers do. Clive stood between us, keeping us apart, and instructed me to take my shorts off. I needed no second bidding.

The second Clive stepped back, the boxing theme was abandoned in favor of a form of freestyle wrestling. I grabbed Sean around the neck and pulled him close, pressing my hard cock against his sweaty thigh. He responded by tripping me up; I landed on my back, with him on top of me. Soon we were sucking each other's cocks, hands grabbing asses, fingers penetrating holes. If this was Sean's first time with another man, he *was* a natural.

Waits kept up a stream of "direction" that was far too repetitive to transcribe here, consisting mostly of the words "yeah," "cock," and "ass," plus a few appropriate verbs. Eventually Clive took off his pants and joined us.

For the finale, I fucked Sean up the ass while he sucked Clive's cock. We took turns coming; I pulled out and sprayed over his back and ass, Clive came copiously in his upturned face, and finally we held Sean up between us in a seated position, slipping fingers in and out of his hole, while he jerked himself off to a messy climax.

"It's a wrap!" yelled Waits, handing us towels. "Pick up your money on your way out. Thank you, gentlemen." We cleaned up and started dressing.

"Right, Ron, what's next?" asked Waits, returning to the office.

"Welcome to the stable," said Clive, patting Sean and me on the back. "If you ever feel like getting together for a spot of rehearsal…"

"I need a beer," said Sean, his face still flushed and sweaty. "Will you join us, Mitch?"

"Sorry, gentlemen. Another time. I have work to do."

I descended the stairs slowly, pondering what I had learned about the British-American Film Company and its boss, Herbert Waits. Where did David Rhys fit in the picture? And Peter Dickinson? How much did Hugo Taylor know about his employers—and how much did his employers know about him?

There was much to consider, but little time in which to do it. I took a bus back to Chelsea. There was barely time to dress for the theater.

# X

BOY WAS PACING THE HALL WHEN I ARRIVED. "WHERE THE hell have you been, Mitch? We're going to be late. You're not even dressed." His bad mood was not entirely due to the hour; he knew all too well that while he had been at work, I had almost certainly been at play.

"Won't take me a moment!" I shouted, bounding up the stairs. I threw off my clothes, rinsed myself fore and aft, and was dressed in my evening wear in moments. We were leaving the house and giving final instructions to the babysitter within five minutes of my arrival.

I desperately needed time to think. If only I had Morgan to myself: he was a good sounding board for ideas, as well as being a top-quality fuck. Or Bertrand, who was proving himself to be an equally serviceable sidekick. What fun the three of us could have...

No! Focus, Mitch, focus!

The cab trundled along the Embankment, while Boy and Belinda chattered about the events of the day, the baby's latest exploits in the nursery, the chances of Boy securing a desirable promotion.

I tried to review the latest developments in what I still thought of as "the case." But with every passing moment, it was slipping further from my grasp. I might as well have been one of the millions who would read about it in the newspaper tomorrow, for all the influence I had on events. If something did not come to light tonight, I would be nothing more than a bit player, a bystander in the drama that had unfolded right under my nose. I might as well forget all my sleuthing pretensions, and concentrate instead on being a good doctor to my patients and a good partner to Vince. He had laughed often enough about my detective mania; this would give him the biggest laugh of all. A murder, two movie stars, diamonds, drugs, a suspicious policeman, even an outrageous dowager, straight out of Agatha Christie. All the pieces of the puzzle were there, and what had I made of them? A muddle. A sperm-soaked mess. I'd fucked it up, in more ways than one, distracted at every crucial point by my restless dick.

I groaned.

"What's the matter, old chap? Got a bit of a headache?"

I smiled and composed myself. "No, Boy. Just trying to work something out."

"Oh, you men and your mysteries," said Belinda. "Now, look lively. We're here."

Charing Cross Road was choked with traffic, pedestrian, horse-drawn, and motorized. The façade of the Garrick was ablaze with electric light, illuminating the names TALLU-LAH BANKHEAD and HUGO TAYLOR in vast red letters. Somewhere the words "The Lady of the Camellias" appeared in much smaller type; nobody was here for poor Alexandre Dumas. Almost as bright were the diamonds adorning the heads, throats, and chests of the audience, now piling into the theater in a fur-wreathed crush. We were just in time, and joined the end of the line.

The five-minute bell was ringing, and there was no time for drinks. We made our way to our box, where Bertrand and Simmonds were already sitting, looking thoroughly awkward in their cobbled-together evening wear. Bertrand was wearing a jacket several sizes too large for him; the sleeves came down way over his hands. But at least his shirt was clean; that was money well spent. They stood up when we arrived and moved to the back of the box—but Morgan soon put everyone at ease. Belinda was as charming as ever; if she had any inkling of the nature of my friendship with her husband, or of the kind of people I associated with, she kept it to herself.

The theater was packed to the rafters. Up in the gods sat the real Taylor and Bankhead fans, those theatergoers who kept the business alive, who sweated and toiled to afford their tickets and repaid the stars even more in terms of their devotion. Further down, the clothes became more opulent, the faces less expressive of eager anticipation. By the time you got to the dress circle and the orchestra, hardly anyone was looking toward the stage. They were all far too busy talking to friends, waving at acquaintances, standing to show off gowns and jewels. In the other boxes people were drinking champagne and eating sandwiches—and casting suspicious, disapproving glances toward us. Frankie must have been delighted at the thought of placing people like us in the middle of all these titles and jewels. I scanned the boxes for a familiar face—and yes, there was the Prime Minister himself, just as Frankie had said, in earnest conversation with a woman who looked about 100 years old, so encrusted with jewels that she might have been wearing armor.

And there, in another box, was another familiar face, beneath a turban and a plume of feathers, above a treasure chest of jewels—Lady Antonia. So she was here. Of course. She would be. The chickens were coming home to roost.

A sudden hush fell over the auditorium, there was a certain amount of pointing and craning of necks, and the orchestra struck up the National Anthem. Everyone turned toward the royal box—just two doors up from us, as it were—and awaited The Presence. Who would it be? King George himself? Queen Mary? The Prince of Wales? Even a good American like me could not suppress a thrill of excitement.

Everyone stood. In the royal box I saw a glitter of jewels, a flash of brass. A handsome young man in naval uniform advanced to the front of the box, waved to the crowd a few times, then took his seat next to a beautiful young woman in a chic silver sheath dress, a diamond necklace at her throat, a white fox fur around her shoulders.

The audience, taking its lead from the royal personage, sat down.

"Who is it?" I asked Morgan.

"Prince George, isn't it? Belinda?"

"Yes, of course it is."

"Which one is he, then?"

"The fourth son," said Belinda. "The bad one."

"Oh!" I began to take more interest. "In what way?"

"Oh, you know. Affairs left, right, and center. They say he dopes."

"No kidding! And who's that with him?"

"Oh, it's that ghastly girlfriend of his, Kiki Preston."

Simmonds and Bertrand practically pushed us out of the way to get a look.

"*Non!* Is that really her? She is quite beautiful," said Bertrand, rather grudgingly. "But you can tell, I think, by her eyes..."

"Tell what?"

"Ah, she is a notorious drug addict! She is known in your newspapers as the Girl with the Silver Syringe."

"You'd kidding."

"She's an American," said Belinda. "Rich as Croesus, of course, but aren't they all?"

"Not this one."

"But for some reason she's taken a fancy to the theater." Belinda lowered her voice. "Apparently, she's appeared in revue."

"And what's the connection to Prince George?"

"Well...the obvious one, I suppose," said Belinda. "Although I'm not sure if she isn't barking up the wrong tree, if you know what I mean."

"What, you mean he's—?"

"*Mais oui*," said Bertrand, who seemed to know all the royal scandal while purporting to despise the kind of prurient interest that fostered it. "He is also said to have been the lover of the Maharani of Cooch Behar. Who, perhaps, provided the diamonds that adorn the neck of Miss Preston."

"You don't say. That's an awful lot of sparklers," said Morgan, clearly impressed. "I hope you don't expect me to give you trinkets like that, old girl."

"I wouldn't be seen dead in them," said Belinda, loyally, casting a lingering look at said sparklers. "I'm quite content with what I've got." She waggled her ring finger, where a tiny diamond shone.

"One day I'll buy you a diamond as big as a plum."

"I don't want jewels, Harry. I just want you."

This was starting to make me feel rather unwell, so I turned my attention to the stage. It was well after eight o'clock by now, and the curtain should have been up. The orchestra was getting fidgety; the conductor was in earnest conversation with someone. I sensed a hitch, as did much of the audience.

People were starting to get restless, when a harassed man in a dinner jacket walked in front of the curtain.

"Your Royal Highness, my lords, ladies and gentlemen!" He held up his hands, and the audience was silent. "We apologize for the late start to tonight's show. This is due to the indisposition of Mr. Hugo Taylor—"

His next words were lost. Groans and cries of "no!" rang out from the top of the balcony all the way down to the front of the orchestra.

"Please, ladies and gentlemen! Mr. Taylor assures me that he will be able to go on, and craves your patience."

There was a burst of applause; again the manager begged for silence.

"We will have the curtain up in approximately half an hour. In the meantime, the orchestra will entertain us with a medley of light operatic airs. And finally, ladies and gentlemen…"

There was a pause, a hush; surely he was not going to announce that Tallulah had gone AWOL?

"Is there a doctor in the house?"

I stood up immediately—one is trained to do so—and announced my presence to the stage. For a moment, all eyes were on me. Even from the royal box.

Hugo Taylor looked ghastly. His eyes were bloodshot, and he was shaking.

The stage manager left us alone.

"What appears to be the matter, Mr. Taylor?"

"I'm not sure. I suddenly got taken very ill… Hello, don't I know you?"

"We were on the train together."

"Thought so. I never forget a handsome face. So you're a doctor, are you? Any good?"

"I haven't killed anyone yet."

"Well, that's a relief. Because I rather think that someone is trying to kill me."

"What gives you that impression?"

"You may remember I was attacked on the train."

"An unfortunate collision with a cocktail cabinet, you said."

"Cocktail cabinet, my arse. That's what that goon from

the studio told me to say, to avoid scandal. Actually, someone crept up on me and hit me over the head. Nearly cracked my skull." He parted his hair to show the wound. "Fortunately, it won't show up on stage, at least I hope not."

"And what happened tonight?"

"I don't know. I was right as rain this afternoon, just the usual nerves, nothing much. I never eat before a performance because I always get the shits if I do. Forgive me if I speak plainly."

"I'd much rather you did."

"So it can't have been anything I ate. I mean, a funny oyster or something." I took his pulse; it was fast and erratic, but nothing too alarming. He was not about to drop dead.

"Have you taken anything? Any medication?" I wondered if he, like his *Rob Roy* costar and, apparently, Prince George's friend Kiki Preston, was a drug addict.

"Certainly not. I'm fit as a fiddle. And if you are driving at what I think you're driving at, no, I haven't sniffed or injected anything, swallowed it, or stuck it up my bum, as I believe some people do. I can't stand all that stuff." He scowled.

"When did you become ill?"

"Just now. Twenty minutes ago. Just before we were due to go on. I have a little ritual when I'm going on stage. I do a few limbering-up exercises, then I wash, and dress, and do my makeup. Then I warm up the voice. There's a lot of words in this, you know, and it wouldn't do to get hoarse in the final act."

"How do you do that?"

"The usual rubbish, la la la la up and down the arpeggios. Peter Piper picked a peck of pickled peppers. A quick gargle with Listerine, to nobble any germs that might be lurking, and, incidentally, to sweeten the breath for my leading lady."

"Do you swallow?"

"I beg your pardon?"

"The Listerine."

"Oh, I see. Well, no. I sloosh it around, one, two, three, and then I spit it into the sink."

"Do you have the bottle here?"

"No. My dresser has it. He's squireled it away somewhere. I usually have a quick glug in the interval."

"Did you use a glass?"

"Why? What's the big emergency?"

"Did you, or didn't you?"

"Yes, of course. I don't swig from the bottle. Here. This is the one."

I took the glass and sniffed it. It stank of mouthwash, of course—but wasn't there just the faintest whiff of almonds? And that could mean only one thing.

"What happened when you became ill?"

"I was just opening telegrams and signing photos, the usual stuff you do before you go on, when I felt terribly weak. I thought it might be first-night nerves, although usually I don't go for that kind of rubbish. Then I felt giddy, and I thought I was going to faint."

"What sort of giddy?"

"As if I was standing on the edge of a cliff, with a great big sheer drop beneath me."

"Vertigo. That makes sense."

"What the bloody hell is happening to me, doctor?"

"You've been poisoned. I'm almost certain that it's cyanide."

"Fuck me! Cyanide! Isn't that rather...well, dangerous?"

"It's extremely dangerous. Not to mention lethal."

"Shit. Am I going to die?"

"No. If you were going to die, you'd be dead by now. You've had a very lucky escape. Can you breathe properly?"

"It's coming back. I felt terribly winded just before you got in."

"Your pulse is slowing down. I think you're going to be all right. But you must go straight home and rest."

"Not on your life. I've got to go on. Can't let the audience down, old chap. First rule of the theater."

"But Mr. Taylor, someone has tried to kill you."

"Well, in that case, the safest place for me is out there, isn't it? I'm on nearly all the time. Perhaps while we're doing Act One, the police could have a little sniff around and see who's trying to do the dirty. It's really most inconvenient, tonight of all nights. We have some rather important guests."

"So I saw."

And, as if on cue, the door burst open and there, looking resplendent in his uniform, stood His Royal Highness Prince George, fourth son of King George V.

"Hugo! Christ! Are you all right?"

"Georgie!"

The Prince rushed toward Taylor, who sat wilting on his chair, much like the consumptive heroine of the play in which he was about to appear, and embraced him.

"Whatever is the matter with him? And who are you?" He looked me up and down, with somewhat more interest than I imagined a royal personage would have for a commoner.

"This is Doctor... Er... I'm sorry, old chap, I forgot your name."

"Mitchell. Edward Mitchell." I shook the Prince's hand. "Mitch, to my friends."

"Well, Mitch. I wonder if you know my friend, Miss Preston? She's American too." He spoke rather like Lady Antonia: *Ameddican*.

"I don't believe so."

"George, for Christ's sake, that's like asking if you know some crofter in the Outer Hebrides just because he happens to be British."

"It's quite possible that I do," said the Prince. "One meets so many people."

When he smiled, he was dangerously handsome—quite as much as Hugo Taylor. What an attractive couple they made...

"Is he ill, Mitch?"

"He's had a very lucky escape."

"Yes, yes, well, enough of that, George doesn't need to hear the gory details. Dodgy oyster for lunch, you know. Nothing serious."

I didn't contradict him.

"I say, do you need a little something to get you through the evening? You know... A little livener..."

"No thank you," said Hugo, rather primly. "You know my opinion of all that."

"As you like it. But I'm sure that the good doctor would agree that cocaine is an excellent stimulant and that its harmful effects have been greatly overexaggerated."

"I'm afraid not, sir."

Perhaps the Prince was not used to straight answers, particularly of the negative variety. He looked quite taken aback.

"There, Georgie, you see? Not everyone shares your taste for danger."

"Well, well. As long as you're all right. I wouldn't want anything to happen to you."

"Thank you, old chap. Now leave me in peace to pull myself together. I trust I will see you at the party?"

"Wouldn't miss it for the world."

"With La Preston, I presume?"

"She is ever at my side."

"How tiresome for you."

"Oh, I don't know. Kiki's fun. She knows how to enjoy herself, I'll say that much for her."

"You play with fire, Georgie."

"One of the very few advantages of being a member of the House of Windsor is that one is flameproof. Toodle-pip."

He saluted, and left.

"Bloody idiot," muttered Hugo. "Now, tell me, Mitch. Am I going to get through this evening, or am I going to puke all over the orchestra?"

"How do you feel?"

"Shaky. Bit of a headache. Like the worst bloody hangover in the world, with none of the fun that goes with it."

"You'll survive. Once you're on stage you'll feel better. And, as you say, no one is going to murder you in full view of the audience."

"I bloody well hope not, unless Tallulah is part of the conspiracy."

"You think there's a conspiracy?"

"Oh, I don't doubt it for a minute. They'd like to get rid of the whole lot of us."

"They? Who are they? And who are 'us' for that matter?"

"The bloody fascists," he said, blotting his forehead with a tissue. "A thoroughly troublesome group of people. They disapprove of the kind of company that George keeps. They don't like the royal family being sullied by a bunch of actresses and foreigners and queers. They don't like queers, you know."

"Ah." That would explain the presence of Lady Antonia in the audience. She was not there to cheer Hugo Taylor, and she certainly didn't look the Bankhead type.

"I am one." He continued making up at the mirror.

"A fascist, or a queer?"

"The latter. There. I've shocked you."

"The only thing that would shock me would be if someone as handsome as you wasn't."

He turned and looked me steadily in the eye. "Ah. I see. Well, in that case, Mitch, perhaps I will see you at the party...and afterward."

"Afterward?"

"There is a little soiree that I have arranged for my intimate friends. What we would call a 'hair down' kind of event. I hope you can come."

"Be delighted. Where is it?"

"A little place in Russell Square. The Rookery Club."

"I have to talk to you," I whispered to Bertrand when I got back to the box.

"And I to you."

As soon as the curtain was up and the play under way—and I must say that Hugo Taylor was in excellent form; no one in the audience would have guessed that he had been a recent victim of attempted cyanide poisoning—I slipped out into the corridor, and Bertrand followed me.

"Something is wrong," I said.

"Yes. For one thing, Bankhead is completely miscast. And the décor—*paff!* So *bourgeois*. Taylor is *pas trop mal*, although he acts with his head, like all English actors, not from the heart—"

"I don't mean wrong with the play. I mean there's something going on here. Some connection with what happened on the train."

"What did Taylor tell you?"

I gave a quick résumé of Taylor's suspicions concerning the British Fascists, and told him where the private party was to be held.

"And that's the very club where Andrews and Rhys used to go. It's too much of a coincidence. Not to mention the fact that that old dragon Lady Antonia, a prominent member of the British Fascist party, who takes an active interest in the private life of the royal family, is here in the audience tonight—"

"The smell of a rat, yes?"

"A great big nest of rats. And I have a feeling that King

187

Rat is none other than our friend, Peter Dickinson."

"To think, I let that man put his finger in my hole." He shuddered with disgust. "*Dégueulasse.*"

I'd heard him use that word in connection with Simmonds, his new love, but thought I unwise to remind him of the fact.

"And what did you have to tell me, Bertrand?" I braced myself for some declaration of passion, or at least a lurid description of their antics at the Regal Hotel, but Bertrand was much more useful than that.

"They have searched the…what is it? *Le chemin.*"

"The chimney?"

"Non… That on which runs the train."

"The track."

"*Ça.* The track."

"And they found the finger?"

"*Non.* Exactly that. They found not the finger, not the knife, in short, nothing at all."

"That's either a lie, or someone has concealed them. Who told you?"

"Thomas spoke to his friend at Kings Cross Station."

"Your Thomas has very useful friends."

"Indeed. More useful than that, even."

"Why?"

"He told him… *Mais, chut!*"

He grabbed me and pushed me through a door that led to the stairs.

"What's going on?"

"Him! Dickinson!"

"Here? Did he see us?"

"I think not."

"What is he doing here?"

"I don't know, but I do not like him."

"You're not the only one."

"Ah! *Enfin!* You have changed your advice, I see."

"There's something wrong. Something too convenient about everything. The way he befriended us…"

"Yes, after one smile you were ready to allow him—"

"And let us not forget, Bertrand, that it was your ass he had his fingers up."

"*C'est vrai.*" He peeked through the door. "It is well. He is passed. He did not see us."

"Now what were you going to tell me? What else did Thomas's friend say?"

"He said that there is another tunnel. A second one."

"You don't say!"

"*Evidemment.* There is the normal tunnel, the one that everyone goes through, the one in which we were stopped the first time. But then there is another one, running in parallel, built into the side of the hill. It is very rarely used."

"What the hell did anyone want to build another tunnel for?"

"In case of emergencies. If a train was stuck, for instance, they change the…*quoi? Les aiguilles.* To change the direction of the things…the tracks."

"Ah. The switch. They change the switch."

"And whoop! The train can go into the second tunnel. Out of the way. And safe from any collision."

"Or, in this case, it can be hidden."

"*Bien sûr.* So you think as I think—"

"That they reversed into the second tunnel—"

"To dispose of the evidence—"

"And we were none the wiser—"

"Because we were so busy fucking—"

We were both speaking at once, the full horror of the situation dawning on us. Oh, we had been taken for a ride.

"We were in the dining car," I remembered, "and the train was going backward, and suddenly we were thrown sideways. Remember?"

"*Bien sûr*. You knocked a bucket of ice into my lap. How could I forget?"

"That was it! That must have been when we went across the switch. And then I found the key to the bathroom and discovered Rhys's body. How could I possibly have realized that we were in a different tunnel when I had that to deal with? And your Thomas—he was so shocked he nearly threw up."

"Thomas knew nothing."

"Are you sure?"

"I am sure. Of that he has convinced me."

"Did he know of the existence of the secret tunnel?"

"No. It has not been in use for many years. They say it was closed down during the war, in case German agents packed it with bombs, and *poof!*"

"But clearly it's been opened up again."

"This is what Thomas supposes."

"But now, I am sure, it is closed again."

"*Peut-être*. But his friend will investigate."

"This friend of his is very useful. Is he trustworthy?"

"I think so, yes. He is like us."

"What's his name?"

"Arthur. Yes, you know him. The little boy." Bertrand made a moue of disapproval. "I think he is a fool. But Thomas says he is not." He shrugged—as he always did when dealing with some unpalatable truth. "It is not for me to choose his friends for him. What am I to him? Just a *divertissement*—"

"For God's sake, Bertrand, the guy's crazy about you."

"About this, perhaps." He slapped his ass. "But for the future—"

"Damn the future," I said. "It's the present I'm interested in. When will Arthur be able to search the tunnel?"

"Tonight, after the last run up to Edinburgh. He will take the mail train south. He has a friend at York—"

"I imagine he has friends everywhere."

"And he will take him down there on a little wagon. He will telegram to Thomas the results, at the hotel."

"So that's what you've been doing all afternoon. I thought you were back at the hotel, fucking."

"Some of the time, *oui, on se baisait.* But also, we work. We pay calls."

"Come on. We can't let Dickinson get away."

"But La Bankhead! Hugo Taylor!"

"I'm sure they'll survive without us."

"Where are we going?"

"Backstage."

It was not difficult to find Dickinson. We skirted the theater, picking up a large bunch of white lilies en route—they had been carelessly left in the foyer, doubtless for collection at the interval by some hysterical fan to fling across the footlights at Tallulah—and presented ourselves at the stage door.

"Flowers for Miss Bankhead's dressing room," I lisped to the door keeper, in what I thought was a passable impression of an English florist.

"Leave them here, sir."

"Oh!" I let my hand flutter around my throat, as I had seen Francis do. "The idea! Miss Bankhead insists that we arrange them personally. *N'est-ce pas, Bertrand?*"

Bertrand let loose a stream of impassioned French, which convinced the doorkeeper that we were indeed of the flower-arranging classes. He waved us in with a barely concealed sneer of distaste.

I dumped the lilies in a fire bucket, and we crept along the corridor toward Hugo Taylor's dressing room. He was on for most of the first act—but a light was burning in the room, and I could hear voices.

We stopped and listened.

"You want it?"

"Mmmmmh…"

"Where do you want it?"

"Up my arse."

"Say please, sir."

"Please, sir."

One of the voices was Dickinson's—and you can guess which. I thought I recognized the other, but I couldn't place it.

There were more sounds of shuffling and slurping, and I got as near to the door as possible—close enough to spy through a crack.

Dickinson stood with his back toward me, his broad shoulders bent forward, one powerful arm working slowly back and forth. Before him, sitting awkwardly on the dressing table among Taylor's pots of powder and paint, his pants around his ankles and his legs raised, was the familiar form of Billy Vain, whom I had met at the British-American "audition." He was holding his pale white ass open as Dickinson worked a thick, spit-slick finger in and out of his pink hole.

"Please sir," jabbered Billy, "please fuck me."

"And what will you do if I do?"

"Anything. I'll do anything."

The little fool; he didn't realize what he was dealing with.

"You understand what will happen if you don't do exactly as I tell you?"

"Yes, sir. You won't fuck me."

Dickinson slapped the boy on the ass—not a playful slap, but a hard, stinging blow. Billy bit his lower lip. "Listen to me, Billy. If you don't do exactly what I tell you to, I'll have you up in front of the beak so fast your pretty little feet won't touch the ground. Do you know what happens to boys like you in prison?"

"N-no, sir."

Dickinson drew a finger across his throat, and made a horrible tearing sound. "Understand me?"

"Yes, sir."

"Good." He pulled his finger out of Billy's ass with a plop; the hole gaped open for a second, and a looked of dazed idiocy flickered across Billy's pretty face. "Now dress yourself, you little pansy."

"Aren't we going to do it?" He stuck his lower lip out, like a sulky child.

"Later, if you acquit yourself to my satisfaction. Then you can have it any way you want it."

"Can't I just...suck it?"

Dickinson cuffed Billy across the face. Bertrand and I withdrew into the safety of an unoccupied dressing room and waited for the coast to clear. Within a few moments, Billy was humming happily next door. I recognized a tune from Noël Coward's *Bitter Sweet*, "If Love Were All."

"What are you doing, Billy?"

I stood in the doorway, trying to look imposing. Billy spun around, obviously hiding something behind his back.

"I... I'm not... Oh, hello, it's you! The Yank! How did you get on with Bertie Waits?"

"Fine. That's not what I'm here to talk about."

"Oh, I suppose you're here to see Hugo." He sniffed. "It's not fair. He gets all the good ones."

"I asked you a question. What are you doing?"

He tidied up a few pots, hung a few clothes. "What does it look like? I'm doing my job, if that's quite all right with you. Now please let me get on. Mr. Taylor will be coming off shortly, and he's got a quick change, and you shouldn't be here in the first place."

"There's no hurry, Billy, is there? There's plenty of time— time for a fuck, for instance."

"Oh."

"I heard you and Mr. Dickinson."

"Did you?"

"And I saw."

"Oh, dear." He actually blushed, which surprised me, but recovered quickly. "Oh, well. Nothing that thousands of others haven't seen on the silver screen, I suppose. Did you like what you saw?" He had stepped closer, and fluttered his eyelashes at me. He wasn't to my taste, but I could not deny that he had a tidy rear end and a very fuckable little hole.

"Sure."

"Want a taste?"

"But Mr. Taylor—"

"Oh, bugger Mr. Taylor. On second thought, don't. He gets more than his fair share as it is."

"Sounds like Dickinson's got you all worked up."

"He has." Billy grabbed the front of my pants, and his eyebrows (plucked, I fear) shot up. "Well! It's my lucky day."

"If I fuck you, will you tell me what Dickinson was saying?"

He scowled. "Oh, I see." His hand fell to his side. "No. I can't."

"You're scared of him, aren't you?"

"I don't want to go to prison."

"Nobody wants to go to prison. But, you see, if you don't tell me what he said, then I shall be forced to say something about the mouthwash."

Billy jumped as if he'd received an electric shock. It was a good guess.

"What did he say?"

"Who?"

"Taylor."

"Nothing. He thought he'd had a funny oyster. Fortunately for him, and unfortunately for you, I am a doctor."

"Pull the other one. Doctors don't make dirty movies."

"This one does. And as a doctor, I recognize the symptoms of cyanide poisoning. Not to mention the smell."

Billy came toward me again, and started entwining himself like a snake. "It's not my fault. I didn't know what it was. Dickinson just told me to put it in something that Hugo would drink." He wrapped his leg around mine, pressing his hip into my groin. "I thought it was a love potion." He was grinding against me like a dancing girl.

"But you didn't know that Taylor would spit instead of swallowing."

"I didn't think. I'm not very bright." His eyes were hooded, his lips parted.

"No, you're not, are you." He knew what he was doing, and I was almost fully hard—and I was tempted to fuck him. I might have done so, were it not for the fact I had left Bertrand in the adjacent dressing room.

"Now listen, Billy, you have a choice. You can do what Dickinson tells you to do—and face the consequences. If anything happens to Hugo Taylor, I will talk, and you will be on trial for murder. Or you can do as I say."

"And then Dickinson will grass me up."

"He won't. He's got too much to lose. He's desperate. He's gambling on your fear."

"Oh, what the hell. He told me to give him this." He pointed to an electric hair dryer on the dressing table. "After a show, Hugo always washes his hair and blow-dries it. I've dressed him before. It's the same every night."

"And Dickinson gave you this?"

"Yes."

"Why?"

"I didn't ask, but I suppose—"

"Exactly." I tugged the wire, which showed signs of tampering. "It's wired up to provide an electric shock the moment it's turned on. It would either kill him, or burn him so badly he'd never go on stage again."

"Shit."

"Shit indeed. I'll take this." I pulled the wire out of the appliance. "Hugo will just have to use a towel tonight."

"He won't be happy."

"Maybe. But he will, at least, be alive. Thanks, Billy."

"You're welcome. Now will you fuck me?"

I'm a believer in fair play. "I tell you what. You've done something for me, I'll do something for you. You can suck it."

"Oh, goody."

"Let me just see where my friend is."

I looked into the empty dressing room where we had hidden.

"Bertrand? Are you here?"

No reply. He must have followed Dickinson. I was about to return to Billy, and his pink, parted lips, when I noticed that the room was full of what appeared to be smoke. I flicked the light switch, and saw a dense white fog—of face powder. The dressing table was in disarray, chairs were turned over—and there was no sign of Bertrand.

I had not heard a struggle, but then, the walls were thick, the rooms soundproofed to prevent noise reaching the stage.

Bertrand's ticket stub lay on the floor, dropped (intentionally?) in the struggle.

But where was Bertrand?

# XI

I TRIED TO KEEP CALM. BERTRAND WAS A RESOURCEFUL BOY; perhaps he had just gone off on his own, looking for clues...

But why was the furniture turned over? Why was the air thick with the spilled face powder? I knew in my heart exactly what had happened: Bertrand had been abducted by Dickinson.

My first impulse was to run out of the theater and look for them on the street, as if I would see Dickinson, cackling like a screen villain, loading the struggling Bertrand into the back of a hansom cab and speeding to his lair. But they would be far away by now, and there was no point in my proceeding alone. I needed help.

I ran upstairs and arrived panting in the box. The first act was just coming to an end, thank God. Belinda, Boy, and Simmonds were all applauding enthusiastically.

"Not your cup of tea, old chap?" asked Boy. He looked uneasy; he must have realized that I'd slipped out with Bertrand, and drawn the obvious conclusion.

"Mitch doesn't go for all that soppy romantic stuff," said

Belinda, with a sly laugh. "You're much more of a man's man, aren't you, Mitch?"

I mustered as much chivalry as I could, but I was in no mood for social pleasantries, even with a woman I esteemed as highly as Belinda.

"Where's Bertrand?" asked Simmonds, looking no more pleased than Morgan. Oh, God, that's all I needed; an irate love rival...

"You'd better come with me."

"Has something happened?"

"Morgan, take Belinda to the bar. We'll meet you later."

"Mitch, what's going on?" His face suddenly brightened. "I say, is there trouble?"

"It certainly looks like it."

"Your young friend... Oh, dear. Has something happened?"

"I'm afraid it has." I restrained Simmonds, who was as eager as I had been to rush into the street. "We must think clearly. Simmonds, come with me. Morgan, take care of Belinda."

"Not on your life. I'm coming with you."

"Oh, Harry!" Belinda cried.

"Come on, old girl. You can entertain yourself. The place is full of people that you know."

"And what will they think if they see me wandering around on my own, without my husband? A very nice impression that will give. Honestly, Harry, the one night we get out and you want to rush off on the tail of—well, I don't know what."

"She's right, Morgan. You must stay here. We don't want to draw attention to ourselves. If they think—"

"They?" Morgan's eyes were blazing. "Who's they? You mean there's a gang? Here? In the theater?"

"I have no idea. But there are too many coincidences. We must be watchful. I need you here, Morgan, behaving completely normally, but keeping your eyes and ears open. See that old bird down there?"

"Who, the one with the chicken's arse sticking out of her hat?"

"Harry!"

"The very same. That's Lady Antonia Petherbridge. She was on the train. Watch her like a hawk."

Belinda peered around. "Oh, yes!" She waved in Lady Antonia's direction; the great lady inclined her head in return. "We know her, darling. She came to the wedding."

"Did she?" Morgan peered around, with a cheery smile on his face. "Oh yes. Her. Spent half an hour telling me that Jews were taking over the banking business."

"That sounds about right."

"She's from a very old family," said Belinda.

"Soft in the head, those old families," said Morgan.

"I want you to engage her in conversation. Keep her busy. Don't let her get away. Has she got her companion with her? Dowdy little woman by the name of Chivers?"

"I can't see anyone, no," said Belinda. "Just a couple of other old dears. Oh, wait a minute. That's Rotha Thing-ummy. You know. The one who's in the papers all the time. The fascist woman. And that's her henchman. I wonder what they're doing here?"

I recognized the faces from the newspapers: Rotha Lintorn-Orman, head of the British Fascist Party, and her "head of intelligence," Maxwell Knight. They were constantly in trouble for their notoriously violent public meetings.

"I imagine they're here to cause trouble."

"Gosh," said Morgan. "Do you suppose they've got rotten eggs in their handbags? You know, to pelt the stage with?"

"Bombs, more likely," said Belinda. "They're complete lunatics."

"Right. Your job is to keep them occupied. On no account

let them out of your sight. Cause a commotion if necessary. Think you can manage that?"

"Of course we can," said Belinda—and I had every faith in her. "But could you give us the tiniest hint of what this is all about?"

"There have been two attempts on the life of Hugo Taylor this evening."

Belinda and Morgan's faces fell.

"And, if I am not mistaken, Prince George could be in danger as well. Our friend Bertrand has been abducted—"

"No!" Simmonds sounded as if he'd been punched hard in the stomach.

"A man was killed on the train, and two others, including Taylor, assaulted. Another man has been arrested for the murder, and a woman has been arrested as his accomplice."

"You mean Daisy Athenasy, don't you?" said Belinda. "It was in the papers. They said she'd been arrested in connection with a motoring offense. I said, didn't I, darling, that I didn't believe a word of it. So she's a murderer."

"She's no more a murderer than you or me. She's been framed."

"Wow!" Morgan's eyes were wide; he was enjoying all this much more than he'd enjoyed *La Dame aux Camélias*. "So what do you want us to do in the second half?"

"Watch the play, of course. If anything is going to happen in the theater, I want you to witness it."

"Oh, God. Can't I come with you?"

"Certainly not," said Belinda, firmly. "Now, Mitch, what happens after the show?"

"We're going to the party, of course. At the Café Royal."

Simmonds and I hurried out of the theater and into the street. Why were we hurrying? There was little we could do to help our friend—but the idea of sitting inactive, while he was in danger, was unthinkable to both of us.

"What are we going to do?" Simmonds looked genuinely stricken. His face, a strange cross between handsome and brutish, was pale, his eyes wide with fear. "Will they...hurt him?"

"I don't know. Dickinson is a very dangerous man."

"But he's the police. Is Bertrand under arrest?"

"Possibly."

"But for what?"

"There's always a reason to arrest people like us, Simmonds."

"But he wouldn't have been—"

"No. I don't imagine he would." Not after the fucking you'd given him, I almost added. "But Dickinson is a senior officer. Who's going to take the word of an impoverished foreigner against his?"

"Not so impoverished, as it turns out."

"What?"

"Didn't he tell you? He went to see his uncle this afternoon."

"And?"

"His father's will is very...favorable."

"Ah. I see. Well, that's good news. I congratulate you."

"Me, sir?"

"I assume that you have some interest in Bertrand's future."

"Not that kind of interest, sir. If you're suggesting that I'm after his money—"

"I know perfectly well which part of Bertrand you're after, Simmonds, and it ain't the pounds, shillings, and pence. Or whatever they have in Belgium."

"Francs, I believe, sir."

That seemed to bring the conversation to an end, and we walked up Charing Cross Road deep in thought, to all appearances like two friends out for an evening stroll. I had no idea where to go, what to do.

"If I might make a suggestion, sir…"

"For God's sake, can we drop the 'sir'? We're not on the train now."

"Sorry, Mitch. I think we ought to check at the hotel, to see if there's a telegram for me."

"Ah, the famous secret tunnel!"

"Yes. Arthur should have had time to have a good look around by now, and he promised he'd send a telegram as soon as possible. It hadn't arrived when we left, but it's nearly half past nine now."

"Good idea. The only thing we can do now is to build the case against Dickinson."

"You really believe that he's behind all this?"

"I have to believe it, Simm— Sorry, Thomas. There is no other possible explanation."

"But you have no proof."

"Not yet, I admit. Just a lot of guesswork. But there's no time to put together a case against anyone else. We just have to take a gamble. If the pieces fit, then we have our man. If not… Well, we're in the dark."

"And Bertrand?"

"We will find him, Thomas. I promise you that."

"Thank you, Mitch."

"And if the pieces of the jigsaw do fit together, and it turns out that Dickinson is somehow behind the murder of David Rhys, then we…well, we…"

"Yes. That is the question. What do we do, exactly? It's not as if we can call the police. He is the police."

"They can't all be rotten."

"You're asking the wrong person. My experience of the boys in blue has not been a happy one."

I had heard this frequently from my friends; I guess I had just been lucky. But I cast my mind back to that long-ago summer in Norfolk, when Boy Morgan and I discovered a taste for detection—and even there, in the tiny village of Drekeham, the police force was riddled with corruption. There was one good copper, my friend PC Shipton, he of the hairy, obliging ass—but there was also the sadistic sergeant and his bullying sidekick Piggott, whose interrogation of an innocent suspect opened my eyes to the unorthodox policing methods rife in the English constabulary. If that sort of thing happened in rural Norfolk, how much more vicious would they be in London?

Yet surely, for every Peter Dickinson there must be at least one PC Shipton. We needed to find a sympathetic friend on the force—someone who could give us access to restricted information.

And in order to find this much-needed friend, I was willing to stoop to any depths necessary.

A plan was hatching in my mind—but first, the Regal Hotel, and Arthur's telegram.

We ran up to Simmonds's room—to the amazement of the porter, who had seen Simmonds leave, satiated, with one man only to return, bounding and eager, with another. With shaking hands, Simmonds tore open the telegram.

TUNNEL CLOSED STOP POLICE GUARD STOP HOPING FOR MORE LATER STOP ARTHUR

My heart sank. I was hoping for the evidence that I needed to confront Dickinson, free Bertrand, and absolve William Andrews.

"Dickinson is covering his tracks," I said. "I'm sure that we backed into the tunnel so that he could get rid of the evidence."

"But who changed the switch?" asked Simmonds. "And why didn't I notice anything? I make that journey six times a week."

"If you don't mind my saying so, you were a little preoccupied. There was blood seeping out under the door. People had already been injured. And I suspect you were thinking of Bertrand—"

"You're right. But you can't just flip the switch over without someone knowing about it. Someone has to know what they're doing. Someone...on the train..."

"Who are you thinking of?"

"Eltham. The engineer."

"Ah, the man in the shed. But why would he do it?"

"Because someone threatened him, maybe. He and Rowson weren't very discreet."

"Rowson being the stoker, I presume. So Bertrand really did see them in the shed at York."

"It wasn't easy for them to be together."

"They worked together, for God's sake!"

"Mitch, have you ever tried fucking while stoking a furnace and running an engine?"

"So the unscheduled stop at York—"

"I'm afraid so. It's not the first time it's happened. I'd warned them, but they wouldn't listen."

"So much for the nonstop service."

"Better than doing it while the train's moving. Eltham might have missed a signal, and then none of us would be here at all."

"Dickinson had been snooping around, hadn't he? He'd have heard about them from someone. You know how people talk, especially if money changes hands. Then he'd put pressure on them, get them to do what he told them to do. When the train stopped south of the tunnel, one of them could have run out and changed the switch manually."

"It's possible."

"And under the circumstances, none of us would have noticed a thing. Just another jolt, and back into the darkness."

Simmonds sat on the bed, holding Bertrand's frayed, torn old shirt. There was a spot of blood on the front, which he rubbed between finger and thumb.

"It's okay, Thomas," I said. "We'll find him."

"I will never forgive myself for hitting him."

"That's the one thing about all this that I still don't understand. What happened?"

"I don't know. I just saw red. I'd wanted him for so long... Oh yes, I'd seen him traveling up and down the line before, always looking so sad, as if he needed a friend. I know how that feels. And when I found that he was traveling without a ticket, I got him into the bathroom, and I just lost my head."

"You tried to stick your cock in his mouth."

"I panicked. I thought it might be my only chance." He looked like a man who has just received a death sentence. "And he looked so shocked, so horrified."

"So you hit him."

"Yes."

"Did you not think of the consequences? Or did you believe that Superintendent Dickinson would cover for you? You can't afford to lose your job, can you. You're a family man, I understand."

"That is correct, sir." His mouth was set in a grim line. "Thank you for reminding me of my obligations."

"I'm just asking—"

"My marriage is over. We stay together for the sake of the children. I see now that even that was a bad idea. It's turned me into the kind of man who...well, does what I did."

"Time for a fresh start, Simmonds."

"Do you believe that's possible?"

"Yes. Otherwise, what's the point of anything? Come on, man, pull yourself together. Things will work out fine," I said, hardly believing it myself. "When this is all over, you and Bertrand have a fine future ahead of you."

"Really?"

"I know you do. But there will be plenty of time to think of that—afterward. Now is the time for action."

Simmonds stood up. "Let's go. But where?"

"We're going to get ourselves arrested."

It wouldn't be difficult, if the stories were true, to find a policeman in the West End of London. The public toilets, or "cottages," as they were known to their habitués, were said to be crawling with them, lying in wait for heedless homosexuals to show a flicker of interest.

But where to go? We needed expert advice.

"Hi," I said to the porter downstairs. He was eyeing us with a typical English mixture of prurience and disdain. I exaggerated my American accent, and leaned on the desk in an overfamiliar way. "How are you doing?"

"Very well, sir," he said, frostily. He must have been used to all sorts of comings and goings at the Regal, and thought it best to maintain a civil distance. "May I help you?"

"My friend and I were wondering where the action is."

"Action, sir?" His nostrils flared, as if I'd just farted. "I don't know what you mean."

"You know." I leaned forward conspiratorially. "Where can we get a bit of cock."

"Oh, really, sir!"

I pulled out my wallet, which worked its usual magic. "I'm sure you know all the places, don't you?"

"Well, there are one or two clubs—"

"I don't have time for clubs. I don't want to stand around sipping a drink and making small talk. What about the parks—or the johns?"

"Johns, sir?"

"You know. Public restrooms. Bathrooms."

"Oh, I see. Well, sir, I believe that Russell Square gardens have their attractions."

"I'm really not a country boy. All that crawling around in bushes."

"And as for the...bathrooms, sir, you might like to head into Covent Garden. I believe that some of the restrooms there are anything but restful."

"I see. And are they...safe?"

"Safe? Oh, I see what you mean. The police. Well, if I were you I would avoid the ones on the Strand. They have a reputation for being rather...well observed, you might say. But other than that—"

"Thank you. You've been most helpful."

He was warming to his theme. "In fact, there's one in Brydges Place that I have always found to be terribly reliable."

"Thank you." I was in a hurry to get going.

"One gets quite a nice class of serviceman in there, and they're really not at all greedy."

"I see." I filed the information away for future use, and pressed the note into his clammy hand. "I thought you might be able to help. You look the type."

"Well! I—" He was about to be offended, but then he glanced at the denomination of the note, and thought better of it. "Happy to oblige, sir. Good night."

"Good night."

"And happy hunting!"

We almost ran out of the hotel. I would have laughed, until I saw the look of concern on Simmonds's face.

"What are we going now, Mitch?"

"Which way is the Strand?"


It was impossible to miss the cottage in question: there might as well have been a huge neon sign on the roof reading QUEERS THIS WAY. There were men hanging around on the sidewalk, casting furtive glances at each other, occasionally going into the little brick building, coming out, hanging around some more, and so on.

I sent Simmonds inside, and told him to station himself in one of the cubicles—preferably one that commanded a general view of the interior. I knew from my own observations that such places usually had holes drilled in the doors by dedicated perverts who must, I suppose, carry carpentry tools with them for such necessities.

I gave him five minutes to get himself settled, then went in. The interior was dimly lit with a single electric bulb reflected in puddles on the filthy concrete floor. Moss was growing in cracks on the wall. The place stank, of course, that powerful combination of piss, shit, and disinfectant that some find an irresistible aphrodisiac. It was not my favorite aroma—but it was not without its charms.

A quick glance around revealed the setup. I was in luck: there was only one obvious policeman in the building. Sometimes they worked in pairs—but obviously vice was so rampant on the West End streets that they were stretched too far, and had to do this important work alone. He was standing at the urinal farthest from the door, almost in the dark, a slim, upright figure in dark clothing. My eyes adjusted to the lack of light. Yes, he was wearing the sort of clothes that an office clerk, a waiter, or a hotel porter might wear, not too dressy, but not obviously rough trade. He looked the type.

Only one of the cubicles was occupied—and that would be Simmonds, rather than another copper lying in wait with handcuffs.

The only other person was standing two urinals up from the young policeman. I'd seen him coming and going outside; he was the sort that I classed as a habitual, indeed compulsive, toilet trader. He glanced at me when I walked in, his face gaunt, as if consumed by lust, and then returned his attention to the policeman on his left. He was heedless of the danger, perhaps aroused by it. It would be doing him a kindness to intervene—and that's just what I did, positioning myself at the vacant stall between them. My action could not have been misinterpreted—had I been a normal "user" I would have selected the urinal nearest the door, leaving plenty of space for us all. My right-hand neighbor let out a gasp of exasperation, and when I turned I was met by a face contorted with frustration and fury. His hand was busy in his groin, palpating a large genital.

"Do yourself a favor, pal," I said, out of the side of my mouth, "and get lost."

"What?"

"You heard me. Fuck off."

"Well!" He put himself away and stepped back. "I've never heard anything so... Oh!"

He stormed out—without washing his hands, I noticed. Was there no end to his depravity? I hoped that he didn't work around food.

When we were alone, I got my cock out and concentrated on pissing. The young man on my left remained in position, and a sidelong glance confirmed that he too was exposed— and not even pretending to urinate. Fortunately for me, I'd not had a chance to relieve myself since we left Morgan's house, and I genuinely needed to go. A powerful stream was soon splashing against the porcelain.

"Aaaaah... That's better."

No response from my left.

"What do you say? Nothing like a good, long piss."

A grunt.

"What's that? Yes or no?"

"Hmmmph."

"You're not much of a conversationalist, are you. Say— what do you think of this?" I arced the jet of piss upward, right to the top of the urinal and then over to the left, into his stall.

"Hey! Watch out!"

"Sorry, copper. Did I splash your boots?"

"What did you say?"

"Copper. I'm right, aren't I? Plain clothes. Vice squad. Shitty job, huh? Literally."

"I don't know—"

"What I'm talking about. 'Course you don't. You just like to spend your evenings hanging out in public bathrooms, letting guys like that look at your dick." I was almost through pissing now, and the flow was slackening. "Unless, of course, you're off duty, and just doing it for kicks."

"Certainly not."

"Ah. I was right, then." I stopped pissing, and shook the drops off vigorously. "So, what's it like?"

"What?"

"Your job. Standing around flashing your cock at queers. You like your work?"

"It's not the best job going." For the first time, he looked at me, and gave a shy smile. He was a good-looking boy, not more than about 21, with a fresh face and blue eyes.

"I guess you drew the short straw, then."

"They always put the new boys on this detail."

"I see. Baptism of fire, huh. Or in this case, water." I kept shaking, in no hurry to put my cock away. It was starting to swell. He said nothing, but looked down toward me.

"So, officer. Are you going to arrest me?"

"No, sir."

"But I'm committing an offense."

"Are you, sir?"

"Yeah." I started obviously masturbating. "This the sort of thing you're looking for?"

"Well... I..."

"Lewd behavior, that's what you call it, isn't it?"

"Technically speaking," he said, his voice a little strained, "you haven't actually committed an offense yet."

"And how would I do that?"

"You'd have to proposition me...or attempt to touch me."

210

"I see." I reached over and grabbed his cock, which was as stiff as a truncheon. "Like this?"

"That sort of thing..." He swallowed nervously, but did nothing to remove my hand.

"Am I breaking the law now?" I squeezed him hard and he gasped, his knees buckling slightly.

"Yes. Definitely."

"And what about you, copper? Are you breaking the law too?"

"I suppose... Oh!... I must be."

"Might as well be hanged for a sheep as a lamb, then." I grabbed his hand and brought it down to my prick. He took it tentatively at first, but when he felt it throb and jump he could no longer resist. He started jerking me. Even in the dim light, I could see that his cheeks were burning, his eyes shining.

We didn't have much time—someone could come in at any moment. I had to move things along.

"Say, seems a shame to just play with it. Why don't you—"

"Yes?"

"Do what the queers do to you?"

"You mean—"

"Yeah, boy. Suck it."

He needed no second bidding; it must have been a nightmare of frustration for him, surrounded by all that available cock, unable to taste a drop, like the Ancient Mariner. He squatted down, never letting go of my prick, and started kissing it, running his tongue over me, unconcerned by the last drop of piss that hung from the slit. I rubbed his short blond hair, drawing him in.

"That's it, boy. Open your pretty mouth and take it."

He did as he was told—and at that very moment, as my head slid along his velvety tongue, Simmonds burst out of the cubicle and caught us in the act. The young copper stopped in midsuck, a look of terror in his pretty blue eyes, his lips stretched around the base of my dick. I held his head in place, and even thrust a little. It was an exquisite scenario.

"Well, well, well," said Simmonds, in his best mean-conductor voice, "what have we here?"

The young copper couldn't reply; I made sure of that.

"Looks like we've got a queer, Mitch."

"Sure does. Look at the way he's sucking my cock."

"Yeah. He likes it, doesn't he?"

The poor boy's eyes were watering now, and I brushed a tear from his cheek.

"Now, Tom, what are we going to do with this young fellow?"

"I guess we should turn him over to the police, Mitch."

"I guess we should. But it seems a shame to ruin such a promising career."

The boy was making various noises in the back of his throat. I stroked his hair, and gently fucked his mouth. I noticed he didn't gag once.

"So, copper," I said, stroking his smooth cheek, "are you going to cooperate with us? Or do you we turn you in?"

He nodded vigorously, which had the interesting effect of working my cock into hitherto unexplored areas of his mouth.

"If I take my cock out, you aren't going to shout for help?"

He shook his head just as vigorously.

"Okay. Here we go." I took my hands from the back of his head, and let him slide off in his own time. A long string of saliva and precum connected us for a while, then he wiped his mouth and got to his feet.

"You're not going to tell on me, are you sir?"

"That rather depends on you. What's your name?"

"Godwin, sir. PC Jack Godwin."

"Well, PC Jack Godwin, you're in luck. We're looking for a young lad just like you."

"What for?"

"Not what you think, although maybe later." I could see that Simmonds was interested; he was looking at the young blond cop with a positively wolfish expression on his face. "We need some inside information."

"On what?"

I heard footsteps; we had been in there long enough, and the hunters were returning.

"Not here. Let's walk."

There was a café on the corner, where we ordered tea.

"Right, Jack. We have a job for you."

"What?"

"I need to find out about a dead man."

"Where did he die?"

"Somewhere between York and Peterborough. Around about Grantham. In a train, in a tunnel."

"That's local constabulary, then. Or Transport Police. I'm Met."

"So's Superintendent Dickinson. Ah, that made you prick up your ears. You've heard of him?"

"Of course. He's big in homicide."

"That sounds like our man."

"What's he got to do with this dead man?"

"If my suspicions are right, a hell of a lot. I need you to find out where the body is. Who's doing the autopsy. Who's handling the case. What's the procedure?"

"If it's a suspicious death—"

"Yeah, I'd say it was suspicious."

"Well, then, there would be a coroner's report and, if necessary, an autopsy."

"How quickly would that happen?"

"Straight away."

"That's what I need. Can you get them for me?"

"Possibly."

"Possibly is no good to me, Jack. An innocent man is going to hang if you don't help me."

"There's very little I can do."

"A murderer is going to get away scot-free."

"I'll do what I can, sir. Where do you imagine the body to be?"

"It may have been taken off the train at Peterborough. It may be in London. Those would be the first places to look."

"Yes, sir."

"And Jack—"

"Yes, sir?"

"If you want another taste of this"—I pulled his hand under the table to my groin—"don't let me down."

He left without even finishing his tea. Would I ever see him again? Would he simply run to his bosses, and land us in jail ourselves? I was counting on luck more than judgment—and he seemed like a good bet. But it was all a gamble. For all we knew, Bertrand could be dead by now—and there was nothing we could do about it. We were laying a trap for Dickinson, stacking up the evidence against him—but how would we catch him? Everything pointed toward him as Rhys's killer—but I could be completely wrong. He could just be a detective with distasteful methods. Maybe I had painted him as a villain out of jealousy; he was doing the work that I would like to be doing. Perhaps he was just an unscrupulous man who didn't much care what people thought of him, not above abusing his authority when it suited him, but not a killer. In which case, I would have egg on my face—and whoever had got Bertrand, I was doing nothing to help him.

These gloomy musings must have shown on my face.

"Chin up, Mitch," said Simmonds. "We'll get to the bottom of this."

"I hope so. But will we get there in time? I have a terrible feeling that something—"

"What?"

"Something is going to happen tonight."

# XII

WE MADE IT BACK TO THE GARRICK JUST IN TIME. THE audience was spilling out onto the pavement, hailing cabs, smoking cigarettes, trying to gain access to the stage door, through which, at some point, Taylor and Bankhead would pass. There were newspapermen everywhere. Somewhere in the melee were Morgan and Belinda, Lady Antonia and her cronies, and God knew who else.

Yes! There was a face I recognized! A handsome young man, short, shifty-looking, jumping up and down to survey the crowd, his hat pushed back on his head. And I recognized his friend too, taller, more heavily built. He had a camera hung around his neck. Where did I know them from? Somewhere recent? I racked my brain. British-American? No. Before that. Of course: the Flying Scotsman. They were the reporters I'd seen talking to David Rhys. The ones Dickinson, in his disguise as a British-American publicity director, had thrown off the train during that fortuitous stop at York.

And here they were again: two more pieces of the jigsaw, falling strangely into place.

They were not difficult to reach. Approaching, I tipped my hat to them, but they ignored me, far more interested in the comings and goings of the glittering first-night crowd.

"I believe I saw you gentlemen on the train from Edinburgh."

I got a scowl in return.

"Still tailing Hugo Taylor, then?"

"What does it look like?" said the shorter of the two. He had very pale blue eyes, which could have been attractive in a less suspicious-looking face.

"I bet you guys would like to hear a story about Hugo Taylor, wouldn't you?"

"Piss off, mate," said the photographer. "We're working."

I suppose that pressmen are bothered constantly by members of the public desperate to get their crackpot theories into print.

"So it won't interest you to know, then, that there was an attempt on his life this evening."

"Bollocks. Hey! Scott! Here comes Lady Antonia! Get a picture of her!"

The cameraman did as he was told. The reporter scribbled in his notebook.

"And there's Cecil Beaton! And Noël Coward!"

"Together?"

"No. We'll say they've cut each other. Get the shot!"

"Someone put cyanide in his mouthwash."

"Please, sir," said Scott, the photographer. "We've asked you nicely to leave us in peace and get on with our job. Now will you take the hint and fuck off?"

"I just told you there was an attempt on the leading man's life. Is that not of interest to your editor?"

"We heard he had a funny turn. Happens all the time. They're all doping, these actors." The reporter barely bothered to look at me, his eyes riveted on the crowd. "We can't write about it. Orders from above."

"Then I shall take my story elsewhere."

"Good luck."

Ill-mannered little prick! I wanted to knock him down. But I sensed that he knew things that might be useful to me.

"Thank you. And tomorrow, try explaining to your editor that you missed a story all about Prince George."

That got his attention.

"What?"

"Prince George. Backstage in Hugo Taylor's dressing room. Displaying a lively concern. Shortly after Mr. Taylor's costar, Daisy Athenasy, was arrested in connection with the murder of a man on the Flying Scotsman."

"You are joking."

"I wish I were."

"Scott, keep snapping. I've got a scoop."

"But Connor, for God's sake—"

"Do as I tell you." Connor, the weaselly little reporter, took my arm and led me aside, while Scott kept shooting, occasionally casting angry glances in our direction.

"Go on, Mr....er...?"

"Mitchell. Edward Mitchell." He took down my name. "Shortly after you left the train at York, a man was killed..." I told him the whole story, and he scribbled.

When I'd finished, he said, "You really expect me to believe that that interfering bastard who chucked us off the train was an undercover cop?"

"Yes. Call your news desk. Perhaps some of the senior reporters will know the name. You're just showbiz—"

"All right, all right. No need to get shirty. But come on, mate. Even if he is a copper, you can't seriously think that he bumped off some bloke just because he was—what? Nobbing some other feller? You've got to have a better motive than that. What do you reckon? Jealous lover? Queer love triangle?"

"No, I don't think that was the reason."

"Then what? Come on, you're wasting my time."

"I think," I said, improvising wildly, "that David Rhys found out something about Hugo Taylor and Prince George."

I made that up on the spur of the moment, to persuade Connor that I wasn't making a mountain out of a molehill—but suddenly it made sense. Of course! If Dickinson was in league with the British Fascists, trying to "clean up" the royal family and remove Prince George from his undesirable connections, then any inadvertent discovery of the royal person's peccadilloes would be a very good motive for murder.

"And where does Daisy Athenasy fit into all this?"

There he had me, but I wasn't going to admit it. There was no point in telling him about Daisy's drug habit, as that was clearly common knowledge. Once again, I scrabbled around for a foothold in the scree of supposition.

I said, "British-American is making blue movies—"

"You don't say?"

"—to make up the shortfall for her box-office disasters."

"Go on."

I felt like saying "I'm going as fast as I can—it takes time to make this crap up!"—but then I had another flash of intuition.

"And they were being blackmailed by Peter Dickinson."

"I thought you told me he was working for them?"

"He was. But I see it all now. They'd agreed to let him pretend to be a British-American employee, on the understanding that he was trying to crack the drug ring that was supplying Daisy. Herbert Waits, her husband, would have wanted to get her off the drugs—"

"Or possibly he wanted proof that she was on them," said Connor, who clearly had ambitions to get out of showbiz reporting and into proper investigative journalism. "That way, he could fire her on a morals clause—and get a very easy divorce. She's been a millstone round his neck ever since she frog-marched him up the aisle."

"And then," I continued, "Dickinson turned on Waits, said that he'd blow the whistle on the studio's secret activities, unless... Unless what?"

"Unless he lets him get to Hugo Taylor."

We looked at each other. Could this possibly be true? Had Peter Dickinson really abused his position that far—to pervert the course of a criminal investigation to his own warped political ends? It was ridiculous. But then, life often is.

I had a buzzing in my ears, flashes in my eyes, and I felt as if I might faint. I suppose it was a form of panic, or euphoria. I have had it once or twice before, when I've realized that I am about to have sex with someone.

"So," said Connor. "Prove it."

There's the rub, I thought. Proof. I had none.

"You have to believe me."

"For all I know, mate, you could be some republican crackpot or religious maniac trying to spread a crazy story about the royal family, or the film industry. We get them every day. I can't publish without proof. This is a risky enough story as it is. The editor will need a cast-iron case, otherwise the legal actions would be fucking horrific. If you can't back it up, mate, you're just pissing in the wind."

I couldn't let him go like this. He was ready to believe me—possibly ready to help—but without proof, I was wasting my time. And time was in even shorter supply than proof. The crowd was surging around the stage door. Hugo Taylor and Tallulah Bankhead would soon be coming out. I had to move. What could I do?

Simmonds suddenly appeared at my side.

"Mitch!"

"Not now, Simmonds. I'm trying to think."

"Mitch, come quickly!"

"What is it? Not Taylor..." I had a sudden, horrible suspicion that the hair dryer had, after all, done its lethal work.

"No. It's Godwin."

Godwin! My cock-hungry little policeman! Back so soon! I followed Simmonds's pointing finger, and there stood PC Jack Godwin, still in plain clothes, accompanied by another police officer in uniform. He was beckoning me over.

"Here's your proof," I said to Connor. "Straight from the horse's mouth."

He followed me over. I shook Godwin by the hand.

"What have you got for me, Jack?"

"It's not me, sir. It's my sergeant here. Mr. Mitchell—Sergeant Shipton.

Shipton? Surely not...

The uniformed sergeant held out a hand. "Evening, Mitch."

"Bill Shipton? I don't believe it!"

"You been corrupting young officers in public toilets again, Mitch?" He grinned, and I remembered our first encounter in that faraway pisshouse on the Norfolk coast. "I may have to take you in for questioning."

I shook his hand warmly; he was even more handsome than I remembered. I was at a loss for words; his sudden presence, here, in the middle of London, at the critical turning point of the entire case, had knocked my sense of reality dangerously sideways—just like that moment when we lurched into the secret tunnel. And once again I was groping in the dark.

But Sergeant Shipton had a light.

"You're looking for a body, I understand from young Godwin here." He laid a fraternal hand on the young constable's shoulder. "No surprises there, I said; my friend Mitch is always looking for a nice body. But in this case I understand it's a stiff. If you'll pardon the expression."

"Very stiff, and very cold."

Shipton pulled out his notebook. He and Connor eyed

each other suspiciously—and with a certain curiosity, unless I was much mistaken. Bertrand would have laughed at me again for assuming that everyone shared my tastes, but I had been right about Shipton, and I'd trained him very nicely during our previous acquaintance...

"Who is this?"

"Mr. Connor, from the—which paper do you represent, Mr. Connor?"

"The *Daily Beacon.*"

"Right," said Shipton. "This is strictly off the record. Do you understand me, sir? If you reveal your sources for this information, you and your editor will regret it very much indeed."

"You're safe in my hands, constable."

I was not mistaken.

"What can you tell me, Bill?"

"Godwin says you're interested in one David Rhys, found dead on the Edinburgh-to-London express yesterday, correct?"

"Correct."

"The death was reported to the Peterborough Constabulary at four P.M."

"That's when Dickinson left the train."

"And an arrest was made shortly after. Mr. William Andrews, on suspicion of murder."

"So what's happened?"

"Well, Mitch, this is where things don't add up. Andrews is in custody, but he's already been moved down to London before any kind of hearing in Peterborough."

"Is that normal?"

"No. It's highly irregular."

"I see."

"And then there's the question of the body."

"What about it? Has there been an autopsy? Have they established the cause of death?"

"No."

"Why not, for Christ's sake?"

"Because, if you'll let me get a word in edgeways, the body has gone missing."

"What? What do you mean? How can a dead body go missing?"

"Good question. The paperwork was signed at the Peterborough police morgue. The body should be there. But when I called them just now, the place was in uproar. There was nobody."

"What—nobody to answer the phone?"

"No, Mitch. No body. No corpse. In short, no David Rhys."

Morgan and Belinda were waving frantically above the throng. I pushed my way through the crowd to meet them.

"Where have you been, Mitch?" Morgan demanded.

"Never mind that. What news?"

"They were watching him like a hawk, Lady Antonia and her pals."

"Who?"

"The Prince, of course. Couldn't take their eyes off him. But thanks to my intrepid wife, they didn't get near him."

"Just a little womanly ingenuity," said Belinda, looking quietly pleased with herself. "I told Lady Antonia that my father had a vast amount of money to invest, and that he was, shall we say, sympathetic to their cause." She shuddered. "None of which is true. Poor Daddy is broke, and he would rather cut his own throat than support that gang of crooks, but there you go. Needs must."

"They seemed frightfully interested in money, didn't they?" said Morgan.

"You can be sure of that. All these crackpot political parties are in it for the money. No doubt they've got Lady Antonia to hock her entire estate."

"Well, those diamonds she's wearing are paste," said Belinda. "A woman notices these things."

"Not surprised, the way you were examining them, old girl," Morgan said. "You practically bit them."

"And didn't she love showing them off? Oh well, kept them busy throughout the interval. No harm done. Hugo and Tallulah got standing ovations. No bullets rang out above the crowd. And, judging by the squeals coming from around the corner, I imagine that they have emerged to face their adoring public." Belinda had a sardonic streak; she was a good foil to the eager, trusting Morgan.

"Oh, I say! Can we go and have a look?" Morgan said enthusiastically. "I'm dying to see them at close quarters."

"You'll have plenty of opportunity to do that later," I said. "We're going to the party."

"I say, are we really? How ripping!"

Sometimes, Morgan was just too preposterously English for his own good. I longed to slap his beaming face with my cock, before stopping his mouth with it. But that would have to wait.

I looked around the corner for just long enough to confirm that Hugo Taylor was alive and well and not covered in hideous burns. He and Tallulah were busy signing autographs and posing for photographs, and I saw the gilded locks of Frankie Laking hovering behind them.

"Let's go and stake out the Café Royal," I said. "I want to watch everyone come in."

We stepped off the pavement—and as we did so, I heard the approaching roar of a car, the screech of breaks, a thump. A black sedan sped away toward the river.

"Oh, my God! Belinda!"

Morgan crouched over his wife, who was sprawled in the road, one leg pointing out at a crazy angle from the knee.

She was alive. Her head had hit the curbstone, but fortunately she'd broken her fall with her hand. Her wrist may have been broken and her leg badly sprained.

"That bastard!" Morgan ran down the road in pursuit of the car, but I called him back.

"Someone call an ambulance! Boy, stay with her."

Simmonds ran into the theater, while Morgan peeled off his coat and jacket to cover his wife, who was cold with shock. His eyes were full of tears. "What happened, Mitch?"

"It could have been an accident."

"But it wasn't, was it? They were aiming at us."

"I don't know, Boy." But I did know. I could see it all too clearly. They had been aiming at me.

I positioned myself at the head of the stairs, where I could watch the guests arriving at the Café Royal. Undoubtedly there was a rear entrance as well, but now I was working on my own, and I couldn't cover it. Bertrand had disappeared, and Simmonds had gone to look for him—pointlessly, I thought, but I could hardly stop him. Morgan was with Belinda at the hospital. Shipton and Godwin had gone to dig out all they could on the Rhys case, while Connor and Scott had returned to the *Beacon* to file what they hoped would be the scoop of the century.

I felt vulnerable. If they—whoever "they" were—were looking for me, I was a conspicuous target. I kept my back to the wall; at least I'd see any attack coming.

"Mitch, you fascinating creature!" I felt a hand on my ass; so much for not being taken from behind. "How delicious to find you here."

"Hello, Frankie."

"And all alone! Don't tell me my luck has changed at last."

"That depends, Frankie."

"Ooh! Sounds promising. What do you want? Money? I don't carry a great deal of cash, but I can usually rustle up something."

"Not money. Information."

"Go on then. Pump me."

"Well, first of all—"

"I said, pump me."

"Oh. I see."

"Fair exchange, and all that." He pouted and started talking like a baby, an affectation of his set that I found utterly disgusting. "If 'oo want Fwankie to spill beany-weanies, 'oo let Fwankie pway wiv your willy."

"For God's sake, Frankie—"

"Otherwise," he said, snapping back to his clipped Mayfair tones, "my lips will remain sealed. In more ways than one. Oh, I say! That's rather witty! I shall have to tell Noël. Perhaps he'll put it in a show."

"Come on, then," I said. "This had better be worth it."

"It will be, dear, on so many levels."

Seldom have I gone to a sexual encounter with so little enthusiasm. It wasn't that Frankie Laking was particularly unattractive; he was good-looking enough, for all his dandification, and I even liked his company in an odd sort of way. But I found his ridiculous air of sophistication extremely off-putting, not to mention the indiscreet way in which he rolled his eyes at all and sundry as he led me to the lavatory.

"Turn a blind eye, Stephanie," he trilled to the attendant, pushing me into a cubicle.

"Yes, Sir Francis." The Royal was known as a haven of tolerance, but I didn't realize just how tolerant it had become.

"Now then, let's see what we've got," said Frankie, dropping to his knees in the cramped confines of the cubicle. I've sucked, and been sucked, in many public conveniences in my time—but this was certainly the most luxurious. The fixtures were marble, the fittings gold. "Oh, I say. What a handsome piece."

He pulled my dick out through my fly, his long, slender

fingers running up and down my shaft as if he were about to play the flute. This was one instrument he certainly knew his way around, and I prepared myself for a virtuoso recital.

"Is naughty man going to stick gweat big fing into ickle Fwankie's gob?" he said, looking up at me and batting his eyelashes.

"Frankie, can the baby talk, or there will be no cock for anyone."

"Hey ho," he sighed. "I suppose I'd better get on with it, then." He sounded so world-weary—it was the fashion among his set to be so—but he went about his business with more enthusiasm than I'd seen him muster for anything. Yes, Sir Francis Laking, baronet, had certainly sucked cock before. He started off with a few preparatory trills and arpeggios, kissing the head, nibbling up the shaft, flicking my balls with his tongue. I shut my eyes, sighed and let him bring me to full erection. And then, when he could see I was ready, he began to play love's old sweet song, a melody of which I never tire. He swallowed me to the hilt, and I gave myself over to him entirely, forgetting even the information that I was supposed to be getting in return. For a moment, I feebly wondered if Frankie had been dispatched by Dickinson or Lady Antonia to get me out of the way. (I really should not have come, I should stop now, protest, resume my watch...) And then his tongue swirled around my helmet, his lips glided down my length, and I stopped thinking altogether.

After several variations on a theme, Frankie squeezed my balls and, sensing that I was about to come, relinquished my cock from his mouth and pointed it straight into his face. One, two, three firm tugs and I was spewing a heavy load into his hair, his eyes, over his nose, mouth, and chin. It dripped off him, and he licked his lips, savoring the taste.

"Well," he said, producing a mauve silk handkerchief from his breast pocket, "that was marvelous." He mopped up the worst of the semen and then, to my astonishment, refolded the handkerchief and replaced it in his pocket.

I left first, splashing my face with cold water, and resumed my position at the head of the stairs. Frankie said he'd follow, with information—but would he?

The guests were arriving thick and fast. What had I missed? Who was here? Why had I been so stupid...?

"I suppose you've figured it all out by now, haven't you?"

"Frankie! I thought you weren't coming."

"What do you think I've been doing for the last five minutes!"

"Oh, I'm sorry—"

"Yes. They all say that. Happy for Frankie to take a facefull, but what do they do for Frankie? Fortunately, I'd saved something to remind me of you." He patted his breast pocket, where the ends of the damp mauve silk square stuck out, rather bedraggled. "A fragrant memory..."

"Next time, I'll remember my manners."

"Next time, indeed. Promises, promises. Anyway, speaking of promises, I never break mine, so here goes. You know all about Hugo and you-know-who, I take it."

"Prince George?"

"The very same, but we call her Princess Saltylips, on account of her distinguished naval career." He rolled his eyes skyward and ran a hand through his golden tresses. "Now, he and Hugo have been carrying on recklessly for years, dear. It's the talk of the palace. I mean, it's hardly the greatest love affair of the twentieth century, because, *entre nous*, they are both complete sluts. But in between *affaires de coeur*, they keep coming back to each other for a bit of how's your father. And when your father happens to be the King of England, and your mother is the divine Queen Mary, that sort of thing is taken rather seriously."

"So the family disapproves."

"Mitch, dear, that's rather like saying that we disapproved of the Kaiser in 1914. It's a thorn in their side, according to my sources, but what can they do? He's never going to be king. Queen perhaps, but... Well, you know what I mean. And as long as he doesn't do anything stupid, they prefer to keep their own counsel. I mean, it's far more worrying when the Prince is running around with Kiki Preston, who can't keep her mouth shut, she wants everyone to know all the details—and, my dear, she knows the mostly ghastly people, drug dealers and spies and communists and God knows what. And the dear Maharani of Cooch Behar, lovely girl, but, well, you know, rather obviously brown. Oh, and of course poor Florence Mills... And his own cousin, so they say, dear Louis Ferdinand..."

"My God. He's a busy boy."

"Well, darling, there have to be some advantages to a title. He can have anyone he wants. Even my own humble baronetcy has gained me a certain cachet among social-climbing queers."

"So his friendship with Hugo is the least of their worries."

"Yes, you'd think so. But apparently, they've taken against him."

"Why?"

"I'm not entirely sure, my dear. It all seemed to be going so nicely, and I'm sure it's not Hugo who's rocking the boat. He's no fool, and he knows a good thing when he sees it. George is a very generous man, you know. Nice little prezzies. A diamond here, a Bentley there, a house in Hampshire, a holiday on a yacht..."

"Maybe I should make a move on him myself."

"You'll have to work your way up. Through me. Start at the bottom." He put a hand over his mouth and giggled.

"So what's changed? And what's this got to do with what happened on the train?"

"I haven't a clue, dear, but I'll tell you this. Suddenly, a lot of people want to stop George from seeing Hugo. It all started before Christmas. Hugo was philosophical. I mean, he has plenty of other fish to fry." Frankie sighed deeply. "I thought at one point he might be interested in frying me, but no such luck. He's got his eyes set on Hollywood. He could do well out there. But suddenly, everyone was buzzing about how deeply distressed the Queen was by her son's friendship with an actor. Oh, it was all over town, like a rash. Someone was spreading the rumor. And you know what the palace is like; they deny these rumors till they're *bleu au visage*, but it usually turns out that they started them."

"You mean Queen Mary herself takes an interest?"

"I can't prove it, of course, but I believe it. And of course you know who her number one gossipmonger is, don't you?"

I didn't, but I had a horrible feeling that my suspicions were correct. "Lady Antonia."

"Yes, dear old Antonia, Lady Petherbridge. Her teeth may have gone, but there's poison dripping from her tongue."

"And she has the ear of the Queen?"

"My dear, didn't you know? She was a lady in waiting for years, simply years, and that's the nearest thing that the Queen has to a friend. Isn't it ghastly?"

"She turned the Queen against Hugo?"

"Probably."

"Why? Because of the company he keeps?"

"Charming!"

"I didn't mean you, Frankie. I was thinking of Daisy."

"Oh, Morphine Mary!"

"And through her, Herbert Waits and the whole British-American operation. If I'm right, then the fascists have been digging the dirt on what goes on in Wardour Street, and they've reported back to the Queen."

"How thrilling! You mean that Queen Mary is just one step away from the grindhouses of Soho?"

"Yes. Small world, isn't it?"

"Perversion makes the strangest bedfellows, does it not? It all makes sense. If the fascists were looking for a way to get rid of Hugo, then that sort of smut would do the trick."

"And if that wasn't working—bang! They'd kill him."

"Quite possibly." Frankie shuddered. "They could do away with any one of us."

"I still don't understand why, though."

"Think about it, dear. Now, I don't pretend to understand politics—there's only room in this pretty little head for one thing at a time, and I think you know what that is—but put yourself in their position. If you were a member of a political party, what could be better than having a member of the royal family on your side, as a sort of spokesman, a figurehead."

"You mean they're grooming Prince George?"

"Well, I would, in their shoes. Not that I'd ever wear those ghastly clodhoppers that Lady A. stomps around in." He shuddered again. "But look at it this way: they want Prince George's patronage, and if he's not willing to give it freely they will use other means of persuasion. So they dig up all the dirt they can find."

"And nobody else must know, or they could discredit him."

"Precisely. Top secret. Highly confidential."

"But surely everyone knows about Prince George's affairs. You said so yourself."

"There's a big difference between gossip and truth, dear, as you must surely know."

"Truth has to be proved. Oh, my God." Another piece of the jigsaw fell into place. "David Rhys had proof. That's why they killed him."

"You see why I play dumb?"

"Frankie, I could kiss you right here and now."

"Go ahead. No one's looking at us. They're all watching Tallulah."

He was right: every head had turned to witness the arrival of Miss Bankhead, strategically timed for maximum impact. She burst through the doors like a drowsy tornado, a fur-draped bundle of potential energy, her heavy-lidded eyes belying the fact that she could drink and screw every man in the place under the table. Hugo Taylor hovered behind her. Every breath was held. Tallulah Bankhead, in her pomp, made Daisy Athenasy look like a very second-rate piece of goods.

The star and her retinue swept up the stairs. Frankie waggled his fingers at her.

"Frankie," she said, in that much-imitated deadpan voice, "thank God you're here. I've been duchessed and marquissed to death."

"Tallulah, let me introduce you to a very good friend of mine, Mitch Mitchell. He's like you, Talloo."

"Bisexual?"

"American, I mean."

The exquisite hand shot out from the furs, the bangles fell back to the elbow, and I was permitted to squeeze the fingertips.

"Chaaaawmed, I'm sure," she said, in her native Alabama accent. "You an' me gonna raise a little hell, Yankee Boy?

"Sure, ma'am."

"This is the man who saved my life!" Hugo Taylor put an arm around my neck and squeezed. "Without Mitch, there might not have been a first night."

"God, darling, how many more people are going to try to murder you? First you were blackjacked on the train, now you've been poisoned in the dressing room. It's a bore. A girl doesn't like to feel that her leading man might just drop dead."

"Darling," said Hugo, "I'm sure they wouldn't even notice. It's you they come to see."

"How terribly sweet of you, Hugo, and how terribly true. Oh, God, look out, here's that wicked old witch Antonia Petherbridge. God, how she stares at me! I swear she's a dyke."

"You think everyone's a dyke, Tallulah."

"Honey, you'd better believe it. Give 'em a couple of drinks and—well, in vino veritas, as the dear Romans said. Which makes me the truthfullest gal in town. And speaking of vino, Frankie, I need a goddam cocktail. Sniff me out something gin-based, there's a dear."

A uniformed waiter happened at that moment to pass by, bearing a silver tray full of drinks. Frankie relieved him of it with a single deft movement, leaving the poor boy gaping with shock. (Hugo Taylor comforted him, I noticed, with a few quiet words, and the lad scurried off, his cheeks aflame, for fresh supplies.)

"Here," said Frankie, "dinky-donkies all round. I do hope they're cold." He tested a glass with his little finger. "Ooh! Lovely and chilly! One for Talloo, one for Hugo, one for Mitch, and—well I never!—two for Frankie. Here's how."

We toasted each other. The martini was cold and smooth and powerful, and bitter, so bitter...

# XIII

I WOKE UP IN TOTAL DARKNESS, A BLINDFOLD AROUND MY
eyes, cords cutting into my wrists and a burning sensation in
my ass. Someone was trying to fuck me.

My first impulse was to struggle, but I knew that would
be dangerous. Something big was working its way into
me—it was the pain that had woken me—and if I moved
I would be in big trouble. I could not see what it was,
but I assumed from the shape, texture, and warmth that
it was a human penis, albeit a very large one. My hands
were tied, so I could determine nothing through touch. I
could hear steady breathing, and I could smell a mixture
of sweat and tobacco smoke and...was it?...could it be?...
lemons.

I was lying on my back on a blanket or rug, over a hard
surface that felt like wood; it was not cold enough to be
stone. My arms were secured at the wrist and held in an
upright position, pointing toward the ceiling. My legs were
also raised, knees bent and pulled in toward my chest, the
calves resting on some kind of support. I tried to move them

and felt the restraints that bound me at the ankle. I was blindfolded and gagged, but I could breathe quite easily despite the discomfort of the position. Fortunately, I have spent quite a lot of time in this position—voluntarily, I might add—and therefore I am used to the strains that it places on the body. I am also used to taking things up my ass, be they cocks, fingers, or inanimate objects, so I knew how to relax my sphincter and reduce the pain.

There was a foul taste in my mouth—something sour, metallic. My tongue was dry and my gums were stinging. I remembered the cocktail at the Café Royal, how bitter it tasted... The cocktail that had been handed to me by Frankie Laking...

Whoever was fucking me knew what he was doing, and was not hell bent on causing me unnecessary pain, which came as a relief. Some lubricant had been used, and nothing was being forced in. As I concentrated on relaxing my ass, it slid in a couple more inches...a couple more...a couple more. This was a very large cock indeed, and despite the unpleasantness of my predicament I could not help but register the fact. My own cock had woken up, it seemed, and was swelling fast.

This had not gone unnoticed.

"Look," said a deep, gravelly voice, "he is getting stiff." There was an accent there, something non-European. Russian, perhaps.

"Oh, for heaven's sake." I knew that voice: Francis Laking, bart. "Some people have all the luck."

"I suppose you'd like to be in his position, Laking." Dickinson, of course; I knew he would be behind it all. But his was not the cock that was fucking me; his voice came from somewhere way over to my right. There were at least four of us in the room, then.

"It's not fair," said Frankie. "Nobody ever fucks me."

"I'm sure Joseph will oblige, for a consideration."

235

"Oh, I can't afford him. I'm sure he charges by the inch."

I felt hands on the backs of my thighs—large, rough hands, pushing my legs back. So it was Joseph who was inside me—Joseph, whose reputation for size was apparently well deserved. No wonder he'd been employed to keep Daisy Athenasy quiet. His hands moved down to my ass and pulled the buttocks further apart.

"I'm all the way in," he said, and he was—I could feel his wiry pubic hair rubbing against my skin. "Now I fuck him."

"Hold on a second, Joseph. Let's see if he's conscious."

Footsteps, hands on my head, the blindfold removed, the shock of bright light. I squinted against the glare, then tried to see where I was. Looking between my bound arms and legs I could dimly make out the huge, hairy bulk of Joseph. Turning my head, I could see a large, dingy room, heavy drapes, some old pieces of furniture, a single overhead bulb.

Hands gripped my head from behind and stopped me from looking around.

"Ah, Mr. Mitchell. Good of you to join us." It was Dickinson.

"What the hell are you doing?"

"I thought you might enjoy our little private party."

"Where am I?"

"You were so keen to get fucked earlier on. I'm going to let Joseph break you in. If you can take him, you can take anyone. Then we'll turn you over to the other guests. After we've given you something to...well, to ease your passage, shall we say."

I didn't like the sound of this; it sounded suspiciously as if Dickinson meant to kill me.

"You won't get away with this, Dickinson," I said, but my wavering voice belied any attempt at bravado. Richard Hannay, the daredevil hero of John Buchan's novels, would somehow have worked free of his bonds, leaped to his feet, and felled his captors with a single blow. I lacked his courage—although I doubt that he was ever pinned down by a huge Albanian dick up his ass.

"Why don't you use your mouth for what it was meant for, Mitch?" Dickinson replied. His fingers fumbled with his fly, and soon I saw his cock looming into view over the top of my head. "Come on—you couldn't wait to suck it when we were on the train. Now's your chance."

Before I had a chance to reply, he pulled my head back over the edge of whatever piece of furniture they had me strapped to, and I was staring straight up at his balls. He slapped me a few times around the face with his cock, which was fully erect, and then rubbed it around my lips.

"You can't do—mmmmf bbblllgggh mmmble—" His fingers pried my mouth open, and his prick filled it. There was very little I could do except try not to choke. I opened my mouth wide, breathed through my nose, and let them fuck me at either end. Dickinson's hands roughly caressed my ears, my face, my lips, while Joseph's huge paws kneaded and slapped my ass. My cock was hard, leaking sticky precum over my stomach. Dickinson took hold of it, squeezed it.

"I've never seen a man go so happily to his death."

That took the wind out of my sails.

"Oh, dear, Mitch. I'm so sorry. You seem to be losing interest." My dick had swiftly deflated, and he gave it a contemptuous flick. "And I thought you were such a stud. I'm sure Frankie would be more appreciative."

The pace of fucking picked up at both ends, and the sheer friction brought my cock back to life.

"That's better. Let's see if we can make him come, shall we? That would be amusing."

"Let me!"

"Go on then, Laking. Have a go."

I recognized Frankie's supple fingers and soft mouth on

my cock. He soon had me fully hard again. There was nothing I could do but surrender to the sensation—and if this was going to be my last fuck, it might as well be a good one. My balls were tightening—Frankie squeezed and caressed them as he sucked me—and I was close to coming. My ass tightened, Joseph picked up the pace of his fucking, and then, grunting, started spewing a load into me.

"Ow! You fucking beast!"

Dickinson had pulled Frankie off my cock by yanking his hair.

"I want to see him come."

He didn't have long to wait, and soon I was shooting jets of spunk over my sticky belly, my ass clamping around Joseph's still hard cock. Dickinson pulled out of my mouth, rested his nuts on my forehead and squirted his own load. The first jet hit my stomach, the second my chest, and the rest was dropped on my face.

"Frankie—you can clean him up."

Joseph pulled out, Dickinson stepped away, and I felt Frankie's tongue lapping at my body, licking up the rapidly cooling semen. He had his hand down his pants, wanking as he went. After a couple of minutes he sighed loudly and fell to the floor.

Dickinson adjusted his clothes; Joseph remained naked except for a pair of boots. He was a magnificent creature, huge and hirsute, his thighs as thick as tree trunks. His dick swung half way down to his knee; even limp and recently drained, it looked huge and powerful.

"Oh, my dear, what are you doing?" Frankie sounded worried. "What's that thing? Put it away, for God's sake!"

"Shut up, Laking." I heard a blow and a yelp, saw Frankie sprawling on the ground. "Get out if you don't want to watch."

There was a sinister clang of metal on metal behind me, the glint of something reflective.

"Now then, Dr. Mitchell, this isn't going to hurt much, as I'm sure you've told your patients a thousand times before. Just a little prick."

Dickinson bent over me again, but this time, instead of waving his cock in my face, he was wielding a large hypodermic syringe filled with a clear liquid. The light from the single naked bulb gleamed on the metal and glass, twinkled at the tip of the cruel steel spike.

"What is it?"

"Something to put you to sleep. A good, long sleep."

"I'm not tired."

"That's as may be, Mitch, but I am. Tired of your interference, your stupid questions, and your damnable ability to turn up in the wrong place at the wrong time. I need a rest—from you and your little friends." He held the syringe up, depressed the plunger. "Say good night, Mitch."

Out of the corner of my eye I saw Frankie struggling to his feet, rubbing his jaw where Dickinson had slugged him.

"Don't be a fool, Dickinson," I said. "People are looking for me."

"Precisely. Isn't that convenient? All my chickens coming home to roost. It's as easy as one, two, three. I couldn't have organized it better myself, Mitch. Thank you for doing my job for me."

"What do you mean?"

"First of all, your little foreign friend. What's his name?"

"Bertrand."

"That's him. A delicious hors d'oeuvre. He certainly got our juices flowing, didn't he, Joseph?"

Joseph chuckled, a horrible low rumbling sound.

"Is he dead?"

Dickinson looked at his watch, scratched his chin. "Hmmm... Probably not quite. He should still be warm. Don't want to put people off, do we."

"What do you mean?"

"And now we have you, thanks to Frankie's special martini recipe."

"You didn't tell me you were going to kill him," whined Laking.

"No, of course not. You thought we were just going to drug him and have a bit of fun, didn't you, Frankie Boy? Thought that would be up your street. Watching me and Joseph fucking your boyfriend here."

"Oh, my God."

"Well, you can't complain. You got a taste, didn't you? Ate it all up like a good boy." Dickinson shoved Frankie with his foot, causing him to stumble and fall again. I heard the sound of retching.

"You're not going to waste it all, are you, Frankie?" Dickinson laughed as Frankie threw up. "Any minute now, Mitch, we expect your friend Morgan to arrive."

"What do you know about Morgan?"

"Plenty. I haven't decided quite what to do with him yet. Shall we let him play for a while, Mitch? Shall we let him fuck a few arses? Or shall we knock him on the head straight away and do what we did to you? What do you think he'd prefer?"

"Morgan's no fool. He won't let you—"

"Oh, I expect he will. He'll do exactly what we tell him to do. Perhaps I'll even let him administer the coup de grace to you."

"He wouldn't."

"Wouldn't he? Not even to save the life of his wife and child?"

I had a horrible cold sensation in my throat and swallowed hard. I told myself I must'nt panic.

"Off you go now, Joseph. You know what you have to do." Joseph grinned as he left the room, closing the door softly behind him. "Joseph is our welcoming committee, you see. As soon as your friends arrive, he will be sure to take care of them. And now, Mitch, much as I enjoy your conversation, it's time to put you to sleep. It's such a shame that you're going to miss out on all the fun that people will have with you while you're unconscious. Just as little Bertrand hasn't got a clue what's happening to him."

"You devil."

"Thank you, my boy. I've been called worse."

"You're a disgrace to the police force."

"That's enough. Take your last look at the light, Mitch, before I switch it out for good."

His silhouette came between me and the bulb, and I saw the gleam on the needle...

And then there was a rumble and a cry and a crash, and suddenly the light was dazzling my eyes again. I jerked my head to the right to see Frankie and Dickinson rolling on the floor. Dickinson held the hypodermic aloft, pushing Frankie's face away with his other hand, but Frankie was crazed—biting, scratching, and kicking. And then the syringe started moving toward Frankie's neck...inches away... Dickinson's thumb found the plunger and guided it home...

A scuffle and a thud, and I saw a swift rolling movement, heard a yell from Dickinson that was quickly transformed into a cry of pain. Both men staggered to their feet. Frankie's nose was bleeding. Dickinson was clutching his throat, grasping the syringe. A small trickle of blood ran down from the needle onto his collar. His eyes bulged, his mouth worked noiselessly as he stumbled around the room like a wounded bull. Then he sank to his knees and collapsed sideways on the floor.

"I never did like that man," said Frankie, dabbing at his bloody nose. "Oh, look what a mess he's made of me. I don't mind rough treatment, but really, this is too much."

"Is he dead?" I asked.

"God knows, dear. Whatever that stuff was, it seems to

have put him to bye-byes. I say, I'm most awfully sorry for poisoning your martini. It seemed like such a fun idea at the time—you know, knock-out drops and all that. A Mickey Finn, I believe you Americans call it. And, well, that great big Albanian ape, and our friend here." He poked Dickinson's inert form with an elegantly shod foot. "It was too much for a girl to resist. And having you at my mercy... Oh, dear."

"Are you going to stand there talking all day, Frankie, or are you going to let me go?"

He paced around me. "Well, I must say I'm tempted to leave you as you are. I mean, it's not every day I have a muscular, hairy young man bound hand and foot..." He ran a hand over my stomach and rummaged in my pubic bush. "But I suppose under the circumstances I had better do the decent thing."

His nimble fingers undid the buckles that held my legs, and I was able to get myself into an upright kneeling position while he worked on the ropes around my wrists. I had been tied down to some kind of medical inspection chair, the sort of thing we use in hospitals for examining women, with stirrups for the legs.

My hands were soon free, and I rubbed my sore arms and legs. Frankie stood with his arms folded, looking at me.

"Oh, it does seem a shame to let you go."

"Come on, give me a hand." Between us, we lugged Dickinson's inert form onto the inspection chair, and bound his wrists and ankles. He was still alive—whatever poison he was administering did not cause immediate death. If he woke up, I wanted to know where he was. He looked good tied up, and I was tempted to take a few vengeful liberties—but there was no time to lose.

"I don't suppose you know where my clothes are, Frankie?"

"Now, that really is too much. You can't really expect

me to let you dress." He sighed again. "It's just not my day. Here." He threw me a small towel, which I could just about wrap around my waist. "Cover yourself with that."

"But I have to go and find Bertrand... Warn Morgan... I can't go out there in a towel."

"Just wait and see, my dear," said Frankie, opening the door. "It's terribly informal."

The corridor was warm and dimly lit, and I could hear a faint murmur of voices from other rooms. We appeared to be at the top of a very old house—above us was nothing but the ceiling and access to the roof, while stairs descended for several flights below. Judging by the general air of dilapidation, and the familiar smell of dust, we were in the Rookery Club. My heart sank. It was here that I had told Morgan to come and find me—and Simmonds, and Shipton, and Connor and Scott. Dickinson may be out of action for the time being, but his agents, including the brutal Joseph, were still at large, ready to pick people off as they entered the building. They were walking straight into a trap.

I crept down a couple of flights, with Frankie behind me. "Stay here," Frankie mouthed, allowing his hands to roam around my chest before he slipped into one of the rooms.

He wasn't gone for long. His face and hand appeared in the doorway, beckoning me in.

"As you can see, Mitch, you're not exactly under-dressed."

The sight that met my eyes was like something out of a Hieronymus Bosch painting. Naked, masked figures, all male, some wearing elaborate footwear, others with artificial phalluses strapped around their hips, wandered through the semidarkness like predatory animals closing in on a kill. Beyond them was a row of wooden cots—at least, that's what they most resembled—in which I could dimly discern human forms in strange contortions. People were positioned at some of these cots, like men standing at a urinal.

"You'd better take this," whispered Frankie, handing me a slip of black silk. "Here. Let me." It was a mask, with slits for the eyes, that slipped over my head, covering the upper part of my face, leaving my mouth free. Frankie secured it at the back. "There. Just like any other partygoer."

"Who are they? All these people?"

"Oh, you'd be surprised... The *haut monde*. Cabinet ministers. Bishops, probably. One doesn't ask too many questions."

"And in the stalls?"

Frankie shuddered. "Darling, I don't know."

"What, you mean—"

"I'd better go. I can see I'm not wanted in here." It's true—he was attracting a certain amount of hostile attention from our fellow revelers. "I shall go downstairs and make polite chitchat. This really isn't my *tasse de thé*."

The moment he left, I was surrounded by masked, prowling figures, who divested me of my towel and led me over to the row of cots. At closer quarters I could see that the cots presented a row of alternate mouths and assholes, all of them, judging by the hair distribution, male. Some were being fucked, mechanically and joylessly, others fingered.

Hands caressed my body, stroking my buttocks, brushing against my cock. Erect pricks were all around me, occasionally touching me.

The other guests—strange word for such sinister creatures—crowded around me, pushing me toward the row of holes, holding me by the shoulders and arms. They lined me up in the middle of the row, in front of what looked like a tasty, hairy little ass. Hands parted the cheeks, slapped them, played with the hole, plied it with Vaseline.

Other hands worked on me, bringing me to readiness, guiding the head of my cock to the target.

I was pushed from behind, and my dick, now hard again, slipped in.

It was a good, tight fit.

Muted applause broke around me, and the revelers went about their own business, seemingly content with my performance.

All I could see of my partner—or should I say victim?—was his ass, and a few inches of hairy thigh. The rest of his body was encased in a wooden construction. I was reminded of the traps out of which greyhounds are released at dog tracks.

I rested for a while, with my dick buried in this mysterious hole. I had managed to get erect, and the warm grip was keeping me that way—but I was by no means in the mood for fucking. The muscles gripping my cock seemed to be clenching and unclenching, as if ready for me. At least he was conscious, and seemingly willing... The clenching was powerful, rhythmic, alternating between long, tight squeezes and short, powerful grips. Short, short, short... Long, long, long... Short, short, short... And then a pause... And then the pattern repeated itself.

I had never come across such extraordinary control before. Almost as if the ass was speaking to me.

Short, short, short... Long, long, long... Short, short, short... And then a pause...

And then again.

At first I couldn't believe it. I waited, not moving my cock, which was rock hard thanks to this pulsing grip.

But yes, here it was again. The same pattern, the same rhythm.

I was being signaled by an asshole in Morse code. And it was signaling SOS.

What should I do? I was seriously outnumbered—and I didn't think that the other guests would join me in a rescue mission. I could, perhaps, tackle a couple of them, but there were at least eight others in the room. I'd be over-powered, and find myself boxed into one of these hellish contraptions—which was undoubtedly Dickinson's plan for me. I would be fucked all night, and then killed. It was not a prospect I relished.

I reached down and caressed the ass I was fucking in what I hoped was a reassuring way. I felt certain, from the texture of the skin, the distribution of the hair, the tightness of the hole, that this was Bertrand. I leaned forward, pressed my mouth against the wooden casing, and murmured "It's okay, little buddy. Mitch is here, and I'm going to get you out of there alive, I promise." I doubt if he could hear me—and the action exposed me to curious glances from either side. I needed help. Bertrand would have to wait. The stalls were all held closed with a long brass bar that passed through metal rings before being padlocked in place at either end. I needed keys—or a gun. Nothing else would do. And I needed manpower.

I mimed an orgasm (and to be honest, that was the best I was going to achieve for a few hours, after my recent draining) and withdrew from Bertrand's ass. Another took my place. Stepping away, leaving Bertrand to further torture, was one of the hardest things I have ever had to do. But I could not betray my feelings, and I was glad that I was wearing a mask.

I slipped out of the room and looked across the landing. Laughter and conversation came from behind the door. I looked in—and there was a full-scale orgy in progress. No cages here, no cruel padlocks—just couches and rugs on which sprawled, perhaps, two dozen men in every imaginable combination. Normally I would have dived straight in, like a little boy finding a swimming hole on a hot summer's day—but for once I was looking not for a dick to suck or an ass to fuck, but for some way of extricating myself and my loved ones from a potentially lethal situation.

A couple of men near me were fucking hard on a chaise

longue, a rickety old piece of furniture covered in faded red velvet and ripped gold brocade, which creaked and swayed with each thrust. I didn't recognize the boy on the bottom—he was a slim, athletic-looking youth with short blond hair. The man on top was naked except for a mask. He was powerfully built, tall and hairy, with a long, deep scar running the length of his left thigh. I recognized that scar; I had caressed it myself only the day before. My soldier from the train—the one with whom I had fucked Bertrand in the conductor's car. The sergeant.

If he was here, he was almost certainly in the pay of Dickinson. I assumed that we had been lured to the conductor's car for a reason—to keep us out of the way. But he had struck me as a decent man, and he was after all a member of His Majesty's armed forces, down in London on royal guard duty. Surely he would help me...

It was a ridiculous gamble—almost suicidal, I now think—but I went up behind the sergeant, clutched his meaty ass, and whispered in his ear, "What do you think the King would say if he could see you now?"

He stopped in midfuck, and looked toward me. His eyes glinted through the slits in his mask and he looked me up and down, uncertain at first, but then, when he reached my dick, recognizing me.

"The American."

Well, apparently my cock had made a lasting impression.

"Sergeant."

"You want to join me?" He moved aside, so that I could see his prick sliding out of the young man's ass.

"Not right now. I need something else."

"You can't fuck me, if that's what you had in mind. I don't do that."

The sergeant, like many of his type I had met in Edinburgh, was remarkably single-minded.

"I don't want to fuck you." This was a lie, but now was no time for honesty. "I need your help."

"Oh, aye. To do what, precisely?"

"Someone tried to kill me."

"Fuck off, man. You're drunk."

"I've never been more sober in my life. Dickinson—"

"What about Dickinson?" The sergeant's cock slipped out of the young man's ass; the empty hole gaped, and the boy looked up to see what was going on. Seeing not one but two men standing over him, he smiled, and starting playing with himself, caressing his balls and fingering his ass.

"He's a killer."

"Bollocks."

"He murdered that man on the train—"

"He did not."

"He tried to kill Hugo Taylor, and me, and he's threatened to kill my friends."

"Prove it."

"Come with me."

He looked from me to the boy, from the boy to me, as if struggling between pleasure and duty. I could take no chances, so I grabbed him by the cock—it was still rock hard—and led him from the room, jerking him gently as we crossed the corridor.

"Well, you've got my attention now, mate. What's this all about?"

"Come with me."

I led him into the other room, where the stalls were still in use.

"Look in the central one."

"Why?"

"Tell me if you recognize what's there."

The sergeant, thank God, lacked manners, and barged up to the stalls, pushing people out of the way and hauling one man straight out of Bertrand's ass. They were about to remonstrate, but when they saw the size of the sergeant, they thought better of it.

"What about it? It's an arsehole."

"Look closer. Doesn't it look familiar?"

"Come on, man. You don't expect me to recognize a bum."

People were forming small, concerned groups around the edge of the room.

"You should. You've fucked it."

The sergeant knelt before the stall, the asshole at eye level. He felt it. He touched it. Finally, he tasted it, delving around with his tongue.

"It's that French lad."

Was it my imagination, or did Bertrand's asshole twitch in nationalistic indignation?

"Exactly."

"And what the fuck is he doing here?"

"He was abducted and drugged. As was I."

A couple of masked revelers were moving toward the door. The sergeant sprang to his feet.

"Stay right the fuck where you are," he snarled. There was a gasp. He strode toward the door and kicked it shut.

"Time to shed a little light on matters." He flicked a switch, and the room was fully illuminated. The partygoers cowered, trying to hide.

Dickinson addressed the room. "I thought this was a straightforward fuck party. But my friend here tells me it's something quite different. Now, does anyone have anything to say?" A couple of men advanced toward him, as if they thought they might get past him. The sergeant picked up a chair and smashed it over their heads. They fell to the ground, their cocks lolling over their thighs.

"Anyone else?" The odds were now considerably reduced. "I thought not. Now, let's see what we're dealing with. Unmask."

Nobody seemed in a great hurry to reveal their true identities, apart from the sergeant and me. We both whipped off the horrible silk strips and threw them on the floor. His face was angry, brutal—but, I thought, honest.

"My name is Sergeant Robert Langland of the Scots Guards," he announced, glaring at the cringing figures, their dicks shriveling quickly. "Our motto is 'nemo me impune lacessit,' which, roughly translated, means fuck with me at your own peril. Now, show your faces."

He picked up a broken chair leg and brandished it like a saber. Nobody doubted that he would use it.

One by one the masks dropped to the floor, and a sorrier bunch of sex fiends I have never seen. Hair was wet with sweat, plastered down or sticking up; I was instantly reminded of Laurel and Hardy. The men were of various ages and states of preservation; some were young and firm, others were running to fat. The confidence with which they'd assaulted those caged mouths and asses had evaporated.

"Well, well, well," said Langland. "What have we here? Your Eminence."

One of the larger, older gentlemen buried his face in his hands.

"And the shadow home secretary, I believe."

"Oh, God," sighed a middle-aged man with a very pendulous pair of balls, "how did you know?"

"You never look at the faces of the men who serve you—but we see yours. That's one of the advantages of a uniform. Now, gentlemen, you have a choice. You can continue resistance, and be sure that, if you survive, your careers will be over in the morning. Or you can help us. What is it to be?" He slapped the chair leg into his hand as he strode around the room. His cock was no longer fully erect, but was still standing out from his thighs, swaying as he walked. Eyes were generally fixed on the chair leg, but occasionally flicked downward.

Langland stopped. "So, Bishop, what's it to be? We look to you for a lead."

"I... I... Well, really... Oh, dear..."

"Good man." Langland clapped him on the shoulder. "Now, how about joining me in some good works, and freeing these poor souls from bondage."

"But how?"

"Where there's a will, there's a way. Hey! Mitchell!"

He had remembered my name; I was flattered. "Yes?"

"There's a fire extinguisher in the hall. Go get it."

"Yes, sir!"

It was a large, metal contraption, so heavy I could barely drag it along the floor. Langland lifted it in both hands, the muscles standing out in his arms, and raised it above his head.

"Stand clear, lads," he said. "We're going in."

The fire extinguisher came down with a smash on the end of the stalls, snapping the padlock and twisting the metal bar almost to 90 degrees. Langland moved to the other end and delivered a second blow. The rest of us moved in to pull the wretched structure to pieces and release its sorry captives.

I will not dwell on the condition in which we found them. Those who were conscious were in great pain, their arms and legs contorted into awkward positions, their mouths and asses bruised and sore. Others were unconscious but still breathing—to them I gave my most urgent attention. One was beyond help. The Bishop knelt over his body, deep in prayer.

# XIV

BERTRAND, THANK GOD, WAS AMONG THE CONSCIOUS, although he was in great pain and terrible distress. I comforted him as best I could, holding him as he clung, panting, sweating, and wild-eyed, to my naked body. I kissed him and rocked him like a baby, wondering if he would ever recover from this nightmare.

Langland was stomping around the room with a look of fury on his face, his mouth contorted in a snarl, his eyes wet with tears. "Wait till I get my hands on that fucking bastard," he said. "He told me nothing of this—nothing."

"Come on. We've got work to do."

We put our masks back on—a necessary precaution—and left the shamed churchmen, MPs, and whatever else they were to look after Bertrand and the others.

Out on the landing, Langland moved silently, like a huge cat. He signaled to the stairs, and we descended swiftly, both barefooted. I couldn't help admiring his huge, solid buttocks as he went before me; I remembered how they'd rippled as he pumped into Bertrand's ass on the train.

Looking down the stairwell, I could see the entrance hall where Marchmont had greeted me; we must now be on the floor above the reception room where we had sat sipping gin only a few hours ago. He had said that the place would be transformed; how right he was!

On this floor there were more rooms—bedrooms, I supposed, for members and their guests—four doors leading off the landing. Anything could be going on behind those doors, and I shuddered at the thought of more nightmarish contraptions like the one we had just demolished upstairs—but Langland beckoned me on.

The party was in full swing in the reception room. Thirty or 40 guests, some fully dressed, others in costume, circulated and talked. They were being served drinks by three naked waiters bearing trays. I recognized them, of course: McDonald, Ken, and the little redhead, Sergeant Langland's brothers in arms. So this was how the guards supplemented their notoriously low wages. Hands swooped in from above to take drinks, and from below to caress cocks.

These details aside, it could have been any cocktail party, anywhere in London. There were even a few ladies present—some of whom, I suspected, may not have been quite as female as they appeared. But there, to my astonishment, was Kiki Preston, Prince George's companion—and, yes, there in the corner, talking to Hugo Taylor, was the royal person himself.

How much did they know about what was going on upstairs?

Marchmont drifted around like a busy bee, gorgeously arrayed in a Chinese silk kimono, glitter on his cheeks and his eyes outlined in kohl. He was certainly the oldest of the Bright Young Things.

Langland grabbed a tray of drinks from the sideboard and motioned to me to do likewise; if we could pose as staff, we might not arouse suspicion. As I circulated, I was groped, grabbed, and poked from all angles. Even Prince George weighed my prick in his hand while taking a glass of champagne, as if he was testing a piece of fruit before buying. Well, that would be something to tell the grandchildren I would never have. Beats dancing with a man who's danced with a girl who's danced with the Prince of Wales: his brother squeezed my dick.

While I was being royally manhandled, Langland was circulating through the room and, between handing out drinks, whispering in his subordinates' ears.

Suddenly, without any signal being given, the lights went out. Several people screamed. I heard a scuffle and a thud, and the lights came back on. Langland and his three soldiers were standing with their backs to the door. Marchmont lay unconscious on the ground—and Langland was holding a key.

"Ladies and gentlemen," he announced, in his gruff Scottish accent, "please do not panic. There is plenty of drink to go round. Enjoy yourselves."

He pushed me out the door. When we were all on the landing, he turned the key in the lock.

"That'll keep them out of mischief," he chuckled. "Now, lads, this way."

They disappeared down the stairs without making a noise, and were quickly lost to sight.

It was time for me to find some clothes. There were enough of them strewn around the landing, hanging from the banisters and even from the dusty chandelier, for me to put together some kind of ensemble. It might not have passed muster in Mayfair, but here at the Rookery it would do. Bizarre I may have looked—a pair of black dress pants, far too large for me, held up with an Old Harrovian tie, a dinner jacket with no shirt, just a stiff shirt front held in place with a celluloid collar, bare feet—but I was no stranger than some of the other partygoers.

Where had Langland gone, and what had he told his men

to do? I had not told him of Joseph, and the danger I feared for Morgan and the rest of my friends. Perhaps Langland had double-crossed me. I felt horribly powerless. Now that the excitement of my escape had worn off, I was groggy and nauseated. I would have been no use at all in a fight.

Holding on to the banister, I made my way slowly down to the ground floor, ignoring the thumps and cries from the reception room. The only way out of there was by the window—and I didn't think many of that crowd would be willing to risk their necks, or spill a drop of blue blood, in the attempt.

And there, standing in the hallway looking somewhat perplexed, was the one person I wanted to see above all others: Morgan. His brow was furrowed, as I had so often seen it when he was wrestling with some (to him) complex problem. Woozy as I felt, it made me smile. I ran down the rest of the stairs with a lighter heart.

"Morgan, thank God."

"Mitch!" He looked up at me, this time with real concern on his face. "Oh no—"

"What is it?"

His eyes widened, and his mouth worked, but no words came out.

"Shit, Boy, have they got Belinda?" I came closer, put a hand on his shoulder. "What's the matter? You must tell me? What is it?"

And then, stepping from behind the curtains like the bogeyman in a child's nightmare, came Joseph. He was holding a gun, and the gun was trained on Morgan's temple.

"Ah, Mr. Mitchell." Joseph's dark face was illuminated by a truly diabolical light, and I half expected to see cloven feet, rather than the heavy boots that composed his entire wardrobe. "You will follow me."

"I'm sorry, Mitch," said Morgan. "He overpowered me."

"Are you hurt?"

"No, I'm—"

"No talking!" snapped Joseph, pushing Morgan toward the final set of stairs that led to the basement. "You come with us, or it will be bad for your friend."

I complied. Joseph ushered us both downstairs, the gun at our backs.

The basement was damp and filthy. Crates of wine and spirits were stacked against walls black with age-old dirt and mold. Candles burned on crude sconces in the wall, casting mad shadows as they flickered in drafts from unseen sources. It was the sort of setting I often dreamed about for the climax to some longed-for mystery, complete with brooding villain. But now, in reality, it was less appealing—even given the fact that my villain was handsome, hairy, and naked. I just wanted to run—out of the cellar, out of the house, out of London, away from all this danger and cruelty and death…

Joseph waved us into a corner with his gun. We stood together, Morgan and I, both shaking with fear. His hand found mine, and we clasped each other for comfort. If we were going to die, at least we would die together.

Time seemed to stop. The basement was silent except for the occasional drip of water, the fizz of the candle wicks, and our breathing. There was the faintest rumble of traffic from the street above. Any second now I expected the calm to be shattered by the crack of a gunshot. Which of us would die first?

Joseph stood there, the gun in his left hand, his cock in the other, idly playing with himself. The power pleased him; he was at least half hard.

"Two little boys," he said. "Two nasty interfering little queers."

"I say," said Morgan, "that's not on."

"Shut up!" Joseph stepped toward us, waving the gun in Morgan's face. His cock was getting harder; this was clearly much more to his taste than screwing Daisy Athenasy, or acting as Dickinson's paid thug. Joseph craved power in his own right, and that might buy us time. For what? I didn't know, but every second of life seemed precious.

"Please, sir," I said, thinking to play to his vanity, "don't kill us. We'll do anything."

"I know what you queers like," he said, stepping back and waving his hips around, so that his huge cock swung from side to side, making a huge black shadow on the floor. "It's this, isn't it?"

I felt this was stating the obvious, but this was no time for smart remarks.

"Oooh, yes, sir," I said, licking my lips. "Let me taste it."

Morgan was stealing sidelong glances at me, obviously thinking that terror had made me flip my lid. I reassured him with a squeeze of the hand.

"You want my big cock, boy?"

I'd heard these lines before, usually from men trying desperately hard to convince themselves that they are really normal, and that their "use" of queers doesn't make them queer themselves. It disgusts me, in the normal course of events—but now it seemed to offer some hope.

"Please," I said.

"You want to suck it? You want to put your lips around it?"

"Oh, yes."

This was having the desired effect, as Joseph was now paying more attention to his cock and less to his gun. Perhaps the blood that was flooding into his dick, bringing it to full erection, was starving his brain of oxygen. Whatever the reasons, he had been effectively sidetracked. I got to my knees and opened my mouth. Morgan, thank God, had understood the plan, and joined me on the filthy floor.

We started kissing Joseph's huge club of a dick, licking his balls, taking him into our mouths in turn, generally behaving like a couple of dogs who are pleased to see their master. Joseph stood there, his feet planted a yard apart, and accepted our adoration as his due. Every so often he would run the gun over our heads, or around our mouths; I prayed to God that the safety catch was on, or this was going to be one hell of a messy blow job.

Every so often, my tongue made contact with Morgan's, and we stole a few kisses. They might be our last...

A splintering crash, a vertical pillar of light, a flurry of movement, and the thud of feet on the dirt floor. Joseph spun around on the balls of his feet, waving the gun wildly at a figure crouching on the ground—it sprang up, and a leg shot out and knocked the gun from Joseph's hand, sending it spinning across the floor to land in a filthy puddle. Joseph yelped with pain and surprise. There was no time to lose. Morgan and I rushed him from behind, leaped at his back, and fell headlong in the muck, with Joseph struggling beneath us.

Who was our deliverer?

Sergeant Langland, of course. Through what appeared to be a hole in the cellar roof but was actually a hatchway, a rope was lowered, and three more men dropped nimbly to the ground. All of them, including Langland, were still naked.

"Leave him to me, Mitch."

We climbed off Joseph's back, and he struggled to his feet, only to be met with another swift kick, this time to his chest. He collapsed, winded, and sat on his ass fighting for breath. The soldiers quickly had him bound. His naked body was covered in mud and grime. Langland picked up the gun and emptied the chambers, scattering the bullets into the dark corners of the cellar. Lacking a sporran, or any handy pouch in which to store the gun, he handed it to me.

"What next, boss?"

My usual answer to this question, when asked by a naked soldier with three naked subordinates leading a bound naked man, would be nonverbal. But the occasion called for action of a different nature.

"Upstairs, I think. It's time to turn the tables on Superintendent Dickinson and the whole gang."

"Have you cracked it, old chap?" asked Morgan, his face still wet from where he had been slobbering (rather enthusiastically, I thought) over Joseph's cock. "Are you going to call the villains to account, and all that?"

I wished I had the confidence in my outlandish theories to say "Yes" with more conviction. In reality, I was improvising wildly, hoping that my tissue of guesswork and suspicion would mesh into a net to catch a killer. Yes, my metaphors were as muddled as my reasoning.

"Follow me," I said, beckoning with the gun. "Langland, Morgan, upstairs. The rest of you, round up anyone else who's still at large and lock 'em in with the others. We'll call them as we need them."

McDonald, Ken, and the redhead disappeared as soon as we reached ground level on swift, silent feet. I led the way to the top of the house, followed by Langland, leading Joseph by his bound wrists, with Morgan bringing up the rear. The time had come to confront Dickinson—if he was still alive.

He was just as we'd left him, his powerful legs strapped to the couch, his arms bound and held upward. I checked for vital signs: he was alive, drowsily conscious, and very cold. I took his pulse. It was sluggish, but steady. Whatever was in that syringe was not lethal, thank God. I did not want a death on my conscience.

"Well, well," he said, in a feeble, cracked voice, "how things change."

"You've got some questions to answer, Dickinson," I said.

He laughed. "Do you have any idea of the trouble you're in? Assaulting a police officer is a serious business—"

"Shut up and listen, Dickinson. We know all about you."

Morgan's eyebrows shot up, and he was about to speak, but I silenced him with a look.

"Oh, dear. I'm frightened," said Dickinson, sounding anything but. "And who is this I see? Sergeant Langland, unless I'm much mistaken. Has he changed sides, Mitch? That must have been expensive."

Langland would have struck Dickinson across the face, but I stepped between them.

"My hero," said Dickinson, the sarcasm in his voice rather undermined by a violent coughing fit. His breath rattled; he had some congestion of the lungs. I'd felt that way myself when I woke. I suspected that he'd used some form of chloroform in that syringe—a dangerous form of anesthetic even in trained hands. Frankie, who had plunged the needle into Dickinson's neck, was not only untrained, but furious. Nobody wants a furious anesthetist.

"So now you've got me where you wanted me all along, Mitchell," said Dickinson when he'd recovered sufficiently. "What are you going to do first? Suck my cock? Eat my arse? Fuck me?" He thrust his groin in the air, and indeed it was an appetizing prospect. But I had a different sort of probing in mind.

"I wouldn't fuck you if you were the last man on earth, Dickinson," I lied. "I just want some answers."

"Fuck off."

"Why did you kill David Rhys?"

Dickinson laughed. "Me? For Christ's sake, you're not going to try and pin that on me. What's the matter? Trying to protect Andrews? That slag's been riding for a fall for a long time. He had it coming."

"Shut the fuck up!" barked Langland, smacking Dickinson around the head. "Answer!"

"I see, it's the old good cop, bad cop act, is it? I'm familiar with the routine," said Dickinson.

"I'm sure you are," I said. "But there's a big difference

here. We don't have to play by the rules. As it is, I'm finding it very hard to prevent Sergeant Langland here from killing you. Don't piss him off any further."

"Langland's a mercenary, a fucking gun for hire—"

Crack! Langland smacked Dickinson hard around the head with the flat of his hand. He coughed again, and lapsed into silence.

"Now, I'll ask you again. Why did you kill David Rhys?"

"I did not kill David Rhys."

"Why did you try to kill Hugo Taylor?"

"I did not try to kill Hugo Taylor."

This was getting us nowhere. I tried a different tack.

"When did you start working for the British Fascists?"

"I don't know what you're talking about."

Langland drew back his arm to hit him again.

"That's enough, sergeant. Let's not sink to his level. Tell me, Dickinson, how did you find out about British-American?"

"Herbert Waits is a fool."

"Ah, at last we're getting somewhere. And I agree with you. He's a fool, and he's made himself vulnerable. Is that where you saw your chance?"

"I don't know what you mean."

"You wanted to get to Hugo Taylor, on the orders of the British Fascist Party. They would pay you a great deal of money to rid Prince George of his undesirable connections."

"This is a fairy story."

"And so you found a way into British-American by blackmailing Waits."

"No comment."

"And then you saw a chance to get Daisy Athenasy out of the way, off the payroll, so that Waits would be even more in your power."

"You read too many books, Mr. Mitchell."

He had a point; I was making this up as I went along, basing my claims on the kinds of things that happened in detective fiction. Well, if Miss Marple could draw her conclusions from her observations of village life, why shouldn't I base my method on an equally implausible source?

I paced the floor, stroking my chin.

"So you had two sources of income, and you played one off against the other. Very convenient, very clever. With Hugo Taylor at the center, a member of the royal family on one side, a drug-addicted movie star on the other... Nobody wanted any of that to come to light, did they? And you made a very healthy profit. Tell me, Dickinson, what do they pay a detective superintendent in the Metropolitan Police? Isn't it enough for you? Do you have such expensive tastes? What do you need the money for? Are you being blackmailed?"

That struck a nerve. "Shut the fuck up, Mitchell."

"I'll take that as a yes. I wonder what for? I imagine you're capable of almost any crime. I'm sure it will all come to light in due course."

"Any minute now," said Dickinson, "my men will be swarming through this house. And then you and your friends are in big trouble."

It was my turn to be sarcastic. "Are the police in the habit of going to orgies?"

He shut his eyes and seemed suddenly tired. Perhaps the chloroform had not quite worn off.

There was a knock at the door, and McDonald stepped inside—still naked, I was pleased to see. He saluted.

"What is it, McDonald?"

"There's a man outside, Sarge, says he needs to talk to Mr. Mitchell here."

"What's his name."

"Thomas Simmonds."

Simmonds! At last! Just as I was running out of theories, here, I hoped, were reinforcements.

"Send him in," said Langland.

Simmonds stepped into the room. "Mitch, thank God." He saw Bertrand lying in the corner, wrapped in blankets, and stepped toward him.

"He's okay. Let him rest. I'll tell you everything later. Now—what news?"

"They've opened the tunnel."

At these words, Dickinson's eyes snapped open.

"And what did they find?"

"I don't know yet. Arthur is on his way to London now. I told him to come here."

"And what do you expect to find in there, Mitch?" asked Dickinson. "All the evidence you want, neatly laid out and labeled? We backed into the side tunnel to avoid accidents. That's all."

"Is this the bastard who kidnapped Bertrand?" said Simmonds, stepping toward the couch to which Dickinson was strapped. "Just wait till I—"

"That's enough, Thomas. We'll have no more violence."

"Oh, go on," said Dickinson, "let him have his fun. How about it, Simmonds? You like picking on people who can't fight back, don't you?"

"Fuck off."

"Not so brave now you don't have your uniform on. Come on, why don't you knock me around a bit, big man? Like your little Belgian friend. You liked that, didn't you?"

He was goading Simmonds into a fury, hoping to provoke some kind of attack.

"That's enough, Tom. Go to Bertrand. He needs you."

Simmonds stood there with his great fists bunched up, his arms held out from his sides, ready to take on an army. He stepped toward Dickinson, and spat copiously between his open legs.

"When Arthur gets here, he'll tell us exactly what you hid in the tunnel," I said. "Now I'm going to ask you again. Why did you kill David Rhys?"

"Give it up, Mitchell. You have no case against me."

"Sergeant Langland—would you ask one of your men to fetch Hugo Taylor? You'll find him downstairs."

Taylor looked superb in his evening dress, as sleek as a thoroughbred stallion, his thick dark hair swept off his forehead, his collar and cuffs as dazzlingly white as his perfect, regular teeth.

"Well! Mr. Dickinson!" Taylor said sarcastically. "I rather wondered what had happened to you. British-American really is going to the dogs. Can't keep the staff from one day to the next."

I said, "Perhaps you can tell us, Hugo, what happened in your carriage yesterday afternoon, when we were stuck in the tunnel."

"After I was biffed over the head, you mean?"

"Just start at the beginning."

"I suppose you want the truth this time."

"That would be helpful."

"Careful, Taylor," said Dickinson.

"You don't expect me to take advice from a man in your position, do you?" Taylor replied. "Now, let me see..." He held his hands behind his back and paced the room, turning every so often to emphasize a point, exactly as if he were delivering a speech on stage. "The porter brought our lunch—steak and mushrooms and potatoes, if I remember correctly. It was remarkably good, although Daisy didn't eat a bite, poor thing. Only one thing she was interested in eating. Speaking of which, hello, Joe! You've been through the wars, old chap!"

Joseph scowled and growled but could do nothing, bound as he was.

"Now, something struck me as queer at the time; there

264

was no steak knife. Usually, they're very good at these things—it always amazes me how they manage to cook so well on a moving train. I mean, I can barely make a sandwich."

"The knife, Hugo?"

"Ah, yes. The knife. I had to use my butter knife to cut the steak with. It didn't matter, as it was very tender, but I must have mentioned something because Joseph said he'd go and give the steward a bollocking. He hadn't been gone five minutes when, bang, the train stopped and the lights went out, and I thought poor Daisy was going to choke herself. Dickinson disappeared, and I went out looking for a lantern. That's when some bugger bashed me over the head."

"Where were you?"

"I was moving down the train, toward third class, hoping there might be lights down there. I couldn't see a bloody thing. I was groping along and I bumped into someone and I said, 'Oh, I'm frightfully sorry,' or words to that effect. We do-si-doed our way past each other and then I got the most frightful crack on the bonce."

"Any idea who it was?"

"None, I'm afraid. Couldn't see a thing."

"Or what they hit you with?"

"It made a bloody awful thud when it hit me, I can tell you. Nearly knocked me out. I put my hand up and felt blood. Somehow I managed to stagger back to our compartment, where someone had had the presence of mind to light a candle. Daisy was there, looking like a frightened rabbit, feverishly chopping out lines of cocaine by candlelight. I sat down and felt pretty bloody grim, if you must know. I took a swig of wine and I passed out for a while, I think. When I came to, I saw Dickinson moving around in the carriage, looking for something, I thought. I had the impression that there was someone with him—Joseph, I supposed—but I couldn't really see. I asked him what the fuck was going on, and he said there had been an accident of some sort. I thought maybe that had something to do with what happened to me. I was confused."

I turned to Dickinson. "But it wasn't Joseph, was it, Dickinson?"

"Of course it was," Dickinson sneered. "Nobody else was allowed in the compartment."

"I think it was David Rhys," I said. "Was that where you killed him? While Hugo was semi-conscious, and Daisy was doped out of her mind? Murder by candlelight."

"Ridiculous," said Dickinson.

Taylor continued, "Now that you come to mention it, there was a struggle, and someone fell to the floor. I didn't really know what was going on. When I came round, you were there, Mr. Mitchell, and the porter. I made up some yarn about how I'd hit my head on the bar."

"Why did you lie?"

"Because I was frightened, if you must know. I had reason to believe that someone was out to get me."

"Had you received threats?"

"I receive threats all the time."

"From whom?"

"Well, they don't sign them, dear boy. But I know who they're from. Rotha Lintorn and her gang of thugs."

"And you knew that they were on the train?"

"I'd seen Lady Antonia, yes. Not that I suspected her."

"Then who?"

"Well, I hate to say this, old chap, but I did rather wonder about...you."

I was rather stung by this, as I'd taken great care over dressing Taylor's wound.

"Please don't be offended. I quickly saw I was wrong. But you get into a habit of telling lies when you're in my position."

"And you're lying now," said Dickinson. "You'd do anything to protect your meal ticket. You're a fucking parasite."

"I don't deny it." Taylor replied. "But you must admit, I do it with a certain amount of style."

"You make me sick."

"Oh, Mr. Dickinson, in your position—and what an interesting position it is, really—I would be very careful about what I said. You wouldn't want anyone to lose their temper, would you?"

Behind his urbane façade, Taylor was reaching the boiling point.

"Thank you, Hugo. You can return to the party if you want."

"What, and miss the fun? Not on your nelly."

"So, Dickinson—you murdered Rhys in the private compartment, and then dragged the body to the toilet, where it would be discovered. You cut his finger off and removed the ring to make it look like robbery. And then you planted the ring in Daisy Athenasy's luggage, to throw suspicion on her, make it look like a conspiracy."

"Mitch..." It was Bertrand, his voice weak. "When we were in the toilet together... You know... In the dark..."

"Yes, I remember."

"We tried to get out. The door was stuck. Do you remember?"

"Someone wanted to keep us out of the way, to make sure we didn't see something. That would have been when the murder was taking place. Dickinson took Rhys into the private compartment. Someone else jammed the door."

"Joseph, I imagine," said Taylor. "He wasn't with us."

"Of course. Who else would be strong enough to hold a door against two people pushing from inside? And then, when the coast was clear, he let us out."

"That's when I found you," said Simmonds. "You were—"

"Yes," I interrupted. Nobody needed to be told what we'd been doing when Simmonds found us. "And the door was not locked."

"No. It was open. I couldn't understand why you thought you were trapped."

"So you didn't need to use your key."

"No. He must have stolen it from me."

"Exactly. Dickinson needed the key so he could lock Rhys's body in the toilet, make it look like a classic closed-room murder. You laid too many false trails, Dickinson. As murders go, this was not well planned."

"Still in the realms of fantasy, Mitchell. Now let me go."

"I thought your boys in blue would have arrived by now, Dickinson. I was rather looking forward to that."

He shut his mouth in a grim line.

"It's all starting to make sense, isn't it, Dickinson? First of all, you blackmailed the engineer to stop the train in the tunnel. That was easy; you knew he had something to hide, and you were quick to take advantage of it. In the chaos and panic, it was easy to get Rhys into the compartment, with a little assistance from Joseph. You killed him—how, I wonder? Lethal injection? That seems to be your favorite method. You made sure we were well out of the way, and then you dumped the body, covering your tracks with a false scent."

"It's an amusing theory, Mitchell, but you're barking up the wrong tree. One thing you are right about, though. Rotha Lintorn, and her British Fascists. They were on the train, and they wanted to get rid of Mr. Taylor."

"Seems I've had a lucky escape," Taylor said.

"You're not seriously suggesting that Lady Antonia and Mary Chivers were responsible?"

"They attacked Taylor," said Dickinson. "They would have killed him if they could. And they were after Rhys as well, but they got the wrong man."

"Andrews?"

"Exactly. They found them together in the dark, and attacked."

"This is ridiculous."

"But they weren't the killers, much as they'd like to have been. It was Andrews who did in David Rhys. Of that I am certain."

"How can you be so sure?"

"Because I saw it."

"What? How?"

"Untie me," said Dickinson, "and I'll tell you."

# XV

"YOU MAY RECALL, MITCHELL, WHAT WE WERE DOING JUST before we stopped at York station."

Dickinson was sitting upright on the couch, rubbing his wrists; the rope had bitten deeply into the skin. Sergeant Langland stood guard beside him.

"I remember well enough," I replied. Oh, what a fool I'd been to let my desire for that man betray me into such a compromising position! Bertrand with his ass exposed, Dickinson pushing his fingers inside him...

"When the train stopped, I went back to our compartment to make sure that everything was in order. On the way, I came across Andrews and Rhys having a heated exchange in the corridor."

"You mean they were fighting?"

"If you like. I didn't catch what they were talking about; I didn't pay much attention to it at the time. I had a job to do. Getting those reporters off the train."

"More witnesses you wanted out of the way."

"Witnesses, yes—but not to what you think. They were

snooping around after Hugo and Daisy, and I had to put up a decent pretense of protecting their privacy—that's what I was supposed to be there for."

"We rather imagined that you'd tipped them off in the first place," said Taylor. "They seemed to know exactly where to find us."

"On the contrary. When I work undercover, I pride myself on doing my job properly. That's why I threw those reporters off at York. Very convenient, that stop. I couldn't have organized it better myself. Oh, but you think I did."

"Go on," I said.

"Hugo and Daisy were all for getting out and stretching the legs. I think we know what the attraction was, Hugo, don't we? Our friend Langland here, and his kilted comrades. Were you going to share them between you?"

"It did occur to me, yes," Hugo replied.

"I tried to dissuade them, but they were out before I could stop them. I went up to the dining car to make arrangements for lunch, and I saw Andrews and Rhys again, disappearing into the toilet together."

"We know why that was," I said. "They were lovers."

"You're a romantic fool, Mitchell. Andrews is a crook. He'd been stealing from the bank he works at, investing money in stocks and shares and creaming off the profits for himself. But he got greedy, and he invested heavily in a diamond mine in South Africa that, unfortunately for him, didn't actually exist."

"You don't say," said Taylor.

"Rhys was the con man who sold him the scheme in the first place. Andrews was desperate; he followed him to Edinburgh in an attempt to get his money back, but Rhys gave him the slip. So Andrews caught up with him on the train."

I said, "You don't seriously expect us to believe that he dragged his wife and children all the way up there just to chase some phony investment?"

"That's exactly what he did. What better cover for getting leave from the bank? Taking the family on holiday. The perfect disguise for a man with something to hide. Wouldn't you say, Simmonds?"

Simmonds glowered at him but said nothing.

Dickinson continued, "When Andrews realized that he wasn't going to get his money back, he panicked. He realized it was only a matter of time before the bank found out about the missing capital, and there was a trail of transactions that led straight back to him. That's when he decided to kill Rhys—the man who knew exactly where the money had gone. And then—who knows? A quick flit across the Channel. There were investments all over the place: Switzerland, Norway, Holland. We knew all about him."

"Is that why you were on the train?"

"Actually, no. I was genuinely investigating a drug smuggling operation. We thought that someone was using Daisy Athenasy as a kind of courier."

"Daisy? You must be joking," I said. "She wouldn't know how to spell the word."

"Daisy Athenasy isn't as stupid as she looks," said Dickinson. "She had her finger in a lot of pies—as Herbert Waits would tell you. But you know all about Mr. Waits, don't you, Mitch? I heard about your performance. Very impressed, was Bertie Waits. You want to watch out, Taylor. You've got some competition. Mr. Mitchell here is an up-and-coming screen idol. With the emphasis on coming."

Heads were being scratched around the room, and I thought it better to change the subject.

"So how did the ring get into Daisy's luggage?"

"Quite simple. She stole it."

"What?"

"She found the body in the lavatory, and she saw her chance. Never could resist diamonds, that girl. And when she couldn't get it off Rhys's finger in the normal way—"

"You're not suggesting it was Daisy who cut off Rhys's finger?"

"I am. Nasty, isn't it?"

"And what did she do with the finger?"

"I have no idea. She may have eaten it, for all I know."

"I doubt that," said Taylor. "She was terribly conscious of her figure."

"She stole the passkey from Simmonds," said Dickinson, "and locked the door after she'd stolen the ring. See? Not as stupid as she looks. I found it in the carriage, and had to get rid of it fast. Hence the little sleight of hand with the champagne bucket. Not my finest moment, I admit, but necessary. Sometimes, Mitch, one is obliged to cover one's tracks. To muddy the water."

Heads were nodding around the room.

"Hang on," I said. "Nobody actually believes any of this, do they?"

"You have to admit, old chap," said Morgan, "it seems to make sense."

"Thank you, Mr. Morgan." said Dickinson. "Someone has their feet on the ground."

"An awful lot of that sort of thing goes on in banks, you see," Morgan continued. "Chap at our place got his fingers burnt. I've been tempted myself. You can make a packet almost overnight. Stocks and shares move so fast. You just take a little punt, and no one's any the wiser."

My case was collapsing like a punctured party balloon.

"Now, gentlemen," Dickinson said, with renewed confidence. "I'm perfectly prepared to overlook all of this if you will let me get on with my job."

"And what exactly is that job?" I sounded like a sulking child who has been deprived of his favorite toy. "Kidnapping and raping young men?"

"Ah, your little friend."

"And me. You seem to forget that you were ready to kill me just now."

"Come, come, Mitchell. You exaggerate. A little bit of fun, that's all. I thought you of all people would be interested in exploring some of the...shall we say, darker corners of the playground? Young Bertrand certainly didn't complain, did you, *mon ami*?"

Bertrand hung his head. Oh, God, was nothing as it appeared to be? Had Bertrand really allowed himself to be seduced by this man into some kind of sexual slavery? He had always said he hated Dickinson—and yet he'd said the same about Simmonds. Was he really just ruled by his ravenous asshole?

"You see, Mitch," continued Dickinson, "things are not always quite what they seem to be. When you've been a detective for as long as I have, you'll understand that. Appearances can be deceptive. Look at Mr. Taylor, here. You'd never think, by looking at him, that he was...the way he is. And he disguises it very well. All those leading ladies and society beauties hanging on his arm. The trouble with you, Mitch, is that you see what you want to see. You want the policeman to be the villain, because I'm a bit of a bastard. I don't conform to your standards. Well, I'm sorry about that, but in my line of work you can't always be the hero."

I felt ashamed. I looked over at Morgan; he was staring glumly at his feet.

"But you were going to kill me."

"Mitch, if I frightened you, I truly apologize." Dickinson slipped off the couch and got rather unsteadily to his feet. "Oof! That stuff is strong! You're not supposed to take quite that much. Fun in small doses, but..." He stumbled and put an arm on my shoulder. I could feel the heat from his naked body as he leaned his weight on me. I could smell once again that unmistakable scent of lemons. God, what a fool I had been! What a meddling, interfering fool!

McDonald appeared at the door again. "Young man to see Mr. Simmonds, sir."

More "evidence" to make me look a fool, I thought. I glanced up at Dickinson—he was a good few inches taller than me—and saw him smiling indulgently.

"Never mind, Mitch," he murmured in my ear. "We'll make a detective of you yet."

The door opened, and in walked Arthur, the porter from the Flying Scotsman.

Dickinson froze.

"Arthur!" said Simmonds, jumping to his feet. "You made it!"

"Yes, sir. Looks like I'm just in time for the fun." His eyes were bulging at the sight of all the naked flesh. "Crikey, it's Mr. Dickinson!" He whistled. "Good to see you, sir."

I asked, "Have they searched the tunnel, Arthur?" I had to know. Everything depended on it. If the tunnel was empty, as Dickinson said it would be, I was not only going to look a fool, but I was also going to have to face the music. I had assaulted a police officer and made some very serious accusations. Knowing Dickinson's unscrupulous methods, that could land me in some very deep trouble.

"Go on, Arthur," said Dickinson. "And be careful that you tell the truth. You know what happens to boys who tell lies."

There was a vicious gleam in Dickinson's eyes, and for a moment Arthur quailed. Doubtless Dickinson had threatened him, as he had threatened us all, with exposure, and with the full weight of the law.

"Well, sir…"

"Yes? We're all waiting, Arthur," said Dickinson. "Remember that whatever you say will have to stand up in court."

"I… I don't know…"

"Arthur, for God's sake," blurted out Simmonds. "Are

we going to live like this forever? Tell the truth, boy, and face the consequences like a man."

Arthur's face was red and he was shaking—but he swallowed hard and spoke up clearly. "They found the body of Mr. David Rhys in the tunnel, wrapped in a roll of blood-stained carpet."

Total silence.

"Anything else?" I asked, barely able to breathe.

"Yes. A knife."

"What sort of knife, Arthur?"

"A steak knife. One of ours. The sort we use in the dining car."

The air seemed thick, and I could hear the blood thrumming in my ears.

"What do you say to that, Dickinson?"

"He's lying. The tunnel is closed and under police guard."

"No, sir," Arthur replied. "If you don't mind my saying so, the tunnel was opened by the order of the police."

"That's impossible."

"What else did they find, Arthur?"

"Nothing."

"No severed finger, for instance?"

"No, sir."

"What did you do with it, Dickinson? Did you keep it as a souvenir?"

Dickinson took a step toward me, and was instantly restrained by Langland and his soldiers.

"Time for you to be tied up again, copper," said Langland, twisting Dickinson's arms behind him. There was a struggle, in which Dickinson's shirt was torn. They soon had him bound again, kneeling on the floor, his wrists and ankles securely tied behind his back, his ripped shirt hanging down from his waist. His torso was huge and powerful and hairy—and even now, I could not look at him without desiring him.

His steel-gray hair, usually so neatly combed, fell over his forehead. He was starting to sweat. I relished every drop.

"You think you're very clever, Mitchell, but you're way out of your depth. You don't know what you're dealing with."

"Oh, I think I do," I said, feeling the reins were back in my hands. "That gang of half-baked gangsters who call themselves the British Fascists. They don't frighten me."

"Then you're a fool."

"Who do you take your orders from, Dickinson? Lady Antonia? Or does she get Chivers to boss you around?"

Dickinson struggled furiously in his bonds, but said nothing.

"I heard her talking to him just before we left Edinburgh," said Arthur. "I was carrying all their luggage—she's a lousy tipper, that Lady Antonia, like a lot of posh folk—and they forgot that I was there. The old lady was making a big fuss about the hatboxes, and so on—but I was behind her, and I heard her maid talking to Dickinson."

"What did she say?"

"Something like 'Have you got it yet?' "

"And what did he say?"

"He said no, he didn't have it yet, but he knew where it was and he'd deliver it before we got to London."

"What did you imagine they were talking about, Arthur?"

"Search me."

"Mr. Dickinson. Can you enlighten us?"

"I never spoke to the bloody woman. The boy's lying."

"You surprise me, Dickinson. I thought you'd have a story already made up. You were in the pay of those people, weren't you? And you had been commissioned to infiltrate Hugo Taylor's intimate circle and steal something from him. What was it?"

"You tell me, Sherlock Holmes."

"I have a suggestion," said Hugo Taylor. "I was carrying

a packet of letters—rather compromising letters, as it happens—that were written to me by a certain person. There had already been an attempt to steal them from my apartment in London, so I took them with me to Scotland, to keep an eye on them, you know."

"Why didn't you just destroy them, if they were so compromising?"

"Because I'd promised a certain person that I would return them."

"Sounds like your boyfriend didn't trust you, Taylor," said Dickinson.

"Can't say I blame him, really," said Taylor. "I wouldn't be the first actor to keep such things as a sort of insurance policy. Awfully useful when the work dries up and we're facing penury in some boarding house for retired theatricals in Worthing. Very handy to have letters from the crowned heads of Europe. Such things have a market value. But I imagine you know that very well, Mr. Dickinson."

"You're a fool, Taylor."

"Guilty as charged."

"So the British Fascists had paid you to steal the letters and deliver them to Lady Antonia," I said. "That explains her presence on the train. She was a glorified messenger, running back to her mistress to deliver a big juicy bone at her feet."

Simmonds addressed Dickinson. "And you didn't want anyone interfering. That's why you instructed all the staff to be on the lookout for journalists snooping around. We thought you were trying to protect Mr. Taylor and Miss Athenasy, but in fact you were making sure that there was nobody to see what you were up to."

"And you were all to ready to oblige, Simmonds," spat Dickinson.

"You threatened me, like you threatened everyone. I was scared, I admit it. I lost my nerve. That's why I...did something that I am deeply ashamed of."

Bertrand put his arm around Simmonds shoulders, and they kissed. Dickinson growled.

"You see, old chap," said Taylor, "something rather nice has come out of all this. Love always finds a way, as we tell people night after night from the stage."

"The minute the police arrive, you are all under arrest," said Dickinson.

"Oh, someone shut him up, for God's sake," said Taylor, his brow lowering. "Sergeant, be a good chap and stick something in his mouth."

Langland, still naked, was all ready to obey—but there had been enough of that sort of behavior, and I asked him to stand down.

"You don't seem to realize who you're dealing with," said Dickinson, once the sergeant's large penis had stopped waving in his face. "I am a detective superintendent in the Metropolitan Police."

"Correction," said a voice from the door. "You were a detective superintendent. You are currently suspended from duty."

All heads swiveled, and we saw Connor, my young reporter friend, backed by his constant companion, Scott.

"Go on, Mr. Connor."

"Does the name Stanley Goldwater mean anything to you, Mr. Dickinson?"

"It rings a bell."

"So it should. You killed him."

Dickinson laughed. "Stanley Goldwater committed suicide."

"Because you drove him to it."

"That's a lie."

"Who was Stanley Goldwater?" I asked.

"He was what's commonly known as a copper's nark," said Dickinson. "A worthless lowlife."

"Stanley Goldwater was the son of a north London

shopkeeper," said Connor. "He joined the police in 1924, at the age of 19. He was, by all accounts, a conscientious and ambitious young officer. Then he left the force in 1927 under something of a cloud."

"Don't tell me," I said. "He was queer. And Superintendent Dickinson, here, found out."

"A deal was struck," continued Connor, "whereby Goldwater would not be prosecuted, as long as he worked for Dickinson as an informer."

"That's how the police operate," said Dickinson. "We have our sources."

"He was your contact in the queer world," said Connor. "He gave you the names of prominent homosexuals, whom you blackmailed. Then, when he tried to break from you, you threatened him with prison."

"That little bugger was quite capable of putting himself in prison without my help."

"And he was so scared that he stuck his head in the gas oven. His landlady found him. There was a suicide note, apparently."

"No, there wasn't."

"Ah, she didn't tell you about that, did she? Kept it to herself. Thought it might come in useful, just in case she'd done the wrong thing. She parted with it, for a price. You've cost the *Beacon* a great deal of money one way or another, Dickinson," said Connor, "but it's worth every penny to send you down."

"You're talking out of your arse, boy. Just because I chucked you off that train. I hate journalists, but journalists with an axe to grind are the worst."

"The note named you, and gave details of your way of working. You made a lot of money out of other people's misery, didn't you, Dickinson? Including your own superiors."

"You're making this up."

"Why else would they turn a blind eye to so much

corruption? We've only had time to explore the tip of the iceberg. I'm sure there's plenty more under the surface."

Oh, how the mood had changed! Everyone was staring down at Dickinson now, disgust on their faces.

"Crikey, Mitch, the bastard almost had me fooled," said Morgan, clapping me on the back. "I thought you'd made a muck-up of things. I'm sorry."

"There's one thing I still don't understand," said Taylor. "Dickinson had every opportunity to grab the letters. I wasn't exactly watching them like a hawk. One assumed, wrongly, that one's possessions were safe, as the studio had provided us with people like you and Joseph. Why didn't you just nab them when my back was turned?"

A voice spoke from the doorway. "Because someone else got to them first."

Another new arrival—and this one completely unexpected.

"Andrews!" I gasped. "How the hell did you get here? I thought you were under arrest!"

"That's the other thing I meant to tell you, sir," said Arthur. "Mr. Andrews was bailed the minute they opened up the tunnel."

"But why?"

The tread of heavy feet approached, and in walked Sergeant Shipton, followed by young PC Jack Godwin, still in plain clothes.

"Because Dickinson's orders were countermanded," said Shipton. "He omitted to mention to the Peterborough Police that he had been relieved of his duties. Impersonating a police officer is a very serious offense, Dickinson."

Shipton stood over the bound former detective superintendent, who looked up at him through damp hair. It was a piquant image.

"He'd got away with it for years," Shipton continued. "Spying on people, blackmailing his superiors. We've all got something to hide, haven't we, Dickinson? And you've got a very good nose for a secret. Your boss, Commander Fleet, for instance. He had a mistress, and an illegitimate child, tucked away in Fulham. Didn't want everyone talking about his business, so he turned a blind eye to the Stanley Goldwater business, when really you should have been thrown out in disgrace."

"Commander Fleet has said nothing," said Dickinson.

"Commander Fleet has authorized me to tell you, sir, that he has decided to take early retirement."

"What?"

"In order, he told me, to spend more time with his family. His real family. What else did he say, Godwin?"

PC Godwin stepped forward and read from his notebook. "He said that he should have stood up to Detective Superintendent Dickinson over the Goldwater affair, and instead of just suspending him for six months he should have chucked him out of the force on the spot. But Dickinson was blackmailing him, and negotiated the lesser punishment. Now Commander Fleet has retired, and handed the case over to his successor."

"I think," I said, "that we can finally piece this story together. Everyone is here. This is what really happened..."

"Oh, I love this bit," said Morgan, rubbing his hands. "When the detective has got everyone into the same room, and suddenly everything becomes clear. I hope it's good, Mitch. I, for one, am completely stumped."

"Me, too," said Taylor. "Come on, Mitch. I've played the part often enough on stage. Let's see what sort of job you make of it."

I paced up and down for a moment, collecting my thoughts, and then began.

# XVI

"PETER DICKINSON WAS SUSPENDED FROM THE FORCE AFTER the death of Stanley Goldwater," I began, trying hard to control the whirl of thoughts and impressions in my brain. "He managed to avoid outright dismissal due to his hold over his superior, Commander Fleet. But he knew his luck was running out, so he started looking for other sources of income and power. He knew about Herbert Waits's operations at British-American, and he accepted a commission from the British Fascists to steal letters belonging to Hugo Taylor. The two jobs fit together perfectly, and Dickinson infiltrated Hugo Taylor's party under the guise of a publicity manager."

"I wondered why we'd suddenly got a new chap on the job," said Taylor, "but British-American are so disorganized that I didn't really bother about it."

"He planned to steal the letters on the Flying Scotsman, and deliver them to Lady Antonia Petherbridge, who, I presume, would pay him handsomely. She had raised the money by hocking her jewelry—she was wearing imitation diamonds. The money was hidden in her luggage—

which is why she sent Chivers to guard it when the train was stuck in the tunnel. She was nervous, and rightly so. I imagine there was several hundred pounds in her carriage, unprotected.

"It should have gone smoothly. Dickinson had taken the precaution of enlisting the support of railway personnel, looking out for any unwanted snoopers and throwing them off the train. He didn't want any witnesses. But two things went wrong. First, Simmonds failed to get rid of Bertrand and me. Second, when it came to stealing the letters, Dickinson discovered that someone else had got there before him. Isn't that right, Mr. Andrews?"

Andrews stepped forward, a picture of composure. I admired his sangfroid.

"Quite so, Mr. Mitchell. David Rhys found the letters in Hugo Taylor's luggage."

"But why was he searching through Taylor's things? That's what I don't understand."

"David Rhys wasn't a diamond merchant," said Andrews. "Nor was he an insurance broker, as he had told me. He was a private detective."

"Of course!"

"He had been employed by Herbert Waits of the British-American Film Company to get evidence of his wife's adultery with this gentleman." He gestured toward Hugo Taylor.

"My God," said Taylor, "he really was barking up the wrong tree."

"How did you find this out, Andrews?"

"I'd followed David to Scotland. I was desperate to be with him. I must have been mad, dragging Christina and the children all the way up there, and then, the minute David was leaving, putting them all on the train again. But love makes us all mad, doesn't it? David was horrified when he saw me. I see why now—but at the time I thought it was because he wanted to break with me. I pleaded with him to change his mind, but he just refused to talk about it. He told me to keep out of his way. We exchanged cross words. I lost my head. I kept trying to catch him, and he kept slipping past me. God, how ridiculous."

"But you caught up with him when we stopped at York, didn't you?"

"Yes. I pushed him into the lavatory and locked the door, and I started all over again, accusing him of using me—and then I realized that he was frightened. He was as white as a sheet. Something was wrong."

"Did he tell you?"

"Yes. That's when he confessed that he'd been lying to me all along about his job. He wasn't in insurance—he was a confidential agent, a private detective, whatever you want to call it, employed by rich clients to gather evidence on crooked employees or unfaithful spouses. He'd done very well out of it. He said he'd gone into Mr. Taylor and Miss Athenasy's compartment while they were in the dining car having their photograph taken. He was looking for evidence of their affair—and he found a packet of letters. He assumed they were love letters between the two of them, so he took them. As he was coming out of the compartment, he ran into someone—he wouldn't say who, but I realize now it was Dickinson—who saw what he had taken and threatened him if he did not give it back. Somebody came along, and David managed to get away, and shortly afterward we stopped at York."

"So, Dickinson," I said, "just after you'd seen Rhys coming out with the packet of letters, you checked up on Bertrand and me, to make sure we hadn't heard anything. You wanted to keep us busy while you got Joseph to sort out Rhys. You were very clever. You knew exactly how to distract us, didn't you? And you were right. I was a fool. I should have listened to Bertrand."

"You knew that we would stop at York, didn't you?" Simmonds addressed Dickinson. "You'd already got a hold over Eltham, the engineer. You knew all about his situation, and you told him it would suit you to break the journey. There would be no need to tell the passengers, you said. He was glad of the chance to spend some time with Rowson, so he didn't ask any questions. Not the cleverest of men, Eltham, and as for Rowson...well, let's just say he's suited to his job. But then you turned the screw on them. You said you knew all about them. When we left York, they were taking orders directly from you."

"I wondered where you were when we stopped at York, Dickinson," I said, "but now I think I know. You were telephoning ahead to the Peterborough police, telling them that there would be an arrest to be made at the station. You omitted to mention that you were suspended from duty, and they didn't ask any questions."

"Peterborough have confirmed as much," said Shipton. "The moment Commander Fleet spoke to them, they admitted their mistake."

"And where was Joseph? Ah, of course—he was looking for Rhys, instead of looking after Daisy and Hugo, as he was paid to do. But of course, you were paying him, weren't you, Dickinson? He was your henchman."

"And there was me thinking that the studio employed him," said Frankie. "You know, as a sort of gigolo. To keep Miss Daisy happy."

"I imagine Joseph also earned extra pocket money from Miss Athenasy," I continued, "but he took his orders from Dickinson. But you couldn't find Rhys when we were stopped at York, could you, Joseph?"

Joseph said nothing; I had seen him catch Dickinson's eye.

"No, because David was in the toilet with me," said Andrews. "He told me his life was in danger as long as he had the letters. He'd opened the packet and realized what he'd actually taken—love letters from a member of the royal family to another man. I thought it was Taylor he was frightened of; I never thought of Dickinson. David wanted to get off the train, make a run for it—but I kept him in there. Oh, God, if only I'd let him go, he might still be alive."

"I doubt it," I said. "Joseph would have caught him."

"But then we started moving again, and it was too late. He was furious with me, said I'd ruined everything. I was desperate to make it up to him—so we came up with a plan. I'd return the letters to Hugo Taylor's luggage, and somehow all would be well."

"And you really thought that would work?"

"What else could we do? The letters would be back where David found them. He'd stay in public, make sure nobody could do anything to him, and then make a run for it at Kings Cross. It seemed like his best chance, and it would have worked—if only the lights hadn't gone out."

"I saw you coming out of the toilet together," I said, "and I spoke to Rhys. He was nervous—and when he saw Dickinson coming, he ran. Straight into Joseph, I suspect."

"That's when I brought Mr. Taylor his dinner," said Arthur. "Do you remember, sir? I had to squeeze past you and Mr. Dickinson in the corridor. Mr. Dickinson checked that everything was all right, and came with me to the compartment."

"Was there a steak knife on the tray when you left the dining car, Arthur?"

"Yes, sir."

"Well, there wasn't by the time it got to me," said Taylor.

"So, Dickinson was already forming a plan. He pocketed the steak knife. Had you already thought of cutting off Rhys's finger, Dickinson? Or did you just think that a sharp knife might come in handy?"

Dickinson's mouth was set in a grim line. He too remained silent.

"Joseph demanded that Rhys return the letters—but now, Rhys could honestly say that he didn't have them. Perhaps he let Joseph search him. The letters were not there, so Joseph let him go. That must have annoyed you, Dickinson."

"That's right," said Taylor. "Joseph came back into the carriage while I was tucking into dinner. They were mumbling about something or other. I didn't pay much attention. Daisy was being a nuisance, complaining about the food, drinking and taking drugs. Then she was pawing Joseph. God, what a woman!"

"And that's when the plan was made," I said. "Joseph went ahead to tell the engineer to stop the train in the tunnel and put the lights out."

"And I thought he was just going to complain that I hadn't been given a proper steak knife," said Taylor. "I say, we've all been taken for the most dreadful ride, haven't we?"

"Dickinson and Joseph acted quickly," I continued. "Dickinson went off looking for Rhys. They heard Bertrand and me in the toilet together, so Joseph jammed the door shut to make sure we didn't get out. Everyone else was too frightened to move from where they were—the train was pitch dark."

"Apart from me," said Taylor. "I went out looking for help, because Daisy was panicking, and I got a nasty crack on the head for my troubles. I thought it was that bloody Lady Antonia or her little jackal, Chivers."

"No," I said. "It was Dickinson. He thought he'd got lucky. In the dark, you and David Rhys look quite similar—both tall, same sort of build and coloring. He blackjacked you, and would have killed you, but he realized just in time that he'd made a mistake and let you go back to the compartment."

"My God, so it was you!" said Taylor. "And you told me to lie about it, to say I'd bumped my head on the cocktail cabinet, because we didn't want any scandal about an assassination attempt. You devil."

"You went back to your compartment, Hugo, and you passed out. Daisy was out of her mind on cocaine. Neither of you knew what was going on under your noses."

"That's when I replaced the letters," said Andrews. "Everything was quiet, so I peeped through the door. I thought you and Miss Athenasy were just asleep. I couldn't see very well, and I was rummaging around for the right bag to replace the letters in. I thought I'd found the right one—there was a shaving kit and so on in there—and I accidentally upset a bottle of aftershave. It went all over the place. Miss Athenasy must have heard, because she started saying something—but I don't think she really saw me. I panicked, and stuffed the letters into the bottom of the bag, and ran."

"So that's why you smelled of lemons," I said. "You'd put the letters back into Dickinson's bag, and in the process you'd spilled some of his aftershave. It's a very distinctive smell, isn't it, Dickinson? Lemons."

"It's Coty's Esprit de Citron," said Frankie. "Lovely stuff. Terribly expensive."

"The sort of luxury one can afford," I said, "when one is a successful blackmailer. And so, after all that, the packet of letters was actually in Dickinson's own bag. But he didn't know that. He believed that Rhys still had them. He was under strict instructions from Lady Antonia to make sure that nobody else learned of the contents of those letters— otherwise her plan was useless. The fascists wanted the letters in order to persuade Prince George to be their spokesman—but if anyone else read them, they lost their power. The damage was already done. And so Dickinson had to kill Rhys in order to silence him."

"And that's why he accused me of the murder," said Andrews. "What better way of silencing me? He'd have me arrested, and then something would happen and I'd die in police custody. That's why I was moved from Peterborough so quickly. I have no doubt that I would have been next, if Sergeant Shipton hadn't released me."

I continued, "Dickinson found Rhys in the dark, and forced him into Taylor's carriage, not knowing that the letters had actually been returned. Hugo and Daisy were both out for the count—"

"I came round for a moment," said Taylor, "and I thought I saw someone moving around. I thought it was Dickinson and Joseph."

"No," I said. "It wasn't Joseph, was it, Dickinson? It was David Rhys. And that's when you killed him."

Dickinson could remain silent no longer. "This is insane! You let me go! Let me go!"

Langland kicked him hard in the gut, winding him.

"How did you do it, Dickinson? Lethal injection? That seems to be your favored method. I suppose you'd hidden all the syringes in Daisy's luggage; she was a well-known drug user, after all. In the candlelight, it wouldn't have been difficult to spike him. Quieter than a gun, less of a struggle than strangling him. You didn't want to wake anyone. As soon as he lost consciousness, you concealed the body."

"*Bien*," said Bertrand, "and since they now have Rhys disposed, Joseph permits us to leave the *toilette*."

"That's what confused me," said Simmonds. "When I let you out, the door wasn't locked. You could have got out yourselves."

"We came down the corridor," I replied, "on our way to lend a hand in the third-class carriages, and that's when we saw Daisy coming out of the compartment. Dickinson and Joseph had already made themselves scarce—figuring out a way to dispose of the body, I suppose. Is that right, Dickinson?"

Dickinson was fighting for breath and could only wheeze.

"I'll take that as a yes. And while we were at the back of

the train, you were very busy. Somehow, you stole the pass-key from Simmonds—"

"He stopped me to ask what was going on," said Simmonds. "He could have done it then. It was dark, and I was preoccupied."

"And then, when the coast was clear, you and Joseph dragged Rhys's body out of the compartment and into the toilet."

"But Mitch," said Taylor, "that's not possible. I would have seen them."

"Good point," said Morgan. "What do you say to that, Mitch?"

"Okay, okay... Let me think. They didn't conceal the body in your compartment, Hugo. Where else could it have gone?"

"Lady Antonia's compartment was next door," said Simmonds. "She and Chivers were in the dining car all the time the lights were out."

"And what better place to hide the dead body than in the compartment of the very woman who had caused you all this trouble? But you couldn't leave it there. The lights would be coming on again soon, and it would be found. You had to put it somewhere secure. Somewhere with a lock on the door."

"But what about the finger, Mitch?" said Morgan. "You said there was loads of blood. If he'd stuck him in the neck with a syringe, he'd be a goner. Why mutilate the body?"

"To make it look like robbery. Remember, Rhys was posing as a diamond merchant. And Dickinson needed to create a plausible motive, in order to pin the crime on Andrews. What better motive than robbery? And in order to distract our attention from the real cause of death, he cut off the finger and took the ring. Rhys still must have been alive when you did that, Dickinson, or very recently dead, in order to have bled so much."

"You monster," said Andrews, turning very pale. Sergeant Shipton sat him in a chair and helped him loosen his collar.

I continued, "The lights came back on, and people started moving around the train, and all the while you were locked in the lavatory with the body of David Rhys. I remember noticing that it was engaged when we went back to the dining car. We walked straight past you. I was hungry, and I was thinking about my lunch. Andrews came back in, and I smelled Dickinson's aftershave on him. I didn't understand it at the time—but it was the one detail that kept nagging at me. If it hadn't been for that, I might have accepted everything at face value. Just that strange smell of lemons, where it shouldn't have been. Oh, Dickinson, you should have been less particular in your choice of toiletries."

"We started to move again when we were at lunch," said Bertrand. "I remember that was when there was an accident with the fish, all over Monsieur Andrews. *Après ça*, no more Esprit de Citron."

"Joseph must have instructed the engineer to move the train forward, so that the switch could be changed and we could reverse into the secret tunnel. There was no time to lose. Dickinson came out of the toilet and locked it with the passkey. It was only a matter of time before it was discovered—but he had to get rid of the evidence. Simmonds saw the blood and raised the alarm, and Dickinson planted the key in the champagne bucket. Why did you do that, Dickinson? I suppose you wanted us to find it. To see the body. To see your handiwork. To get the whole train in a panic, talking about murder."

"Now I have a confession to make," said Sergeant Langland—who, the reader may recall, was still naked. "Shortly after the train had reversed into the tunnel, I encountered Dickinson in the corridor, and he gave me a very large sum of money if I would keep this young gentleman"—he indicated

Bertrand—"occupied at the back of the train. I suppose he'd seen the way that me and the lads had been looking at him, and to tell you the truth we'd been taking bets as to whether we'd manage to fuck him before we got to London."

Bertrand looked stunned.

"We didn't mean you any harm, lad. We just thought you looked like you might be able to accommodate four randy Scottish soldiers."

"*Oh, ça alors...*" said Bertrand, blushing, but he said no more.

"So Bertrand was out of the way at one end of the train," I said, "and you had me occupied at the other, didn't you? Very clever, Dickinson. You played on my vanity quite brilliantly. I was very excited about being the detective superintendent's right-hand man in his investigations. You knew exactly how to play me, didn't you? Getting me all hot under the collar. Yes, I would have done anything you told me to do. If only it hadn't been for that damned smell of lemons. I was ready to swallow everything—quite literally. But something didn't fit. Something made me step back at the critical moment."

"Thank God you've got such a keen sense of smell, Mitch," said Morgan, his eyes shining with admiration.

"And while everyone was busy, Joseph removed the body from the toilet, wrapped it in the carpet, and concealed it in the tunnel. As soon as it was done, he ran along to the engine, told the engineer to move on, and then reboarded the train himself, unobserved.

"And to think," said Andrews, "while I was in the dining car telling you about how I fell in love with David Rhys, that man"—he pointed to Joseph—"was disposing of his body like a piece of meat."

"You accused Andrews of killing Rhys, and all the while you had his blood on your hands," I said. "God, Dickinson, what can you say to deny this?"

Dickinson said nothing and hung his head. The room was silent.

And then, suddenly, Andrews sprang to his feet, screaming. "What did you do with his finger? You bastard! What did you do with his finger!"

He would have killed Dickinson with his bare hands, but Shipton and Godwin quickly stopped him. There was a struggle, and then he went limp.

"Oh, the finger," said Dickinson, suddenly looking up with a strange new light in his eyes—truly a glint of hell, I believe. "Can't you guess? Come on, all of you. You must have figured that out by now."

We looked at each other—Arthur, Bertrand, Simmonds, Taylor, the police, the soldiers, the reporters—as if someone must surely know the answer.

"Fools! Fools!" screamed Dickinson. "You will never find it!"

"*Attendez!*" said Bertrand, struggling to his feet. "I think I have the answer."

"Yes? Go on!"

"When we were together in the carriage, Mitch—you, me and Dickinson—he use his fingers on me."

"And me too," said Arthur. "When I went to serve lunch in the carriage, Mr. Dickinson took certain liberties with me. The same ones. With his...fingers."

"And when I saw you in the dressing room at the theater with Billy Vain," I said, "you had your fingers up his ass."

"A pattern emerges," said Frankie. "I wish I could contribute, but..." He sighed. "He never so much as laid a finger on me. If you'll pardon the expression."

"Sergeant Shipton," I said, "when you speak to the pathologist, please suggest that he inspect David Rhys's rectum. I think he will find—"

"Mitch!" said Morgan. "For God's sake! Spare poor Andrews the details."

Andrews looked very green, and swallowed hard.

"Peter Dickinson," said Shipton, getting to his feet, "I am arresting you for the murder of David Rhys."

"I say, Mitch," said Morgan, as Shipton and Godwin put the cuffs on Dickinson and Joseph, "you've played a blinder, old chap. I'm most awfully impressed."

"I would give anything to turn the clock back, Boy. I should have done something to prevent it."

"No good crying over spilt milk. Come on. Let's get out of here. I get the feeling everyone is keen to—well, you know. It's been a long day.

I looked around the room. Simmonds was embracing Bertrand, Connor was holding Scott's hand, Frankie and Arthur were surrounded by naked soldiers, and Shipton was looking at Godwin in a way that made the young constable blush.

They led Dickinson and Joseph away, amid much shouting and swearing.

"You've been through the wars, old chap," said Hugo Taylor, sitting beside William Andrews and putting an arm around his shoulder. "I don't think you should be alone tonight."

Andrews looked up into the famous, handsome face—the face that so closely resembled that of his dead lover that Taylor had almost been murdered in his place—and burst into tears. Taylor held him, and we left the room.

# XVII

MY COCK PRESSED AGAINST MORGAN'S TIGHT PINK RING, and for the first time in two years he opened up, sighed, and let me in. He lay on his back, still looking up at me with the look of amazed admiration that he'd worn ever since that hellish night at the Rookery Club—a look that had lasted all through his daughter's christening, and which I'd caught across the dinner table all evening. Belinda didn't notice, or if she did, she said nothing. She busied herself with the child and went to bed early; she was still in pain from being knocked down by the car, her arm in plaster. The christening had been a trial for her, but she'd managed superbly.

Morgan and I stayed up for a while, talking over the case, finishing our brandy and cigarettes. Then we went to my bed and gave ourselves to each other.

I fucked him gently at first—I was so sickened by the violence and hatred that we'd witnessed that I couldn't bear the idea of inflicting pain on anyone. I could not rid myself of the image of Dickinson, in cold-blooded fury, hacking the finger off Rhys's dead body and shoving it up his ass. He seemed, by doing so, to express his contempt for all of us—not just for men who love men, but for all who use sex not as a weapon but as a way of giving and receiving pleasure.

Gradually, however, I picked up pace, and fucked him as hard as he wanted me to. His eyes closed, his head fell back over the edge of the pillow, and I kissed him hard on his exposed throat as I pumped my load into him. He came, as he often had before, without touching himself.

We lay glued together for a while before I dismounted and lay beside him, our arms around each other's shoulders, smoking a cigarette.

"So—back to bonnie Scotland tomorrow, Mitch."

"Yes. Back to reality."

"I'll miss you."

"I'll miss you too, Morgan. But we have our own lives to lead, don't we? Our real lives…"

"I suppose so." He shifted around, as if trying to get comfortable, and we smoked for a while in silence, passing the cigarette back and forth.

"Do you ever wonder, Mitch, what things might have been like if they'd… You know. Turned out different."

"What do you mean?"

"If you and I had been together."

"Of course I do."

He propped himself up on one arm and looked down at me, his hair falling into his eyes. "And what do you think?"

"I think it's pointless to even dream about it, Boy. Things are the way they are. You have Belinda, I have Vince. We both have responsibilities."

"I know we do. But I can't help wondering…"

"Are you really prepared to throw everything away just because you like the feel of my cock up your ass?"

"It's not just that, Mitch, and you know it. That's a rotten thing to say."

"So, what? You love me?"

"I don't know. Maybe. Things are certainly fun when you're around." He sat on the side of the bed, suddenly self-conscious. "I say, I'm sure I've got some more fags somewhere. I'm gasping."

"Listen to me, Boy." I knelt behind him, pressing my hairy torso against his long, smooth, naked back. "You don't want to throw everything away on my account. Look at the pain you'd cause to Belinda, your little girl—your family. Look at the dreadful mess that Simmonds is in, leaving his family so he can be with Bertrand."

"But once that's all over, they'll have each other."

"And look at poor Andrews. He's got nothing."

"I don't know. I think he's got Hugo Taylor."

"For a month or two, maybe. A year at the most. Then Taylor will tire of playing that role, and he'll move on to someone else."

"You don't paint a very rosy picture of your way of life, Mitch."

"I'm just trying to spare you from unnecessary pain. I'll always be your friend. We can always have times together, like this." I put my arms around him and kissed his neck. "You know how much I...care for you."

"But do you love me, Mitch?"

No, I was about to say—I love Vince. This time tomorrow, barring any further adventures on the train home, we would be reunited. What would I tell him of the adventure of the secret tunnel? And of all that had happened to me along the way—including this final strange moment with Morgan?

"Well?"

Morgan turned to face me, and we looked deep into each other's eyes. My cock was stirring again, and suddenly tomorrow—and Scotland—seemed a very long way off.

# About the Author

James Lear was born in Singapore, expensively educated in England, and has worked in the theater and the British intelligence services. After a misunderstanding with the authorities, he has lived quietly in London, where he devotes his time to writing and helping local youth. *The Secret Tunnel* is his fifth novel. Other titles include *The Back Passage* (Cleis Press), *Hot Valley* (Cleis Press), *The Low Road*, and *The Palace of Varieties* (Cleis Press). Find out more at www.myspace.com/jameslearfiction.